I0564353

BANSHEE'S BREATH

A CASTOR'S GROVE YOUNG ADULT
PARANORMAL ROMANCE

A.J. RENWICK

1

BEATRICE

None of the Blackwells were dead yet, but it was only a matter of time.

Their banshee had shrieked on Friday morning.

For most covens, the herald of death would've been a somber occasion. The Blackwell Matriarch had decided to throw an impromptu party.

"Tabitha does know that she's the most likely to die, right?" Beatrice asked as she climbed out of the van. Her short pink heels sunk into the mud and the hem of her new dress brushed against the grass. "I mean, she's over a hundred and thirty. That's old! Even for a Matriarch."

On the driver's side, her brother Albert groaned in response and slammed the door. Visiting the manor always put him in a foul mood and having to squeeze into an old suit of their father's did nothing to improve it. At least his tie was a vibrant red.

Beatrice's dress was new, but gray, with sleeves a tad too long, even by witching standards. Unfortunately, the options had been limited in the plus-size section of the store, and her attempts to convince the dress to turn pink had failed. Clothing had a tendency to resist magical impressions.

"Or maybe that's exactly why Tabitha's gathered us here," Beatrice theorized as she trudged toward the driveway. "The banshee visited her dream and confirmed that her death was imminent."

Albert beat her to the back of the van. He lowered the ramp to allow their grandmother, Gigi, to wheel herself out.

"And now, Tabitha wants us all to tell her how great she is and heap praise on her while she's still alive instead of waiting until her funeral," Beatrice continued.

"Of course, you'd think that," Albert muttered, staring down and tugging at his too-tight shirt as though he could force the buttons to lay flat over his stomach.

"It's not the worst theory," Beatrice said, ignoring her brother's comment. "I mean, that's what happens in King Lear. Granted, that doesn't end well, but only because—"

"Darling?" Gigi reached the bottom of the ramp with a loud *thunk.* She rolled her weight and the wheelchair onto the drive and crooked a finger toward her granddaughter.

Beatrice leaned over. Loose brown waves fell over half of her face. With the long sleeves, she couldn't even quickly tuck it back behind her ear.

Gigi grabbed Beatrice's lips and pressed them shut between her index finger and thumb.

Albert let out a loud and uncalled for cackle.

Beatrice would've stuck her tongue out at him if she could, but she had to settle for an annoyed glare instead. *And he calls me immature?*

"Don't run your mouth. Not tonight. It's too important." Gigi released her grip and continued wheeling herself up the drive.

What does that mean?

Beatrice desperately wanted to ask, but she knew the question would only give her brother ammunition to mock her, so she clamped her mouth shut and decided to remain quiet until they reached the manor.

Four of the Blackwell servants met them at the bottom of the stairs. They carried Gigi to the front door. A broomstick would have simplified the issue, but their Matriarch detested anyone flying through her house, and, for all its wealth and glamor, the Blackwell Estate was not wheelchair accessible.

The property consisted of fifty acres of woods, sectioned off from the surrounding city by large black walls. Enchantments ensured that the humans of Castor's Grove could look at the monstrosity of wealth in their city and somehow think nothing amiss.

Several houses existed on the estate: a massive greenhouse, old windmills, smaller homes for less preferred relatives. Among all the buildings, however, the Blackwell Manor was the crowning jewel. It rose out of the trees like a castle from a gothic fairytale. It boasted four towers, seven stories, and over a hundred rooms.

Beatrice had never stepped foot beyond the first floor.

Nor would she tonight.

The party was held in the Manor's ballroom, which was large enough to hold Beatrice's entire house. Constellations shifted on the ceiling. Gargoyles in the form of dragons, griffins, and misshapen cherubs prowled above the stone pillars, their eyes glowing in the flickering light of the torches on the walls. A grand piano in the far corner filled the room with a waltz. Witches and warlocks danced in the center on a wooden floor or stood on the edges, observing and sipping champagne.

As always, Beatrice and her family were the last to arrive. They were the only ones who didn't live on the Estate.

"Oh look!" A high-pitched, nasal voice stage-whispered from beside the door. It was their distant cousin, Debby, making a point of talking to her sister loud enough for them to hear. "The Barely-Blackwells are here."

Beatrice's jaw clenched. It wasn't fair. Just because her mother wasn't a Blackwell didn't mean she wasn't an equal member of their coven. She was ten times the witch either of her cousins was.

"Are you talking to us?" Albert scowled as he marched toward them. Even in his ill-fitting suit, his broad chest and pulsing forehead vein made a menacing display though he was more likely to lose his voice screaming than hurt anyone.

Beatrice went to follow her brother, happy that they were on the same side for a change.

Gigi grabbed her arm. "He can handle them. Come, push me further in. And keep an eye out for anything unusual. Our Matriarch loves a performance. Do you see anything?"

I thought I wasn't supposed to speak.

With some effort, Beatrice swallowed the retort. Compelled by her own curiosity, she followed her grand-mother's instructions and studied the members of her coven as they strolled through.

In the far corner, whispering and ignoring Beatrice as usual, were her first cousins: Rett, Gabriel, and Elle. The two brothers seemed to be fawning over the fair-haired girl, probably praising some potion she'd brewed. Everyone believed Elle to be the most talented young witch in their coven.

Which was ridiculous. Beatrice's spells were twice as powerful. Where was her admiration and praise?

Apparently going to Linda. The middle-aged woman wore a tasteless red-sequin dress, which made her shine like a bleeding disco ball in the center of the dance floor. Her feet stomped on her partner's toes, but he smiled through the pain, ravishing her with compliments. As Tabitha's successor, that was all Linda ever heard from the other members of the Blackwell coven.

Meanwhile, they stared at Beatrice with their noses upturned like she hadn't showered.

"I don't see anything worth my attention," Beatrice informed her grandmother. "You should've let Albert bring Oliver."

It was only a joke, meant to ease the strange tension that Beatrice sensed building in her grandmother, but it drew an exasperated sigh from the old woman.

"You need to rid yourself of this childish crush you've developed on your brother's friend. Oliver Wyrmwood is a snake and the last thing that should be on your mind tonight."

Really? Because daydreaming about Oliver seemed a lot more pleasant than interacting with her coven.

"I don't like him," Beatrice lied, glancing around out of habit to ensure that her brother wasn't standing nearby. "But he is cute. You can't argue with that."

Or perhaps she could because *cute* was an understatement. Oliver had been built like a Greek statue and dipped in bronze. He had broad shoulders, short dark curls, and a jaw to make hearts melt.

Oliver had befriended Albert when they first started middle school, and a year later, Beatrice had fallen hopelessly in love with him.

Her first day of sixth grade in a human school, she'd made the mistake of talking to her classmates about magic. They'd all thought she was crazy and teased her all the way until lunch. She'd probably have been bullied for the rest of middle school.

But Oliver stepped in to save her.

He'd marched over and informed them all that he believed in magic too and that he could show it to them. He plucked a white lily from the earth and turned it black before their eyes. The other kids gasped and ran off shouting.

Oliver gave her the flower, and Beatrice's heart had skipped a beat.

She still had the lily, preserved by an enchantment and hidden in the basement.

"It's not his appearance that bothers me, it's his character." Gigi's voice, soft but annoyed, pulled Beatrice from her memory. "You're a romantic. And Oliver Wyrmwood is no Prince Charming."

Beatrice gasped. It wasn't what her grandmother had said, she'd heard Gigi's thoughts on Oliver a hundred times before.

Something had just touched her arm.

Beatrice looked down in time to see a bluish-gray blur, streaking across the floor and bouncing onto others. It must've been Bean, Tabitha's familiar. Beatrice had always liked him more than their Matriarch.

"I found what's out of place," Beatrice announced, a smile spreading across her face. "Do I win a prize?"

Gigi frowned at her, clearly confused.

But before Beatrice could say more, a loud cough echoed through the ballroom. It brought a stifling silence.

The piano ceased; the dancers froze; conversations died mid-sentence.

A platform rose from the back of the room. The Matriarch stood in its center, a small old woman, buried in a thick layer of black fur. Red heels peeped under the bottom and her face, like a pale moon, rose from the top.

Behind Tabitha, Linda's sequins assaulted the eyes of anyone who happened to glance in her direction. She smiled and waved as though she was a contestant in a beauty pageant.

Beatrice immediately averted her gaze to the third person on the platform. It was Wilburn, the coven's lawyer. His sharp green eyes glared down at the rest of the Blackwells in the room. They landed on Beatrice, and his scowl darkened.

"My beloved Blackwells." Despite her shriveled appearance, Tabitha had the powerful voice of a career woman in her forties. "These past seventy years, under my leadership, our coven has become the most powerful in Castor's Grove. Now, I suspect that I am about to die."

She paused, waiting for any murmurs of dissent. None came.

"And so, I must leave you in the hands of a new Matriarch. One who can guard my legacy."

Linda's smile broadened, and she moved as if to step forward.

"The most powerful witch amongst us."

Linda's foot froze in mid-air. Not even she was conceited enough to believe herself the most powerful of the Blackwell coven.

"That's right. I'm dispensing with this city's ridiculous notion of female primogeniture and returning to the old ways. The title of Matriarch will pass to the most powerful witch."

Whispers filled the room. Heads began to turn. Most went to Elle.

Only Gigi's went to Beatrice.

"She will step forward upon my passing." Tabitha tapped her cane for silence once again. "You will know her by the card she carries in her sleeve."

The Matriarch looked out across the room. Her eye caught Beatrice's gaze, and her lips curved into the slightest hint of a smile.

Or maybe that was Beatrice's imagination. She did have a tendency to let it run wild.

But she couldn't resist indulging in the fantasy, at least for a moment, that the Matriarch had seen something special in her.

Heart pounding, Beatrice's hand searched for the pocket that had been sewn into the too-long sleeve of her dress. Her fingers latched around the compartment, and she froze.

There was something inside.

2

OLIVER

The first hints of daylight streaked soft pinks through the dark sky. A sheen of ice, covering the walls of the Blackwell Estate, picked up the color and cast the dark stones in an eerie glow that seemed half shadow and half sunshine.

"Some there be that shadows kiss; such have but a shadow's bliss," Oliver muttered, staring out the window.

He'd borrowed the line from *The Merchant of Venice*, repeating a message found by a prince who'd chosen the wrong casket.

Luckily, his mother, Lucille, had little interest in literature, so she didn't recognize the reference. She parked opposite the estate's large wrought iron gates, leaned over, and attempted to comb her son's curls with her nails. "You understand the significance of this meeting for us."

It wasn't a question, but Oliver assured his mother all the same. "You've been grooming me to impress the Blackwells since I was eleven. How could I mess this up?"

"By refusing a proposal to Beatrice."

Oliver grimaced. As a warlock, his only job was to marry

into a powerful coven and elevate his own family's social standing. His mother had lofty ambitions, and he wanted to make her happy.

But few things would be worse than marrying Beatrice Blackwell.

She had almost no impulse control, talked constantly, and had a talent for being annoying. His last year at Dashmoor, she'd stalked him between his classes, crashed one of his dates, and managed to scare off most of the girls who'd been interested in him. Oliver had also had more than one of his shirts go missing while spending the night at Albert's house. He suspected he knew where to find them.

"I'll marry literally any Blackwell besides Beatrice."

"Then I've raised a fool." Lucille stopped fussing over her son's appearance and got out the car, slamming it closed with her generous hips.

That hardly seemed fair.

Oliver followed, stepping out of the car and into a chill winter breeze. He didn't know why his mother had stopped outside the front gate. The instructions he'd been given were to go around the back.

"It won't impress anyone if I marry Beatrice. She's barely a Blackwell."

Against witching conventions, Beatrice carried her coven's name through the male line. Her mother, Delilah Shivering, was a woodswitch from beyond the city. It had been the scandal of the decade when Archibald Blackwell chose to marry her.

"Tabitha allowed them to remain in her coven for a reason," Lucille said, as she opened the trunk of her car. "You shouldn't underestimate Beatrice's talent."

"I don't." The problem was that neither did Beatrice. He'd never heard another witch make more outlandish claims. "But even if she's the most powerful witch in the city, I'd still be miserable being married to her."

"What does happiness have to do with marriage?" His mother withdrew a wooden box, the same dark, rich brown as her skin. A green depiction of the Wyrmwood snake had been stamped on the top.

"You're making a delivery? I thought Tabitha refused to purchase anything from us."

Lucille slammed the trunk. "Worry about your own appointment."

"Aren't you going to drive me to the back gate? It'll take ages to walk."

"Good thing you're early."

It was a punishment for saying that he wouldn't marry Beatrice.

Oliver refused to give his mother the satisfaction of knowing that the walk bothered him. He smiled, did the top button of his coat, and vanished from her sight.

The Wyrmwoods were not a powerful coven, but they had two closely guarded, highly lucrative recipes that saved them from utter irrelevance. Invisibility enchantments were the legal one.

Oliver crossed the road, leaving the urban storefronts to approach the massive black walls of shadow and sun and begin his long walk around the estate's perimeter. When he reached the corner of the wall, he stopped and looked back at his mother.

She whispered through the gate to a tall, elderly man in a dark suit.

Is Wilburn Blackwell buying something from us?

Oliver doubted his mother would be impressed if he turned around to ask.

Instead, he continued his trudge along the property's

Eastern wall. The slow, plodding pace was his secret, silent rebellion against the ostentation of the Blackwell Estate. Who needed fifty acres in the middle of a city? Oliver's family lived on the top floor of a two-story building, sandwiched between significantly taller apartment complexes near downtown. Maybe he occasionally complained about noise traveling from his sister's bedroom, but it was a prime piece of real estate, the perfect size for a family of four.

Still, Lucille dreamed about hunting in the Blackwells' woods or dancing in the ballroom. Oliver was her ticket in.

A tall blonde ran out from an alley. Her hair streamed behind her as if caught in the wind, and black heels flashed beneath her long white dress. Instead of turning to run down the street, she barreled toward the Blackwell's wall, and stopped only a few feet ahead of Oliver. She muttered a curse and turned her head to either side as though checking for witnesses.

Oliver's jacket hid him from view.

Satisfied that she was alone, the blonde pressed her hands to the wall. Her shoulders rose as she sucked in a breath, then fell as she released a sigh against the stone.

A moment later, she passed through as though it wasn't there.

———

Oliver gaped at the space where she'd just vanished.

That's impossible. Did she just undo Blackwell magic?

Oliver stepped forward to investigate. A haze covered the stones where she'd breathed. He raised his hand to test it, and his fingers went straight through.

Somehow, the blonde had made it so that the stone no

longer existed, carving out her own secret way into the Blackwell Estate.

Could I—?

Oliver stepped through the stones and onto the property. The hum of magic that had let him know he was invisible winked out, and the world around him transformed from urban streets to wild forest. He peered through the trees, looking for the pale blonde. She'd vanished.

Pity.

Tracking her would've been an excuse to skip his meeting. Even his mother couldn't object to him missing it for such a noble goal. After all, if he apprehended the intruder, Tabitha might hail him as a hero. He doubted the blonde had any noble intentions breaking into the property.

Wait. What was I thinking following her in the first place?

Oliver had no delusions of greatness. Warlocks didn't receive the same formal magical education as witches. He wouldn't stand a chance against someone powerful enough to walk through a protected wall.

Of course, neither would most of the Blackwells.

I have to warn Tabitha, don't I?

Oliver groaned, but he quickened his pace, keeping to the shadows of the wall. He unbuttoned and rebuttoned the top of his jacket, but the magic refused to work. Oliver remained stubbornly visible.

A row of several average-sized houses lined the edge of the woods. They were home to some of the more distant coven members. Despite their humble exteriors, the Blackwell wealth would be on display within.

A round face peered out one of the windows, a teenage boy with dark brown hair and thick brows. He shared his features with most of the Blackwell coven, but Oliver recognized his former friend. Gabriel lacked the brains of his family, but he'd always been kind and easygoing as a child. The fact that they no longer spoke wasn't his fault.

Oliver raised his hand, wondering if to tell his former friend about the blonde. Then he caught a glimpse of Gabriel's eyes.

He looks bewitched.

Was it the blonde? Had she done something to him?

Oliver shuddered. He really did need to warn Tabitha.

Any fears about an unwanted engagement vanished from Oliver's mind as he ran toward the manor. Even racing, it took him another five minutes to clear the trees and arrive at the Blackwell Manor. He'd been instructed to use a servant's entrance around the side. Long vines hid the small door. Oliver brushed them aside and turned the handle. It was unlocked.

He climbed three flights of stairs in complete silence. Then, the voices of two girls whispered through the stones.

"It's probably a joke. Or Tabbie's finally cracked and gone mad."

"Mom says Wilburn will put a stop to it, no matter the cost."

Oliver almost paused. Blackwell gossip could be worth a few dollars to one of the tabloids.

"Well, don't say that now given—"

"I know what I'm saying, Libby," the second girl snapped. There was a slight pause. "You don't have the card, do you?"

The first girl laughed, a hushed, nervous giggle. "Seriously? You're asking me? Check with Elle."

The second girl scoffed. "She's not the one who's actually talented."

Their words became too muffled to understand as Oliver continued his ascent.

Near the top of the seventh flight, he heard someone approaching from the opposite direction. Oliver stepped to the side, heart thumping. He hoped he was about to see a servant and not a mysterious blonde in a white dress.

"Squeak!" Something small and gray charged toward him in the dark.

What the hell?

The creature bounced onto his foot, biting his ankle through his pants.

Oliver winced, jaw clenching to hold back a shout. It was more from shock than pain. Had the Blackwells started training guard rats?

Oliver leaned down and grabbed the animal's tail. He plucked it from his leg and dangled it before him.

The creature answered the question: what would it look like if we combined the DNA of three different rodents? The thing had the tail of a rat, the nose of a shrew, and the ears of a rabbit.

Macrotis lagotis.

More commonly referred to as a bilby, a marsupial native to Australia. Any sensible scientist would have insisted it had no right running around Castor's Grove. But magic didn't care much about the laws of nature.

Bean squeaked in protest, and Oliver rested the familiar back onto the floor. The marsupial raced down the stairwell, sniffing at the air.

Did Tabitha send him to attack me or is she expecting someone else?

It was an unsettling thought. Oliver climbed the final flight of stairs to the top of the tower. A single black door, with the Blackwell cauldron emblazoned in its center, stood ajar.

Oliver peered through.

Tabitha Blackwell sat in a large crimson armchair wearing a long black witching gown. Her green eyes stared without blinking at the wall ahead, half-moon spectacles threatening to drop from the tip of her nose. A red slash burned like a smile on her neck, drooling blood onto the dark fabric.

She's dead. Someone slit her throat.

The blonde in the white dress stood beside her.

———

Holy shit.

The blonde looked up. Oliver caught a glimpse of her eyes for the first time. They were prisms, colors swirling in a rainbow within her irises.

She's a banshee.

Oliver didn't know if to cry in relief or scream in terror.

Banshees were powerful creatures. Their breath had the power to undo magic. It was this ability that allowed them to help the souls of Castors, the magical inhabitants of the city, separate from their bodies and move to whatever lay beyond.

Unless someone attempted to prevent them from performing their assigned task, banshees weren't a threat.

The conclusion was obvious. The girl before him hadn't killed Tabitha. But someone else had.

Vomit rose in Oliver's throat. He shut his mouth and swallowed it. The taste made his eyes water.

"Seriously?" The banshee dropped her arm from Tabitha's body and turned to a large desk. An assortment of files lay on top of it in neat piles. One of them had his name in printed block letters: *O. WYRMWOOD.*

Within would be the details of whatever arrangement

Tabitha had invited him there to discuss. Probably a proposal. Probably everything his mother wanted for him.

The banshee pushed it aside as though it were meaningless. She grabbed a black notebook, emblazoned with the Blackwell cauldron and silver letters that read *Agenda*.

"Oliver Wyrmwood? Meeting at Sunrise?" The banshee opened the book and shook the page in his general direction.

Oliver's tongue was still heavy with the taste of vomit.

"You're early," she snapped, taking his silence as confirmation. Her prismatic eyes grew wide. She gasped and covered her mouth with a hand before running toward him.

Oliver would've run too if his feet would let him.

The banshee stood before him, and he prayed she wouldn't breathe. "You can't be here!" she shrieked. "I was five minutes late thanks to the ridiculous size of this estate. The time of death will be all wrong now. They'll think it was you!"

Oliver prided himself on his ability to be polite and charming in even the most stressful social situation. He opened his mouth and squeaked. "What?"

"Are you slow?" The banshee rolled her rainbow eyes. "Run!"

Finally, his feet listened.

3
BEATRICE

"And then, when I checked, there it was." Beatrice pulled the card from the pocket of her sweatshirt and rested it on the cafeteria table.

It was the Queen of Spades, but from Tabitha's personal deck. The pattern on the back showed the coven's cauldron on a rich sea of crimson. A small ruby glittered in each of the four corners. The queen herself had been painted with the large frame, round face, and deep brown hair characteristic of the Blackwell coven. She held a cane in her hand. A gray rodent-like creature sat on her shoulder.

Eva put down the calculus notecards she'd been studying and picked up the Queen. She offered a polite smile. "Looks just like you."

"Is that it?" Beatrice stared at her friend as she reached for the math notes again. She knew that as an angel, Eva had to maintain a healthy distance from witches' affairs, but she'd expected more of a reaction than that.

Beatrice grabbed the index cards and put them into her pocket, so the witch would focus on what was actually important. "I just told you I'm going to be the next Blackwell Matriarch."

"Oh, so you are going to accept her offer?"

"Obviously." Being Matriarch wasn't something a witch refused. Even an angel should know that. "I'd get control of the Blackwell Estate, access to all the covens' wealth, and ownership of the grimoire."

"I didn't know you wanted any of those things."

"Power, money, and the recipes for incredible spells?" Beatrice held the Queen before her friend, waving it to emphasize its significance. "Eva, every witch wants those things."

"But you can make your own spells. You're a genius savant. Isn't that what you're always saying?"

Only because it was true.

Brewing potions and crafting spells required an understanding of the essential nature of each ingredient. One mistake or slight miscalculation and the magic could go haywire with tragic results. Most witches refused to experiment with new recipes, and each coven guarded their most powerful spells in their grimoires.

But Beatrice's mother had grown up as a woodswitch. Her family had been hunted by humans and hadn't had the luxury of hoarding and perfecting spells for generations. She'd taught her daughter to recognize the essence of flowers, herbs, and roots. Gigi had instilled the proper techniques for enchanting items, using magic to imbue them with power so that they could be crafted into spells or brewed into potions.

It made Beatrice bold in a way that other witches weren't. Luckily, she had the raw magical capability to support her experiments.

She'd often dreamed of using her talents to become a

traveling witch. Castor's Grove was the capital of the magical world, but there were places beyond where witches and fairies and vampires still lived. Many of them had no access to the vast trade networks of the urban areas and still struggled to hide and blend among the humans. A traveling witch, capable of improvising spells, could do a lot of good, have incredible adventures, maybe even save lives.

But that was probably just Beatrice's romanticism running away with her again.

Anyway, being a traveling witch wouldn't impress all the Blackwells who'd turned their noses up at her family. Becoming Matriarch would.

Mr. Harris, a short, balding man who'd gone wrong somewhere in life and ended up teaching mathematics to disinterested high schoolers, approached their table. He cleared his throat.

The girls turned toward him. Eva gave her usual bright smile. Beatrice shoved the Queen into her pocket and tried to mimic her friend's expression. She suspected she came across less as cheery and more as sarcastic.

Please tell me he didn't see the playing card and think we were gambling.

"There's been some bad news from your family, Beatrice. Your great-great-grandmother—" He paused and frowned, brow furrowing as he tried to figure out if he'd made a mistake.

"She died?" Beatrice guessed. She sighed in relief that Mr. Harris hadn't come to confiscate the card, then realized that it was entirely the wrong reaction to a death. But she hadn't been close to Tabitha. Beyond general polite exchanges, she didn't think they'd ever even spoken.

So, while Beatrice felt a twinge of sadness over the old

woman's passing, a guilty excitement and unexpected panic were growing much stronger beneath.

I'm going to be the Matriarch now. It's happening.

Mr. Harris nodded. "I'm terribly sorry. Your uncle's come to speak with you."

———

Wilburn Blackwell waited in the courtyard. He stood, hands clasped before him, back straight, staring at Beatrice with a keen pair of eyes the color of a lime. They were his only shared resemblance with the rest of the coven.

Behind him were two burly men, dressed in the deep purple uniform of the Castors' police.

Why are they here?

"I trust your teacher managed to deliver the news." Wilburn's gaze flicked to the retreating Mr. Harris as though he was a rat instead of a human.

"With a great deal of compassion and sensitivity," she said, feeling the need to defend her math teacher from Wilburn's judgment. "Are you delivering the news to all of the coven in person? Dreadfully kind of you."

She tried to keep her gaze from flicking to the two policemen.

Wilburn's thin lips curved into a smile. It looked unnatural on the old man, whose deep wrinkles alluded to a lifetime spent frowning. "I am here in my position as executor of our late Matriarch's will. As you might be aware, she left certain stipulations as to who was to succeed her. You have the card."

It wasn't a question. The executor held out his hand expectantly for it.

Beatrice flicked her eyes to the policemen behind him.

Perhaps they were there to ensure everything happened legally. She reached for the card.

There was a squeak and something gray leaped from the executor's pocket and onto his hand.

Bean chomped down on Wilburn's fingers.

"Ach!" The executor screamed and muttered a curse. He pried the bilby off his hand and dangled him in the air by his tail. "Useless familiar. You should've perished with your master and died an honorable death. It'll be a pleasure to bury you alive."

The familiar squeaked in protest.

"You can't do that. That's beastly!" Beatrice objected, forgetting about the card. She stepped forward and tried to grab Bean from the executor.

Unfortunately, age had done nothing to stoop Wilburn's body. He was over six feet tall with long, spidery limbs, dangling the familiar out of Beatrice's reach.

"I understand that you were raised among humans—" The executor paused, wrinkling his nose as though the very word tasted bitter. "—with more delicate sensibilities. But it is customary among witches. A familiar should die alongside their master. To survive them is a mark of shame. Bean abandoned her when she needed him most. Now, give me the card, Beatrice, or how shall we be certain that you were chosen as Tabitha's successor."

Beatrice looked at the familiar dangling in the air above her. He seemed to be shaking his head.

Wilburn's up to something. Beatrice couldn't give him the card. But she couldn't leave the poor bilby in his grasp either.

"I'll trade you. For Bean."

The executor's eyes narrowed. "You're in no position to make demands."

Wasn't she?

Beatrice crossed her arms and met the old man's gaze.

He gave a haughty sniff and lowered the familiar. "The card."

She smiled and put her hand into her pocket. She felt the grooves of the rubies on the back of the Queen, and then her fingers flicked to the card beside it, full of Eva's calculus notes.

Math is boring. Wouldn't you rather be a beautiful playing card like the one beside you? Beatrice forced her will into the cue card and pulled it from her pocket.

Not a perfect replica. The queen was too thin, and a yellow sheen remained.

Wilburn snatched it from her without inspection. Beatrice grabbed Bean at the same time.

"There's your proof, officers," Wilburn said, his scowl turning into a sneer as he pocketed the fake Queen. "She's the one responsible. I wouldn't doubt that treacherous creature helped her."

Bean bared his teeth and hissed in response.

Beatrice held him protectively in her arms while she glared at the executor. "Responsible for what? I just gave you proof that I'm our coven's next Matriarch."

"Precisely. Which gives you motive. I always knew accepting woodswitches into the coven was a mistake."

"Sir, please, we'll take this from here." One of the officers stepped forward, placing himself between the executor and Beatrice. There was a sergeant's badge pinned to the collar of his uniform. He looked at her with a pair of deep brown eyes, set like caves beneath a protruding brow. His expression was serious, his voice deep and grave.

"What's your relationship to a warlock by the name of Oliver Wyrmwood?"

4

OLIVER

Oliver stood in the shadow of a suit of armor forged in the shape of a massive wolf. The sign beside him claimed that the item had once belonged to a werewolf. However, given that werewolves had little use for armor and the metal's dull appearance looked suspiciously like plastic, Oliver suspected that it was just an old prop from a C-list movie.

The Museum of the Mystic never did worry about authenticity with its displays. Its title was a misnomer. The residential-two-story house had been transformed on the bottom floor, but its owner, an eccentric writer who had styled himself Marvalo Moon, continued to live on the top floor. He wrote travelogues in which he claimed to have traversed the globe and encountered a variety of mystical creatures.

The magical community tolerated Marvalo purely because he'd managed to get everything about them wrong. Misinformation helped them hide in plain sight. But it didn't mean they enjoyed seeing it on display.

Most Castors avoided Marvalo's museum as if the

writer's ignorance was contagious. That made it the perfect place for Oliver to hide.

The bell at the front of the door chimed.

"Ah, another customer," Marvalo's voice trilled. He gave Oliver a suspicious glance from the corner of his eye before hurrying from what had previously been a dining room.

He'd been happy to let Oliver walk around when he'd first showed up in the middle of the day, but as the hours ticked on, even the author began questioning what could possibly be so interesting among his collection of titles that were mostly subpar puns.

This would be so much easier if my jacket hadn't stopped working.

It was the stupid banshee's breath. Oliver should never have walked through it.

Of course, if he was going to start listing regrets, he should never have gone to the meeting with Tabitha in the first place.

I'm a wanted man now. I can't stay in the city.

The police were already looking for him. His mother had messaged to inform him that a pair of them had shown up at the shop asking questions. But that wasn't what scared Oliver. It was the fact that one of the Blackwells had been with them.

The wealthy coven was ruthless and vindictive. Once the group decided Oliver was guilty, they were unlikely to offer him a chance to explain.

They'll be out for blood.

And given the Blackwells' influence, no one would stop them from exacting whatever punishment they saw fit.

Unless they can't find me.

Oliver held his breath and slunk along the wall, trying not to think about what would happen if Marvalo's new customer was a Blackwell. He peered around the corner, just as the owner continued his spiel.

"Good afternoon to you, young miss. Are you here to experience the unknown world of the Mystic that lurks beneath the surface of our own? Only fifteen dollars."

There was a giggle followed by a frustrated sigh as Sophie rummaged in her pockets.

Oliver breathed a sigh of relief at the sight of his sister, flat-ironed hair already starting to frizz despite the clip that held most of it in position behind her head. She still had on her uniform, with only a loose lime green hoodie to disguise her.

Maiden, Mother, and Crone. She'd make a terrible secret agent.

A sudden ache squeezed Oliver's chest. He'd been so focused on escaping that he hadn't stopped to think about what he'd be leaving behind.

When will I see her again? Or Mom, even Dad? What about Al and Beatrice?

Not that he'd miss Beatrice, obviously. But Oliver had known her for almost nine years. He took it for granted that she'd always be around, chattering about something in his ear.

But there would be no more familiar faces once he fled.

Oliver slapped his fist to his chest, trying to force it to stop aching. If he got sentimental now, he risked clouding his judgment.

Just think of it like a spontaneous vacation that I need to plan very fast.

Oliver stepped out from behind the corner. He waved to his sister, flicked his eyes toward the bathroom, and slipped in.

It was a former powder room with a toilet, sink, and a

single large window. Marvalo had hung an alleged phoenix feather on the wall. If Oliver had to guess, it was actually a peacock quill dipped in red dye.

A moment later, the door opened and Sophie stepped inside.

"You didn't tell me there was an entrance fee. Hope you're planning to refund my fifteen dollars," she muttered, rolling her eyes at the feather before she lowered the toilet lid and dropped the backpack onto it.

"You won't have to share your inheritance. Consider it a fair deal." Oliver intended it as a joke. But the very real possibility that he might never return to Castor's Grove didn't seem quite as amusing now he'd said it out loud.

Oliver opened the backpack, rummaging through to see if his sister had managed to bring everything he'd requested.

"I really thought you were going to come home engaged to Beatrice," Sophie said. She sighed as she tried to squash herself into the space between the sink and the wall. Her shoulder hit the bottom of the mirror. She winced and settled for sitting on the counter instead.

"Me actually killing Tabitha would be more likely." Once again, Oliver's joke fell flat.

"You protest a suspicious amount when it comes to Beatrice."

Something about Sophie's tone suggested that she wanted him to inquire about the meaning of her statement. But Oliver didn't have time. He double-checked the pockets of the backpack.

Change of clothes. Notebook. Passport.

Everything he needed to escape the city.

A dark green scarf had been tucked near the bottom of

the bag. Oliver pulled it out and tossed it over his shoulders.

"That's not for keeps," Sophie informed him. "You have to give it back."

Oliver looked at his younger sister. Her lips were set in the permanent pout she'd developed this past year, but her eyes were watery.

"Once I'm settled somewhere, I'll find a way to send word to you without the police noticing."

Sophie blinked, staring at the dyed peacock feather instead of her brother. "Any idea where *somewhere* would be?"

"Not yet." Oliver noticed a tear starting to drip from his sister's eye. He wiped it away with his thumb and gave her a smile. "Hey, don't cry over me. I'm going to see the world."

He smiled, trying to reassure himself as much as his sister.

There was a level of freedom that came with being a wanted criminal.

Gone was any chance of marrying into the Blackwells and fulfilling his mother's dream. He couldn't take over any business from his father. He would never be able to elevate his coven's status and win wealth and prestige within the city.

So what was keeping him here?

Oliver could do what he'd always dreamed. Forget about marriage or a degree in finance. He could explore the world, become a traveling warlock on the run from the law. There was a hint of romanticism to the idea. Maybe he'd even write his own novel as he went. On his own, he doubted that he had the power to pull off such a feat, but with his sister's scarf, he might stand a chance.

"Well hurry up and go then." Sophie pushed his hand away. "It's hot in here."

So much for a heartfelt goodbye. Oliver rolled his eyes. "Take off your hoodie if you're hot."

"I don't want to."

Are all fifteen-year-old girls this impossible?

"Then don't." Oliver turned away from his sister, pulled the passport from the bag and stuck it in his pocket.

"Fine. Happy?" Behind him, Sophie unzipped her lime green hoodie.

"Positively delight—" The sarcastic retort died on his lips as Oliver looked at his sister. "What is that?"

He put his hand on Sophie's chin and pushed it up so that he could see the marks on her neck. Just above the white collar of her uniform, someone had burned the word *worm* into her skin.

Not the most inspired insult.

"Who did this to you?"

"Who do you think? Two of the Blackwells at school. They all think you killed their Matriarch. Their coven's out for blood. You didn't think they'd leave the rest of us alone, did you?"

"This is illegal, Sophie. You need to report this."

"You seriously think the Blackwells are going to get in trouble?"

The bell at the front of the museum chimed.

"Ah, good day gentlemen, how can I assist—" A sudden thud suggested Marvalo had dropped to the floor.

Oliver exchanged a look with his sister. The Castor's police must've tracked her.

A loud knock came on the door.

"Occupied," Sophie shouted back. She pushed Oliver toward the window.

He shoved it open, grabbed the backpack, and knotted his sister's scarf. Its magic caused Oliver to vanish from sight as he climbed out the window to the lawn beneath.

Invisible, he ran down the street, heart pounding in his chest as he tried to figure out where to run.

Not the airport.

Oliver had been a fool to think he could flee the city and travel the world. The Blackwells were after his family now, and they wouldn't stop until the Wyrmwoods were crushed.

Unless Oliver found a way to clear his name.

5

BEATRICE

A glowing white liquid bubbled in the cauldron before Beatrice.

She stirred it with a long, black spoon. Clockwise three times, widdershins thrice. It was crucial that she keep count.

But Beatrice had been struggling to focus since her discussion with the police.

They claimed that Oliver had murdered Tabitha. He'd been seen on the property that morning, and her time of death coincided almost perfectly with the start of his scheduled meeting.

And for some reason, they thought Beatrice had something to do with it.

"Stop," Gigi snapped, grabbing her granddaughter's wrist.

They were in their potions den, otherwise known as their house's basement. It featured unpainted cement walls, exposed pipes, and no electricity, which suited the witches. Newer technology floundered whenever magic was used nearby, and even electricity could be finicky.

Firelight trapped within floating crystals lit the base-ment. It cast an orange glow on the many ingredients, stacked on shelves across the walls. On one end, glass jars held every type of bird feather, dishes displayed brightly colored reptile scales and an assortment of tongues, tails, and toes, which Beatrice trusted had been ethically sourced from the already deceased. Another corner resembled a plant nursery more than an unfinished basement, with flowers and ferns thriving despite the dark.

Beatrice's favorite section contained an assortment of glowing liquids and insubstantial solids with more exciting labels, like *fairy's tears*, *werewolf's fur*, and *dragon's whispers*. Unfortunately, such ingredients were significantly more costly and beyond their current budget.

That'll change once I'm Matriarch though. I'll have access to the best of everything.

Beatrice looked down at the mixture that Gigi had stopped her from stirring. Her grandmother was right. The liquid was starting to turn gray. Oops! Beatrice rested the spoon on the cauldron's edge and plucked an eagle's eye from a nearby jar.

"Focus on what you need from it."

"I know," Beatrice snapped. She might be a little distracted, but this wasn't her first scrying potion.

Beatrice focused on the index card she'd given to Wilburn, remembering how it had looked before and after she'd disguised it with magic.

Did the executor really think she'd killed Tabitha? After the Matriarch had chosen Beatrice to succeed her?

And what motive could Oliver have possibly have?

She thought of the sweet twelve-year-old boy who'd saved her from her tormentors back at Dashmoor.

There was no way he was capable of murder.

Beatrice dropped the eagle eye into the potion before her mind could wander further.

"You added that very quickly." Gigi snorted and flew higher so that she could watch the eye dissolve in the liquid as its essence spread. The old woman had abandoned her wheelchair at the top of the basement steps and taken a broomstick instead. She hovered on it now, her large frame taking up almost half the length of the handle.

"Do you want to do it?"

Gigi snorted again. They both knew that she did not. The last potion the old woman brewed had cost her the use of her legs. A single wrong ingredient had wreaked havoc on what should have been a simple immune-enhancing recipe she'd intended for her late husband. Worse, the mistake had petrified a previously gifted witch. Gigi had performed nothing but the most basic of impressions and enchantments since.

But she did delight in backseat-brewing through Beatrice.

"You'll need the hair of a manananggal to create the connection."

The half-bat, half-woman was the only magical creature with the ability to split itself in two, which made its hair a requirement to bind items from afar.

Gigi kept it hidden in her secret stash. She claimed it was because of the potential danger. Stories claimed witches had attempted to use the hair to replicate a forbidden potion that would allow the drinker to split themselves in two. Gigi didn't want Beatrice anything overly ambitious just to win the praise of the coven.

But even Beatrice wasn't bold enough to try a forbidden spell. Certain magics had been outlawed for a reason. Ripping yourself in two seemed like a recipe for madness.

The bigger temptation—and likely the real reason Gigi kept the manananggal hair behind lock and key—would be using one to scry on Oliver.

Which would also have been a gray area of the law. Beatrice liked to think she'd have resisted the temptation.

Bean bounced onto the plastic folding table, which they'd covered with a black bed sheet to make it look more appropriately witchy. The bilby held a glass vial tucked beneath his chin.

He squeaked and dropped it with the rest of the ingredients.

Four long black strands curled within.

Beatrice held back a delighted laugh as she picked up the hairs. "Did you break into Gigi's private stash to fetch these for me?"

Bean nodded, big ears shaking with him.

"You're so clever!" Beatrice grinned and rubbed his chin with a finger.

Gigi scowled and shot the familiar an annoyed look. "The coven's going to have a difficult enough time accepting you as Matriarch. You won't have won yourself any friends saving him."

"So?" Beatrice didn't care what the rest of her ghastly coven thought. She uncorked the glass vial and removed one of the strands. "I like Bean better than all of the others put together."

"That familiar failed to protect his master. Not only did he let her get murdered, he wasn't even there when she died, or the banshee would've taken his soul too."

Bean's ears drooped. His head hung in shame.

"Probably because Tabitha had sent him on a mission, and he was being an excellent familiar the same way he always has been," Beatrice said, dropping the hair in the potion and turning on her grandmother. "And you all want to reward him for over a hundred years of service by burying him?"

Gigi held up one of her hands in a gesture of peace, probably because she sensed a rather long lecture incoming if she didn't fold first. "I'm not saying that's what I would've wanted. Some of our customs are a little on the barbaric side. But why couldn't you have let someone else step in and save him? He's the pickiest eater I've ever encountered, and a thief too. And you've already got the police asking questions. It's bad enough they think you might have a connection to that Wyrmwood boy. Let's not throw in a conspiracy with a difficult familiar."

"Oliver. He's slept in this house before. You can say his name."

"And I'll be certain to remind your parents what a mistake that was when they return from their trip next month. Honestly, what a time for them to decide to visit Delilah's parents. They don't even have reception in the woods. Now, finish your potion before it starts to sour."

Beatrice gritted her teeth and swallowed her arguments. Her grandmother was right. The scrying spell needed tending.

She added the final few ingredients, stirring until the liquid turned from white to translucent. Once it was ready, she poured it on the waiting mirror.

The glass bubbled and popped.

Beatrice dropped one of the other math cards onto its surface. The mirror absorbed it and flattened once more.

The two witches and the familiar all leaned over, watching the scene that began to unfold on the glass.

Linda and Wilburn appeared. She held the card in the air and yelled. The mirror showed images not sounds.

Beatrice attempted to read Linda's lips before abandoning the effort and studying the rest of the scene. Behind Wilburn stood a dark pedestal with a large black leather tome. A bright red ruby shone in its center.

Gigi muttered a curse. "They're trying to steal the grimoire."

But obviously, their attempt had failed. Linda tossed the card onto the floor and stomped on it like a petulant child.

"You need to bind it before they find another way to break past Tabitha's protective spell," Gigi said, getting so close to the mirror her nose almost touched. "Can you tell what room they're in?"

She reached for the mirror, likely hoping to maneuver the vision. But, before she could touch the glass, the scene shifted.

A twelve-year-old Oliver laughed as a group of human children ran off. Then he turned to the mirror, grinned, and held out a black lily.

Gigi slammed her fist down, shattering the glass. Bean squeaked and took cover under the edge of the cauldron.

"We can make another scrying potion," Beatrice offered, pulling the broken mirror away from her grand-mother before she could do any more damage. "I got distracted thinking about Tabitha's murder that's all. I don't think Oliver did it. I mean, we have the strongest protection spells in Castor's Grove. No one can enter the estate with ill intent except one of the Blackwells. Doesn't that mean it must have been someone in our coven who's responsible?"

Gigi inspected a piece of glass that had wedged itself into her palm. She pulled it out with her teeth, glaring at

Beatrice as she did. The old woman's eyes succeeded in being cold and fiery at the same time.

"You can play detective, or you can become the most powerful witch in the city. But you can't do both at once."

Or could she?

Beatrice fetched an unenchanted broom from the corner and began to sweep the broken glass. "Gigi, what's stopping me from marching up to the Blackwell Estate, brandishing the card, and demanding I be taken to the grimoire?"

"Wilburn. Linda. Her daughters." The old woman held up her hand listing off angry family members on her fingers. "Even knowing it was Tabitha's wish, I doubt more than a handful of coven members will offer their support."

Because they hated Beatrice for being a Barely-Blackwell, for saving Bean, for daring to have more power and talent than most of their children.

"What if I could make them like me?" Beatrice suggested, a smile spreading across her face.

"How?"

"I could bring them Tabitha's killer."

6

OLIVER

Oliver clung to the leafless maple branch with one hand as he leaned forward. His heart pounded in his chest. It was his dorm. There was no reason to feel nervous.

Other than the fact that the police could be waiting within. One of the Blackwells certainly was.

Yeah, but it's Al. He's my best friend. I can trust him.

Oliver knocked on the window.

A light turned on within. Albert had been studying in the dark. Again.

He opened the window and stuck his head out, looking around.

"It's me." Oliver grabbed the window ledge and swung himself up, almost knocking Albert over as he climbed through.

It had been less than forty-eight hours since Oliver had been in their dorm, yet it felt like a lifetime. Clothes, sheets of paper, and empty boxes of chewing gum covered Albert's half of the room. Yet, it was the tidier of the two sides.

Oliver's dark green sheets had been stripped off his bed

and left in a wrinkled pile on the mattress. His lamp lay smashed on the ground with his books flung open and thrown around it.

"Maiden, mother, and crone," Albert said. He wiped his brow and shut the window. "You shouldn't be here. They've got officers all around campus looking for you."

"Are they the ones who wrecked my stuff?" Oliver undid the scarf so his friend knew where to look. He walked over and picked up one of his books from the ground: a collection of Keats' poetry. Oliver closed it and tried to smooth the cover down. "No one has any respect for the classics."

Albert shoved a pile of his clothes aside so he could sit on his bed. He pulled a stick of gum out and began chewing. "I'm serious, dude. This is dangerous. They think you killed Tabitha."

"But you know I didn't." Despite the confidence in his voice, Oliver's chest tightened.

His friend snorted. "The rumor going around is that you were angry because she wouldn't let you marry my sister. I'd be more inclined to believe you murdered Tabitha if it was the opposite." He held out the pack of gum.

Oliver's eyebrows rose as he took one of the offered sticks. That was news to him. "That's ridiculous. I wouldn't marry your sister if I was dying, and it was the only way to save my life. Who'd you hear that from?"

"Rett and Gabriel. They've been keeping me in the loop."

Oliver made a face as he unwrapped the gum.

"They're not so bad. I don't know why we stopped hanging out with them."

"They stopped hanging out with us." It happened almost the moment that Rett started high school. It would've been easy to dismiss his withdrawal as a normal part of growing up. After all, what high schooler wanted to hang out with kids in grade seven? But Gabriel was a year younger than Albert and Oliver. There was no reason for his older brother to keep him away too.

Unless Rett had realized that proper Blackwells were too good to be around a Wyrmwood.

Stupid thing to feel bitter about now.

But apparently, Oliver hadn't buried his childhood resentment as deep as he'd thought.

"Glad to hear they've accepted you into their fold. Rett still a pretentious show-off?" Oliver turned and opened his closet, only to find it empty.

That wasn't a good sign.

"Police took most of your stuff," Albert said, standing and coming to the closet with him. "I can give you some of mine. Might make you harder to track."

Oliver nodded and stripped down to his boxers.

"I thought you'd have been halfway to Europe by now. This is your chance to escape and see the world, isn't it?" Albert threw some of his shirts toward him.

Oliver pulled the one that smelled the cleanest over his head. His friend knew him too well. "Your coven is coming after my family."

"Bastards. Of course, they are."

"I need your help, Al," Oliver admitted, putting his hand in the pocket of the sweater and finding a set of gum wrappers. He tossed them in the bin. "I have to find a way to clear my name and keep my family safe."

Albert winced. "I know. But the police are already suspicious of me, and so are some of my coven. Rett had to jump in and defend me earlier today, or I could've been in shit too. Other than clothes, I don't see what I can do."

It was a reasonable response, but it stung all the same.

"Maybe you could tell your new bestie to call your coven off my family too," Oliver spat.

Albert shot him a look. "That's not on Rett. Wilburn's in charge until we have a new Matriarch."

"Linda hasn't bonded with the grimoire yet?" Not that she was likely to be any more sympathetic to Oliver's plight.

"It's not going to be her. Tabitha changed her will. Linda's irrelevant now."

Oliver froze in the middle of buttoning a pair of pants that were both too short and too large. "So who's the next Blackwell Matriarch?"

"The most powerful witch in the coven. Whoever the hell that is. No one seems to know, but it's got everyone even more on edge than usual. Then Beatrice went and rescued Bean, which is only pissing them off more because half the coven wants him dead for failing to be by Tabitha's side when she was murdered. Which seems a bit extreme, but granted he is a familiar—"

"Wait," Oliver interrupted his friend. Albert could ramble almost as badly as his sister, but what he'd said had just made something click in Oliver's brain. "Beatrice has Bean?"

"Yeah. She saved him from Wilburn apparently. He went to her school with the cops and Bean was there or something. I don't know. But listen, Ollie, you can't come back here. It's too risky. For both of us. You need to keep your distance."

Oliver nodded, barely hurt that his best friend was casting him aside. It didn't matter. He'd thought of a way to clear his name.

Unfortunately, it meant asking Beatrice for help.

7
BEATRICE

Hamburger juice dripped from the familiar's pointed nose onto Beatrice's notes.

She slid her book over the plastic-covered table. It wobbled under her weight. Either the legs were wonky, or the floor was slanted. Judging from the rest of the place, Beatrice guessed both.

She and Bean sat in the corner of a greasy fast-food restaurant less than a block away from The Blackwell Estate. Its owner was evidently not a creative genius. He'd named his establishment *Very Good Food*. It was too on the nose to be considered witty, but it did at least live up to its name.

"Not sure it's the *only* place worth eating at though," Beatrice noted, taking a bite of pizza.

Bean took a break from his ravenous massacre of the burger long enough to squeak and shake his head.

Beatrice had thought, given the bilby's size, that the single hamburger might keep him for the day. But she'd severely underestimated how much a familiar could eat.

"Well, better you have an appetite for this place than

sushi." She waved to the waitress, letting her know to come over when she had a minute.

While she waited, Beatrice wiped the cheese grease off her fingers and picked up her pen. She clicked it against the bottom of her chin, staring down at the page in her notebook.

She'd created a list of suspects. Oliver's name was written at the top, but only because Beatrice wanted to officially eliminate it.

What would Albert think of that when he saw her list? Or would he want to see it at all?

Beatrice had no idea why her brother suddenly wanted to meet, but she'd suggested here, and he'd agreed.

"What can I get for you?"

Beatrice looked up to see that the waitress standing over her with a big, slightly exaggerated smile. A plastic nametag pinned to her white shirt read *Kenya*.

The waitress reached a hand behind her head. Beatrice thought she was going to adjust the short ponytail of natural curls at the back. Instead, she pulled a pencil from somewhere within and took a notepad from the band of her blue apron.

Beatrice glanced down at the cheap, plastic menu and pointed at several of the items. "To go."

"Throwing a party?"

"Excuse me?" Beatrice was about to inform Kenya that she was actually just very hungry and that the waitress had no right to judge her eating habits. Then she realized that Kenya was staring at the list of names in her notebook.

Oops. Beatrice swallowed the defensive tirade she'd been preparing to unleash.

"Blackwell. Blackwell. Blackwell." The waitress repeated the surname as she looked at the list. Her brow furrowed in confusion as though she were trying to remember something. "You live in that massive mansion, right?"

She pointed out the door in the general direction of the estate.

"Did you guys already run out of burgers? I just dropped your weekly delivery off on Friday. At least, I think I did..." Kenya trailed off as though she couldn't quite recall. Then she noticed the bilby devouring his burger. A smile, considerably more genuine looking than the one she'd greeted Beatrice with, spread across her face. A moment later it turned to concern.

Beatrice hoped the waitress wasn't one of those humans whose aversion to animals overpowered the familiar's magical ability to blend in.

"He didn't get sick, did he?" Kenya asked.

Odd question. Not at all what Beatrice had expected her to say.

"Not anytime recently. He's got a strong constitution for a bilby. Handles pizza and hamburgers better than the average one." At least, Beatrice assumed that was true. She'd never researched the Australian marsupial's actual diet. Seeds, probably?

"Oh good." The waitress put the notebook to her chest in a gesture of relief. "Where's his owner?"

Murdered. And now her insane family wants to murder Bean too.

Probably best not to throw all that information on a Grover though. That was the common name for the human inhabitants of Castor's Grove, whose brains already had to work overtime to find creative ways to rationalize the numerous magical happenings that they accidentally encountered.

"My great-grandmother." Beatrice left off one of the greats for simplicity. "She passed away. Bean is mine now."

"Thrilled to hear it."

At the sound of the voice coming from the chair opposite hers, Beatrice's heart skipped a beat.

She turned her head toward it.

Less than a second later, Oliver Wyrmwood appeared as if out of thin air.

It seemed impossible but being on the run from the police had only made the warlock more attractive. A light sheen of sweat glistened on his bronze skin, highlighting the lines of his aquiline nose, and two days' growth of stubble emphasized a strong, masculine jaw. Even the thin red lines in his dark eyes gave him a hungry, dangerous look that excited Beatrice.

She could've done without the oversized gray sweatshirt that looked like something out of her brother's closet, but even that stopped bothering her when Oliver rolled up the sleeves to reveal the muscles of his forearms. He combed his fingers along his close-cropped curls and smiled.

Beatrice wiped her mouth with the back of her hand just in case she'd started to drool.

Then, her brain kicked in.

Oliver was wanted for murder. Her coven wanted him dead. He couldn't be here.

"I'm so sorry." Kenya pressed her notepad to her chest, staring at Oliver with a slightly dazed expression. "I can't believe I didn't see you sitting there." The waitress laughed awkwardly, or was it a flirtatious giggle?

Beatrice sat up, suddenly on alert.

Kenya tucked and untucked the pencil behind her ear. The nervous gesture seemed to have suddenly developed after Oliver appeared. "Can I get you something for your... date?"

Oliver smiled up at her a bit too charmingly. "Actually..."

"No, that's okay. We're leaving." Beatrice slammed a twenty onto the table and grabbed her notebook.

Kenya raised an eyebrow. "I thought you wanted like ten more burgers to go."

For Bean! Not for me!

The waitress was making Beatrice sound like a glutton.

"I'll come back for them later!" Beatrice stood, grabbed Oliver's hand, and pulled him out of his seat. Bean shoved the few remaining crumbs of bread into his mouth, then bounced after her.

"I was hungry," Oliver muttered.

Beatrice spotted a side door near the back of the restaurant and dragged the warlock toward it.

"You're also a fugitive," she reminded him as they exited into a back alley beside a large green trash bin. "And this place is popular with the Blackwells. Do you have any idea what they'd do if they saw you? Why would you even come here? Are you looking for Albert?"

Oliver spun her toward him, using the hand that she was still holding. He pressed a finger to her lips.

Beatrice's cheeks grew hot. She stared up at the warlock with his perfect skin and dangerous eyes. Her mind raced with a hundred different questions, none of which seemed to match.

Had he killed Tabitha? Was she about to be next? How did he still smell good? Had he showered? What would his stubble feel like against her cheeks?

"So there is a way to get you to be quiet." Oliver smiled and lowered his finger.

Rude!

Beatrice tugged at the edges of her pink sweater and hoped that she wasn't blushing. She wasn't certain if to be disappointed that he hadn't kissed her or relieved he hadn't murdered her.

Relieved. Murder was the more likely of the two.

Though it pained her to admit, Beatrice wasn't delusional. She knew Oliver didn't see her as anything more than Albert's annoying younger sister.

Which made this a rare opportunity to show him that she was mature and sophisticated.

Beatrice crossed her arms and stuck her tongue out. "You're lucky I'm not screaming for the police. I could get arrested just for talking to you. They already think I'm involved."

"I know. I'm sorry." His eyes flicked to the ground. It actually looked like he meant it. "But I'm innocent, B, and I can prove it. There was a witness to the murder."

Beatrice followed Oliver's gaze.

He was looking at Bean.

8

OLIVER

Tabitha Blackwell's funeral took place three days after her death.

In traditional fashion, the service had been scheduled for dusk. In the meantime, her body lay on display in the center of the Pentacular Chapel. From sunrise to sunset, Castors would visit and lay offerings around her. The norm was to leave enchanted items and incantations rumored to guide the deceased in the afterlife. These gifts would be buried with the corpse at the day's close.

In order to avoid theft, most witches brought their offerings later in the day.

It was still morning when Oliver untied his scarf, opened the Chapel's large black door, and crept inside.

Magic was strictly forbidden within the five walls. While Oliver had never been particularly religious, he thought it best not to tempt fate more. He cupped his hands, made the three moons of the Maiden, Mother, and Crone, and bowed his head. He offered a single prayer.

Please, let this work.

In the center of the chapel, on a large pentagonal dais,

Tabitha's body was on display. Black velvet lined her coffin and a cauldron had been engraved into the dark wood. Small, shimmering diamonds glittered around the edges, stealing the color from the floating candles and reflecting the firelight onto the floor.

Normally, the sparkling display of wealth would've held Oliver's complete attention. But today, he had another purpose.

Two, in fact.

He reached his hand into the pocket of Albert's too small jacket and retrieved a rolled-up paperback.

"Boo!"

Oliver whipped his head around, body preparing for a fight before his brain registered the voice.

Beatrice stood a foot away, already in her funeral attire. She'd chosen a long black witch's dress with the customary sweeping sleeves. This one cinched tight beneath her chest, highlighting a smaller waistline than her size might have suggested. She'd undone several of the top buttons by the collar, creating a distractingly low neckline.

Oliver's eyes flicked lower before he caught himself. He was aware, vaguely, that Beatrice no longer looked like the middle-schooler with braces and pigtails, who'd spent over an hour telling him about her favorite boy bands. But Oliver didn't appreciate the reminder that she now carried her weight in exactly the way he liked. He couldn't find Albert's little sister attractive.

At least she's still just as annoying.

Beatrice smiled. "Fancy meeting you here."

She said it as though they'd planned this. Which Oliver most certainly hadn't.

"What're you doing?" Oliver demanded. "I thought we

agreed to meet me after the wake tonight. Are you stalking me?"

"Well, someone thinks highly of himself."

Oliver spluttered for a moment, fighting the urge to ask if she wasn't the same witch who'd memorized his senior schedule so she could be hovering in the correct hallways as he walked between classes. He did still need her help.

So Oliver tried a different approach. He crossed his arms and gave her a concerned look. "You should be with your family preparing for the funeral. Don't you think it looks suspicious if you're missing?"

"Wilburn doesn't want me anywhere near, and Gigi thinks I'm at school."

Which still doesn't explain why you're here.

"Anyway, you're the one who's wanted by the police and strolling around in broad daylight," Beatrice argued. "Why are you here? Are you leaving an offering for Tabitha?"

Before Oliver realized what she was doing, the witch plucked the paperback from his hand. She held it up, looked at the inscription within, and smiled.

Oliver snatched it back. "Don't you know it's bad luck to steal someone's offering?"

"I was just looking." Beatrice continued grinning at him. "You know, I left a book for her as well." She pointed into the large coffin where a few gifts had already been placed.

Oliver looked down at the book in question. It was a large tome of fairytales. He scoffed. "Really? She was over a century, not five years old. What's she supposed to do with that in the afterlife?"

"I imagine she'd read it. Same as yours," Beatrice said, crossing her arms and sounding huffy.

Oliver snorted. He'd brought Tabitha a copy of *The Styles Affair*, an Agatha Christie mystery that centered around solving the murder of an old woman. Reading it might bring her soul a sense of closure.

It was not at all the same as a book of fairytales.

He added his offering to the coffin, careful to rest it as far from Beatrice's own as possible. As he did, he glanced at the few other items within: a bouquet of flowers, a gold coin, and a tarot card.

"Did you see who left these?"

Beatrice stepped closer. Her hips brushed against the side of his leg, and he immediately shifted away. Unlike Oliver, who had a sense of propriety, the witch rested her hands on the open coffin and leaned against it like it was a table.

"The blue iris and the Janus coin were already here when I arrived. But I don't suppose you're concerned about those. A symbol of justice and a representation of a two-headed God who guides people through significant transformations are both understandable gifts."

Maiden, Mother, and Crone, she likes to hear herself talk.

"And the tarot card?" Oliver attempted to speed up the process.

Beatrice smiled like she'd been hoping he'd ask. "The wheel of fortune. A symbol of karmic retribution. Not a normal offering for someone who was murdered."

"I know that." Oliver clenched his jaw, hating the way the witch was milking having information that he didn't. "Who left it?"

"Linda."

Oliver's brow furrowed for a moment. Belinda Blackwell, or Linda as her family called her, had been Tabitha's heir. But, according to Albert, the coven had now abandoned female primogeniture.

Could Linda have killed Tabitha for revenge?

There was no sense wasting time studying clues in a coffin. If everything worked as it should, Oliver would know the identity of the murderer soon enough.

He just needed a strand of Tabitha's hair.

His hand reached toward it.

"Squeak. Squeak." Bean bounced up and down by their feet.

"Someone else is coming," Beatrice translated. She grabbed Oliver's hand and pulled him away from the coffin toward a closet near the entrance. "We have to hide!"

9
BEATRICE

Hiding in a small closet with a wanted criminal while someone came into the Pentacular Chapel was not ideal.

But Beatrice found it very difficult to be upset.

She and Oliver squeezed into the narrow closet. The warlock had to crouch in order to fit. His feet touched the wall, and Beatrice stood in the space between his legs.

Their chests pressed against one another. Beatrice felt Oliver's muscles through the ill-fitting clothes. The scent of soap lingered on his skin. A slight tilt of her head would rest it in the crook of his broad shoulder. The stubble on his chin would brush her forehead.

And if he leaned down, they'd be in the perfect position to kiss.

Which likely explained why Oliver stood like a statue with his chin tilted up. The muscles in his neck trembled. He seemed determined to hold the position and had glued his eyes to a spot on the ceiling.

What's he so afraid will happen if he looks down at me?

Maybe he could hear Beatrice's heart pounding in her

chest and assumed she'd take advantage of the situation. Her feelings for him weren't exactly a secret. But if he'd been so concerned about squashing into a closet with her, he could've broken the rules and used his scarf to turn invisible.

Beyond the closet, came the unmistakable scrape of the Chapel's heavy iron door as someone pushed it open.

Beatrice leaned forward, pressing herself further against Oliver. His lips moved, but his eyes remained toward the ceiling as though he were muttering a silent prayer. Another time, Beatrice would've tried to read his lips, but at the moment she was more concerned with spying.

With her body angled just right, Beatrice had a clear view of the dais, through a thin crack in the closet's door.

A pair of flat crimson shoes peeped from beneath the hem of a long black dress as someone stepped up to the coffin. Beatrice recognized the profile of her cousin Elle.

Though their parents were siblings, they'd never been close. Elle was four years older and never had time for the precocious kid who'd wanted to yammer on about every animal found on the Blackwell Estate. The distance had bothered Beatrice less as she aged. Elle cared too much about impressing their parents, and she preferred gossiping with Rett to spending time with other witches.

"I'm sorry for lying to you," Elle said, addressing Tabitha's corpse. Her hands twisted around one another in the air before her. "But I promise I'll make you proud. I am learning." Silver flashed in the air as she pulled something from the sleeve of her gown.

Is that what I think it is?

Before Beatrice could be certain, her cousin dropped the offering into the coffin, turned, and left.

A moment later, Bean returned, squeaking to assure them that the coast was clear.

Oliver pushed her out of the closet, and Beatrice ran straight to the dais. She slipped her hand into the coffin and pulled out a sprig of silver leaves.

It is silverbloom.

The magical plant was worth a small fortune. Its leaves had healing properties that could overcome even the most powerful toxins.

"What are you doing? That's bad luck." Oliver arrived at her side a second later. He grabbed Beatrice's hand and forced her to release the plant. "Come on. We need to get out of here."

The warlock plucked a few gray hairs from Tabitha's scalp. He muttered an apology as he pulled a handkerchief from his pocket and began to fold the strands within.

Beatrice watched, simultaneously impressed and bemused. "I've already got a strand and a sample of blood. What did you think I was doing here before you arrived?"

Oliver stopped his folding. He looked up at her, eyebrows high. "You took a sample of what?"

Beatrice pulled the vial from the pocket of her sleeve and waved it for him to see. Viscous red liquid pooled in the bottom. A strand of gray hair rose from it like the stem of a flower. "We'll need both for a memory expulsion spell."

"The Malices only said—"

"You spoke to the Malices?"

Oliver gave her a look like she was crazy. "Obviously. My coven might be able to brew some questionable under-the-table forgetting potions, but the Malices specialize in memory-based magic. Who else would be able to figure out the recipe we need?"

"I would." Beatrice pressed her hand to her chest. When

Oliver had spoken to her yesterday about extracting Bean's memory, she'd assumed he also wanted her to brew the required enchantment. He knew she was gifted with brews and spellcraft, didn't he? Beatrice was certain she'd told him.

"No way. This isn't some chance for you to show off. My coven is on the line."

"Exactly." How could he trust the Malices to help him over her? That stung Beatrice more than she could bear.

Oliver put the handkerchief in his pocket and gave her the stern, annoyed look that he'd copied from Albert, then began moving toward the door. "I don't have time to argue about this. Just bring Bean tonight as planned."

"No." Beatrice crossed her arms and refused to move.

The warlock stopped and turned back to face her, his expression torn between frustration and distress.

It made Beatrice's stomach turn to know that her actions were upsetting him, but too bad.

"I don't trust anyone else to cast a spell on Bean. Either I do it, or no one does."

10

OLIVER

An hour later, Oliver was still cursing the witch in his head.

What a stupid ultimatum!

Honestly, how massive was Beatrice's ego that she thought she could brew a memory potion better than the Malices?

Every coven had its specialty, and it stuck to it. He knew the Blackwells were powerful. Their rise among the covens had been largely due to a heightened magical capacity in many of their witches. They'd made their fortune casting large-scale protective spells, which guarded most of the magical buildings in Castor's Grove. The amount of raw power required to secure such large areas was unthinkable to most witches. And if that weren't intimidating enough, the Blackwells were known for finding ways to bypass the magic of other covens.

It was all very impressive. But a memory expulsion spell was an entirely different ball game.

"Then, we add the reflected light caught from a lens, and trace it into a pentagram thrice within the liquid,"

Beatrice said, staring down at the cauldron as she moved the large metal ladle through the potion. "Funny how much we like threes, isn't it?"

Bean squeaked in agreement from where he'd perched himself near the edge of the cauldron.

They were in Beatrice's family's unfinished basement, which they'd turned into a makeshift potions den. Normally, Oliver would have been delighted at the opportunity to come down and get a glimpse of the different items the family hoarded. If he could've given his mother information like that, it would've earned her praise for at least a month.

But now, Oliver groaned and pressed his hands over his eyes, wishing he had another pair to block his ears as well.

Beatrice insisted on narrating everything as she went, which was another issue. If she was so confident in this memory expulsion spell, why was she letting him learn it? Did she think that just because he was a warlock, he wouldn't be able to replicate it?

Probably.

And she was right. Oliver had never mastered even the basic skills that warlocks learned. His mother claimed his will was too weak when it came to impressions. Whenever he tried to change the pattern on a leaf or the color of a petal, his head ached and slammed against an imaginary wall, and he inevitably abandoned the effort.

Beyond that, Oliver could enchant both objects and actions, but he had no concept of how to combine them to craft spells or brew potions. Only his sister, despite being four years younger, had been shown any of the Wyrmwood recipes.

As his mother had explained: *Imagine if we taught you and then after you were married, you shared the secrets with your new coven? We'd lose all our spells if we started teaching them to warlocks.*

"Three drops of Tabitha's blood, enchanted with the memory of her death," Beatrice informed him as she closed her eyes and then dropped them in.

The cauldron's brew hissed and emitted a thin stream of smoke.

Beatrice frowned, and Oliver straightened from where he'd been leaning against the wall.

"Did you mess up?"

"No." Beatrice stirred the cauldron, thrice in either direction. There was a line between her eyebrows. "You saw Tabitha's body. Could you tell how she'd died?"

"Knife across the throat. Does that make a difference? Why're you waiting to ask now?"

"Relax." Beatrice leaned forward and took a deep breath through her nose. She nodded at the scent.

Oliver inched forward and inhaled. He couldn't smell anything.

"I'm just thinking about the silverbloom. It's weird that Elle would leave something so valuable, don't you think?"

Was that what the silver leaves had been?

Botany was the one subject, magical and theoretical, that eluded Oliver most. He hadn't recognized the leaves in the Chapel and learning that they were silverbloom now did little to help him.

Oliver gave a noncommittal grunt as he wracked his brain, searching for details on the topic.

It's a magical plant. I know that much.

Of course, even a Grover could guess that given the glowing silver veins in the leaves.

Beatrice, normally happy to carry a conversation on her

own, had chosen this moment to stare at Oliver in expectance of an answer.

"Your coven is rich. You hemorrhage money without thinking." Oliver wanted the topic dismissed before he embarrassed himself. "Did you finish the potion or not?"

"It's finished. I'm just letting it cool before I give any to Bean. You wouldn't want him to burn his mouth."

The bilby sat up on his haunches and nodded his pointed nose in agreement.

Oliver pressed his lips together. Familiars weren't little children who needed to be protected from a sip of hot liquid. He suspected that Bean was just taking his new master's side.

Annoyed, Oliver stepped forward, took the large spoon from the side of the cauldron, and scooped up some of the liquid. Trails of pale blue and bright red twisted within a clear, almost gelatinous substance. He brought his lips closer to the edge and blew.

Beatrice stared at him, eyes wide as though he were doing something unthinkable.

"What? I thought we were ensuring that Bean didn't get an ouchie." He was fairly certain that his sarcasm was obvious, but the familiar squeaked with apparent delight at having someone cater to him for a change.

Maybe he would prefer not to burn his mouth.

Oliver grimaced, suddenly feeling like a bit of an ass for assuming otherwise.

"You sure you want to give this to Bean?" He passed the spoon to the witch, stomach turning as a sense of foreboding replaced his previous annoyance.

Everyone knew how dangerous an improvised potion could be. Just the slightest miscalculation and... well, it was best not to think about the many ways that this could go wrong.

Beatrice looked at the familiar. "You trust me, don't you?"

The bilby nodded. A long, thin tongue wiggled out of his mouth, licking at the air in anticipation.

Oliver closed one eye and crossed his fingers.

Beatrice brought the spoon to Bean's mouth. He licked it for a few seconds, then his eyes glazed over.

The bilby's tongue withdrew. He rocked on the edge of the cauldron, threatening to fall in.

Finally, an image appeared in the air above his head.

It was Tabitha, sitting in the chair of her study. They watched from Bean's perspective, seeing everything he did from his perch on the desk.

Oliver grabbed Beatrice's shoulder. He couldn't believe it. Her potion had actually worked. He owed her an apology.

In the vision above the familiar, Tabitha rested the file in her hand down on the table. When she turned back, a slash appeared in her throat.

But there was no sign of the knife and no sign of another person. Just an empty space where the killer should've been.

11

BEATRICE

"I knew this wouldn't work." Oliver groaned and ran his hand over his head.

Beatrice registered the motion in the back of her mind. Her focus remained on the memory, still playing above the familiar's head.

In the vision, Bean leaped from the table to Tabitha's lap. He inspected the slash in her neck and waited for a few minutes, likely for the banshee. But when there was no sign of her, the familiar left to chase after the killer.

He ran down a single flight of steps before encountering a pair of boots in the passage. Their owner picked him up, and Oliver's face swam into view.

"Oh great, so your spell picked me up, but not the actual killer." The warlock's voice grew loud and annoyed.

The memory vanished and Bean's eyes cleared. The familiar shook his head and dropped back onto all four paws. He raced along the edge of the cauldron and jumped into Beatrice's hands.

"Are you okay?" She rubbed one of his large ears, feeling

the familiar tremble. It wasn't a memory he'd enjoyed experiencing.

"You're lucky he didn't explode," Oliver said. "Can we please just go to the Malices now and get a proper expulsion spell?"

What was he talking about? "I just performed one."

"Obviously not a good one." Oliver scoffed and looked around the room for his jacket and scarf. "We couldn't see the killer."

The warlock stormed over to the table where he'd dropped his things and shoved an arm through Albert's coat. He tossed the scarf over his neck.

A scarf that let him turn invisible.

"We saw exactly what Bean did that night."

Oliver turned toward her, leaving his scarf untied. "What are you suggesting?"

He knew full well what she meant. "The killer was invisible."

The warlock's eyes narrowed. "You're reaching, Beatrice. Your potion failed, and you just can't accept it. Even I know Tabitha didn't allow your coven to purchase anything from mine. You really think there's a witch that would've had both an invisibility spell and access to the Blackwell Estate?"

"We know at least one."

Oliver froze. His voice was quiet, but hard enough to cut glass. "You think I killed Tabitha."

It was an easy conclusion to reach. An invisible assailant slashed Tabitha's throat, and a moment later, a Wyrmwood appeared. Two and two was almost always four.

But Beatrice wouldn't be accusing just some Wyrmwood. This was Oliver.

The boy who'd spent half of the summer with them for the past eight years. The boy who wouldn't break the rules and use magic in the Pentacular Chapel. The boy who'd saved her when she was eleven years old.

Of course, Beatrice didn't think Oliver was guilty. But why didn't he have the same faith in her? Why couldn't he trust her when she told him that her spell had worked?

"Wow. You really do." The hard edge dropped from Oliver's voice. It cracked and trembled.

He turned away before Beatrice could see his expression, but she knew that her hesitation had stung him more than he'd admit.

"Oliver, I didn't—" she called after him, but he was already on a broomstick, disappearing up the stairs. "Wait!"

She ran to the corner of the room where she'd leaned her own broom. Bean jumped onto it with her, and they chased after the warlock. Unfortunately, broomstick racing had never been Beatrice's thing.

Oliver disappeared into the darkness at the top of the stairs. There was a flash of light as he opened the cupboard door. A heavy thud followed.

What was that?

Beatrice didn't bother to get off her broom. She flew straight into the kitchen.

Oliver lay face down in the center of the floor, a stream of blood trickling from his forehead into the grooves of the white tiles. Beside him, sitting in her wheelchair, blowing the last specks of blue dust off her open palm, was Gigi.

Beatrice almost fell off her broom.

"Something told me to come home early," the old woman said, patting her hands together and closing her eyes to avoid the dust.

Beatrice watched the magic powder float to the floor, and her breath caught. "What did you do to him?"

"Don't tell me you're worried about the boy who killed our Matriarch," Gigi snapped at her granddaughter, glaring at her with a piercing green gaze. "It's sleeping powder. I purchased some from Elle."

Beatrice climbed off her broom, able to breathe again. "He's bleeding. Do we have something to patch him up?"

Gigi's eyes narrowed. "A cut on the head is nothing compared to what this boy has coming if he's found guilty."

There was something ominous about the old woman's tone.

"The coven will want him to suffer for what he's done. They'll be here for him soon."

"You called them?" Beatrice stared at her grandmother in disbelief.

Gigi rubbed her nose with the back of her hand, careful to avoid the powder. "Why're you looking at me like that? It was your idea. I thought you'd be happy. Once you turn in Oliver, the coven will welcome you with open arms. Just give them a story about how you lured him here."

Beatrice's eyes flicked to the old landline on the counter beside her grandmother. "Right now?"

Gigi shrugged, picked up the phone, and wheeled it over to her.

Hands trembling, Beatrice dialed.

A deep voice answered on the other end.

12

OLIVER

Oliver awoke with a sharp searing pain on the side of his forehead and the twang of eighties guitar in the background. He cracked an eye open and found himself staring out a car's window.

Residential homes gave way to large art deco style buildings, then a classic Victorian manor before returning to high-rise apartments. The architectural disaster was an obvious sign that he was still within Castor's Grove, but it wasn't a part of the city Oliver recognized.

He groaned and pushed himself away from the glass.

"Finally." A deep voice snorted from beside him.

Oliver turned to the vehicle's driver.

He was a man with broad shoulders, a mop of curls, and a prominent brow.

Oliver was confident that he'd never encountered him before in his entire life, which begged the question: *why am I currently in a car with him?*

The last thing Oliver remembered was Beatrice accusing him of murder. For some reason, her losing faith in him had hurt worse than anything so far. He'd flown up the stairs, suddenly desperate to be alone. But had he made it to the kitchen?

Something silver rattled in the cupholder of the dashboard. Oliver lifted it. A wolf's head had been pressed into the metal of a large silver pin. Beneath, in bold capital letters shone the word *SERGEANT*.

"You're with the Castor's Police." Oliver was beginning to understand what had happened.

Beatrice had turned him in.

Oliver laughed, chest tight. The situation was funny in a pathetic kind of way. After all, a girl who'd had a crush on him for years thought he was capable of murder. What did that say about his character?

The werewolf sergeant shot him a look. Oliver swallowed the manic laughter before more escaped. He must have looked insane.

"I'm Sergeant Amos," the driver introduced himself. He took one hand off the steering wheel and lowered his radio before returning to the recommended ten-and-two position. "You're a hard man to find, Mr. Wyrmwood. We sent out a lot of PSAs, on Castor and Grover channels. Why didn't you come down to the station?"

The car stopped at a red light. Oliver considered opening the door and jumping out but decided against it for a few very good reasons: he suspected the child lock was on, doubted he could outrun a werewolf, and had no interest in angering the police further.

"I had no idea you were looking for me, Sergeant," Oliver said, deciding to play dumb and innocent. "I don't watch much television."

Amos snorted. "Or speak with your family and friends.

Cut the crap kid, you know why you're here. Tabitha Black-well was murdered three minutes prior to the time you were scheduled to meet. And eyewitnesses report seeing you running from the estate. But listen, I'm not judging. Maybe you had a good reason for getting rid of the old witch. Heavens knows the Blackwells aren't known for their generosity of spirit."

Does he really think playing the understanding cop is going to get me to confess? Like I haven't seen that technique in a dozen shows.

Not that it mattered. Oliver was innocent, and no matter what he said, no one was going to believe him. Maybe it would be better if he just went to prison. Perhaps the Blackwells would consider that punishment enough and leave the rest of his coven alone.

One of the purple cubes that marked the Castor's Police Force Buildings appeared on their right. Oliver waited for the sergeant to slow and turn into the lot.

Amos sped right past it.

That didn't make sense.

Oliver watched the cube shrink in the rearview mirror.

Maiden, Mother, and Crone! Where was the officer taking him if not to one of the police stations? Ironvault, a prison exclusively for Castors, was to the North, and they were traveling West, toward a more rural section of the city. Oliver had heard stories of corrupt officers beating people to death on the edge of the woods out there.

It would be very much on brand for one of the Black-wells to bribe a policeman to murder Oliver.

Which meant convincing Amos of his innocence might well be a matter of life and death.

"The banshee was late. Whoever killed Tabitha met

with her just before I did. Check her agenda and you'll find the real killer."

Amos kept driving West. "What agenda?"

"The one on her desk." Oliver distinctly remembered the banshee reading from it. "Isn't that how you know what time our meeting was?"

"The estate's executor gave us a copy of her day's schedule from his notes. Is that what you mean?"

"No, that's not—Wilburn?"

Amos nodded. "That's the one."

Oliver could've slapped himself. He was such a fool. How had he missed the obvious before? He'd told Beatrice that no Blackwell would have been able to turn invisible, but that wasn't true. Tabitha would never have provided the funds necessary to purchase a Wyrmwood spell, but it wasn't unheard of for warlocks to pursue careers beyond their coven. Wilburn was a lawyer, with his own independent source of income.

"He's the killer. Wilburn got something from my mother just before I went inside. It must've been an invisibility spell. That's why we couldn't see him."

Beatrice's potion had worked after all. Oliver might feel guilty for doubting her if she hadn't handed him over to a corrupt police officer.

"By *we*, are you referring to yourself and Beatrice Blackwell?"

"Yeah. Why?"

"What exactly is your relationship?"

"Nothing. She's my friend's sister." Oliver waved away the question. "Are you listening to me about the other stuff? Wilburn's guilty. I'm innocent. Take me to a station. I'll give a statement."

A dark expression crossed the werewolf's face. "Sorry, kid, but I'm afraid I can't do that. The Blackwells want you in their custody, and they're willing to pay a ridiculous amount to have someone deliver you. More than most people can resist."

13
BEATRICE

That evening, Beatrice was even more of a pariah among her coven than usual.

Throughout the service, she caught family members giving her dark looks from the corners of their eyes, whispering to companions with murderous expressions. It sent shivers through her arms and made the hairs stand on alert. She worried what might happen during the wake.

But the Blackwells wouldn't attack one of their own, even a barely-Blackwell. Instead, Beatrice flitted through the moonlit gravestones like a walking witch-repellant. Every time she drew close to a group, they dispersed, scattering in the wind like the falling snow.

And she didn't even have Bean for company. Attending the funeral would've been too risky for the familiar, and at any rate, she'd sent him on another task.

Underneath the long branches of a leafless hickory tree, another solitary figure kicked the snow with his shoes and stared down at his phone screen, desperately tapping it to

try to make the technology work despite the magical inter-
ference.

Beatrice approached her brother. "Any word from
Oliver?"

Albert's thick eyebrows lowered as he glared at her.
"No, and there won't be any. You betrayed him."

That wasn't true.

"I saved him." No one was around, but she leaned in
and whispered just the same. "Gigi wanted to hand him
over to the coven."

"That's exactly what you've done. You just took a more
roundabout approach that's still made everyone hate you."
Albert scoffed and began tapping at the screen with such
force that it was a wonder it didn't shatter. "You're stupid,
but you're not naïve. You must know half the police are on a
Blackwell payroll."

Beatrice wrapped her arms around herself, hugging her
red winter jacket tighter around her dress. There was a nip
to the air, but it wasn't the cold that bothered her. With no
official Matriarch, Wilburn controlled the coven and its
purse.

What if Sergeant Amos is working for him?

But there was no sense panicking about it now. Beatrice
had taken precautions. She had a plan.

Solve the murder. Save Oliver. Get the grimoire.

Not necessarily in that order.

"Don't worry about Oliver. I'm handling things," Beatrice assured her brother.

Albert turned to her, his green eyes cold. "Is that what
you call this? The coven is going to kill Oliver, and it will be
your fault."

Beatrice's breath felt suddenly trapped in her chest. She
hugged herself tighter, and her lips started to tremble. She

wanted to scream at her brother for being cruel and not trusting her. But if she made a scene at the wake, it would only infuriate the coven more. Instead, she turned and stormed off.

A witch's wake consisted of a curious mixture of mourning and revelry. Coven members wept and prayed to the crone before Tabitha's tomb. Others crowded the refreshments table to boast of the offerings they'd left. And in another section, two young witches—Bailey and Mae— had gotten the idea to display colorful, smoke-crafted visions.

Beatrice slowed to watch. Bailey caught her looking and nudged Mae. The smoke shifted to show Oliver being ripped apart limb by limb. Beatrice covered her mouth, swallowing and willing herself not to throw up.

Someone grabbed her shoulder and turned her away from the display. "Our coven can be so barbaric at times, can't they?"

Beatrice's older cousin, Rett stood before her. He offered a sympathetic smile. It might even have been genuine. Impossible to say with Rett. Gigi used to joke that he could talk straw into gold.

The twenty-one-year-old was the son of Beatrice's Aunt Elba, her father's older sister. Tall and gaunt with sand-colored hedgehog spikes for hair, only Rett's eyes—a brilliant, striking green—matched with the rest of the coven. But it made no difference to his popularity. What Rett lacked in fat, he made up for in brains.

As a child, Beatrice had considered his word to be law. They all had. She'd been so jealous when Rett would take his brother, Albert, and Oliver off on imaginary adventures and leave her behind with Elle. Then, Rett had grown up, recognized the insignificance of a Wyrmwood and a barely-

Blackwell, and added Elle to his retinue instead. Everything he'd done since set him up to be one of the most eligible warlocks in Castor's Grove—charming their relatives, working in the Blackwell greenhouse, and studying actuarial science at university so he could follow in his father's highly lucrative footsteps. Rett hid it, but his ego must have been massive.

"I heard you helped the police catch Oliver," another voice said. A round face with rounder eyes and ruddy pink cheeks popped out from behind Rett's shoulder—his brother, Gabriel. "That was clever."

"Thanks," Beatrice said. She appreciated someone finally agreeing that she'd made the right choice, but it might have felt better had it been someone else.

Rett had stolen all the brains and charm and left none for his younger brother. Gabriel was good-natured but dullwitted. He still followed his older brother with almost fanatical devotion. He wasn't the only one.

"Where's your other lackey?" Beatrice asked, turning her head to search for Elle.

"She's—" Gabriel started to answer, but Rett slapped his brother's chest.

"You're funny, B." Rett moved his arm from her shoulder. "But if anything, it's the other way around. Elle might be in charge of all of us soon." He winked, then whispered something to his brother before disappearing into the crowd.

Gabriel's shoulders fell, likely disappointed to be left behind. He looked at Beatrice. "I saw the banshee crossing the Estate on the night Tabitha died. Want me to tell you about her?"

"Oh, um..." It was sweet that her cousin wasn't avoiding her like everyone else. But Beatrice had already heard from

Albert how attractive the banshee was rumored to be. She didn't need a description from the source.

And Beatrice was significantly more curious about Rett's last comment.

"I have to go to the bathroom." She smiled through the lie and patted Gabriel's shoulder. "But before we separate, does Elle want to be the next Matriarch?"

"She has the card," Gabriel muttered, somehow managing to stare through Beatrice instead of at her. "But don't tell Wilburn. He'll force her to give it to Linda."

That's impossible. How could Elle have the card when it was still safely in Beatrice's basement? Maybe Gabriel must've made a mistake.

"Our secret." Beatrice linked her pinky with her cousin, then wandered deeper into the graveyard in the direction that Rett had vanished. She suspected that Elle would be with him, and Beatrice suddenly felt it vital that they speak.

Around the back of the Pentacular Chapel, the crowds thinned, the sky darkened, and the gravestones blurred with moss and age. Here were some of the oldest tombs in Castor's Grove, dating back three hundred years to the founding of the city. Stone gargoyles and marble statues guarded their slumber.

"It wants leaves. You just need to feel the summer warmth within you." Rett's voice drifted on the wind through the tombs.

Beatrice crouched behind a sculpture of a griffin. When she peeped under the wing, she could just make out Rett and Elle amid the graves ahead. They were staring at a maple.

"It's freezing cold," Elle snapped. "I can't imagine it's summer when there's snow falling on my nose."

"Of course, you can." Rett's tone was soothing. He held

out his hands as if trying to comfort her. "Just close your eyes and—"

"Stop it! I'm telling you, I can't! Gabriel was right. I should never have lied about the antidote. About any of it. This whole situation is a mess."

Rett reached forward and tried to comfort her, then suddenly, their heads whipped toward Beatrice.

Crap. How did they see me?

But it wasn't her.

A tall, beautiful blonde, dressed in a loose white gown and heels despite the snow, stepped out from among the tombs. Her hair streamed behind her, blowing in the opposite direction to the wind.

She looked down at Beatrice with prismatic eyes and a bored expression. "Blackwell coven, correct?"

Beatrice nodded.

"In the future, try to stay on the estate when there's a murderer on the loose. Makes you a lot easier to find." The banshee massaged her throat for a moment, before muttering further objections. "And a graveyard, really? I mean, how macabre. And gross. I thought I saw a rat earlier and almost ran. Luckily, it was just a shadow, so I've stuck around to warn you after all."

Beatrice stared at her. *Does she mean—*

The banshee opened her mouth and let loose a loud, mournful wail that sucked the strength from the witch's body.

—someone else is going to be killed.

14
OLIVER

It was difficult to tell what time it was.

Oliver pulled the dark cloth away from the window to catch a glimpse of outside.

"Come away from there."

He turned back to Amos. The sergeant sat on a plastic chair, shoveling noodles into his mouth straight from the takeaway container.

Not that there was much choice. The small, dusty apartment lacked anything as fancy as a plate. A few plastic forks and spoons in a pair of drawers, an old drip coffee maker, and a small, whirring mini fridge represented the kitchen in the studio apartment. Beyond that, a plastic chair provided seating beside a narrow bed, which worked double-time as the sergeant's table.

Oliver's eyes narrowed as a bit of sauce dropped from Amos' fork onto the corner of the sheet. At least now he knew the source of the bed's orange stains.

"You really think the Blackwells are trying that hard to find me?" Oliver asked. He crossed the small space and searched the pair of drawers, hoping to find a napkin.

Amos wiped his mouth with the back of his sleeve, making Oliver's search moot. "Themselves? Probably not. But I told you, there's a generous reward for anyone who brings you in."

Oliver nodded. The sergeant had explained the situation in more detail when they'd arrived at the safehouse. There had been several incidents the past few days, nothing serious yet—a warlock with a head injury from a bar fight, a witch cursed with misfortune, a small fire in a cauldron store—but the Wyrmwood coven were the afflicted party in every instance.

Amos' theory was that people were targeting them in an attempt to get information on Oliver's whereabouts. Unfortunately, *people* included Castor's Police officers.

"And my family?" Oliver had asked Amos about bringing them to the safe house with him.

"Still can't find them." The sergeant crumpled the empty container in his hands, pressing it into a ball. "Think they've gone into hiding on their own."

Or they'd had the misfortune of encountering an officer with less integrity than Amos and were in the hands of the Blackwells all like now. Oliver's chest tightened at the thought.

The sergeant tossed his empty container toward the trash can near the door. It fell in, and Amos grinned, turning to Oliver.

"What about the agenda?"

The sergeant's smile fell.

"If you get it, you can solve the case, and then the Blackwells will leave my coven alone."

Amos sighed and wiped his hands on his knees. "You're putting a lot of faith in an old lady's calendar."

Oliver frowned. The term *old lady* seemed rather lacking

when talking about the former Matriarch of one of the most powerful covens in the city.

"I've put in a request for a search warrant of the estate. If that comes through not even the Blackwells can..."

Oliver stopped listening. He knew perfectly well what *if* meant.

"Let me go," Oliver said, interrupting the sergeant. "If you can get me past the gates, I can find the agenda. Maybe even the knife Wilburn used to kill Tabitha."

Amos raised his eyebrows and stood. "I don't think bringing in the murder weapon is going to convince anyone of your innocence."

"But you could run tests on it, couldn't you?" Oliver said, his mind running with the idea. "There are witches in your department. You must have ways to trace the weapon back to the killer. If I could find it, you could prove Wilburn is the murderer."

Amos' prominent brow furrowed for a moment. He shook his head. "What you're suggesting is illegal. Even if you're right, the evidence would be inadmissible, and I could lose my job. And you know what'll happen if the Blackwells catch you on their property? Nah. It's too risky. Eat the noodles I brought you, and leave solving the case to the police."

He put a hand on Oliver's shoulder and guided the warlock to the now unoccupied plastic chair.

Oliver tried to resist. He didn't want to sit down and eat cheap takeout. His family were in danger. If he didn't clear his name and fix things, who would? Amos seemed decent enough, minus his poor table manners, but even the sergeant hadn't trusted the Castor's Police enough to take Oliver to the station.

"Eat." Amos forced Oliver onto the seat and shoved the

container of noodles into his hands. The sergeant raised his eyebrows in an almost paternalistic expression. A lecture was incoming.

A knock at the door saved Oliver.

Amos' body straightened and broadened. His eyes burned with a sudden amber light beneath the brown. When he opened his mouth, his canines had grown large and ferocious.

He pushed Oliver onto the floor behind the bed. The noodles spilled beside him.

"Stay down," the sergeant mouthed. He put a clawed finger to his lips and went to the door.

Oliver's heart pounded. Who was on the other side? A corrupt policeman who'd followed Amos? A hitman ordered by the Blackwells?

"Nice to see you again, Sergeant! I trust Oliver is still in the safehouse where you brought him last night."

Beatrice?

Relief flooded Oliver. He almost smiled, then he caught himself. He refused to be excited about Beatrice Blackwell of all people. She'd accused him of murder and handed him over to the police.

Of course, Oliver had been a bit of an ass. Her enchantment had worked and instead of being grateful, he'd acted like a fool. If he'd stopped to think for one minute, he'd have remembered the exchange between his mother and Wilburn.

Did he owe Beatrice an apology, a thank-you, or both?

But there was an even more pressing question.

"How in the name of Selene did you find this place?" Amos demanded.

There was a squeak, followed by a giggle.

"Bean drove in the car with you last night. I sent him to keep an eye on Oliver. So, where is he? In the bathroom?"

Oliver sighed and pushed himself up from behind the bed. He waved.

A relieved grin spread over Beatrice's face. The expression emphasized her cheeks, making them even rounder. Oliver hated to admit, but with her pink hoodie and high ponytail, the witch actually looked cute. Bean sitting on her shoulder and twitching his ears didn't hurt.

Somehow, Beatrice managed to barge past Amos and into the apartment. She ran her finger over one of the drawers, frowned, and then noticed the mess on the floor beside Oliver.

"Advantages of a familiar," Amos muttered, rubbing his hand over his forehead. When he turned, his eyes and teeth looked normal again. "Shame you've got loftier things ahead. You and the rodent would make an impressive addition to the police department."

"Bean's a marsupial," Beatrice corrected him. "But, yes, I daresay we would."

Oliver rolled his eyes. The last thing Beatrice needed was compliments on her stalking capabilities. He didn't want her honing those talents.

Or maybe I do. If Amos was corrupt, Bean might've been able to help me escape.

It was seeming increasingly likely that he owed Beatrice that apology.

The sergeant's phone buzzed in his pocket. He pulled it out, then glanced at the two teenagers before him. "I have to step out for a second and take this. Don't..." He trailed off, apparently uncertain what precisely it was that they weren't to do.

Once Amos left, Beatrice knelt on the floor before Oliver. The position struck him as far too suggestive. He had a vivid recollection of her body pressed against his in a cramped closet and jumped back, only to hit his head against the wall.

Bean gave him a funny look before bouncing from Beatrice's shoulder onto the floor. The familiar sniffed the noodles, and his nose wrinkled in distaste.

"Can probably salvage some of it," the witch said, for once not paying attention to Oliver. She set the container straight, holding the edges to avoid getting sauce on her fingers, and attempted to scoop the noodles with the plastic fork.

Now she's helping me clean?

Yeah, there was no way Oliver could avoid it.

He crouched on the floor next to her and swallowed his pride. "Thanks, B. Not for cleaning up noodles, or I mean, not just for the noodles. For the memory expulsion, and sending Bean to look after me even though you thought I was a murderer, and—"

"I never thought that. I was upset because you didn't think my potion worked."

"It did, though!" Oliver admitted. "And it's helped me crack the whole case."

"Oh? That's good to hear." She stopped cleaning the noodles and looked up at him. The dangerous flash of an idea sharpened her eyes. Her face was incredibly close. "So you sort of owe me a favor, right?"

Oliver pressed his lips together and leaned back, trying to put as much distance between them as the small room would allow.

Beatrice moved closer again.

Oliver's mind flashed back to the cupboard in the Pentacular Chapel, then further into the past. He recalled a thirteen-year-old Beatrice hanging mistletoe around her house. And the realization struck him: *She's going to ask me to kiss her.*

He'd refuse, of course. Albert would kill him. And it wasn't like kissing Beatrice had ever been on Oliver's own personal to-do list.

But I do owe her.

And really, there were worse requests she could make. Beatrice was annoying, but not unattractive. It had taken all his effort in the cupboard not to react to the feeling of her pressed against him—soft in all the right places and smelling like vanilla.

Beatrice had unzipped the top of her hoodie revealing the top of a white shirt beneath. Her necklines kept sneaking lower. Not that Oliver was paying attention. He really wasn't.

Suddenly hot, Oliver brought his eyes up to hers. He waited for the question he was certain would come.

Or maybe the witch wouldn't bother asking. Beatrice's face drew closer. She tilted her head. Their cheeks brushed, and she whispered in his ear, "I think I know a way into the Blackwell Estate."

15
OLIVER

Beatrice waited for him before a large delivery truck with the letters VGF stamped on the side. The wind blew her long, dark hair, and the sunlight caught the strands, highlighting a dozen different shades of brown. Despite the sprinkling of snow, she wore no coat, only a traditional witch's dress, pink and lacy. The neckline formed a low V-shape, revealing the pale skin of her cleavage, pushed together in its center.

She caught him staring and giggled.

Oliver pulled his eyes up to her lips. They were pink like her dress.

"Are you ready?" The keys appeared in Beatrice's hand, and she spun them around her finger.

"Wait, you're driving?" That didn't make any sense. Weren't they supposed to sneak in? How could Beatrice have the keys?

"Or you could." She stepped forward, a smile playing on her face. "If you prefer to be in control."

"Well, it'd be safer than trusting you with it. Do you even

have a license?" It seemed like the kind of thing that Oliver should know.

"I'll give you the keys. But you have to give me something first." Beatrice waved the keys, then tapped her lips with one of them.

Now that gesture, Oliver understood.

"Fine. But only to get the keys." He stepped forward and pushed Beatrice against the truck. She stepped onto the bottom of the wheel, giving herself an extra few inches of height so that their bodies pressed together the way they had in the Chapel's closet.

The witch tilted her head back, smile still playing on her pink lips.

Oliver leaned forward and kissed her.

It should've been short and quick.

But for some reason, he didn't pull away.

Suddenly, he was looking at the scene as a third-party observer. Oliver saw one of his hands tangle in Beatrice's hair. The other pinned her wrists to the truck. Her body rippled against his in excited waves.

The witch's eyes opened, and her gaze turned toward Oliver. Not the him who was making out with her, but the disembodied him watching.

It made absolutely no sense, because—

———

Oliver's eyes sprang open seconds before his alarm sounded.

It was morning, but the covers on the safe house's windows made it impossible to tell.

He rubbed his eyes. Behind his lids, images from his dream taunted him.

Damn it.

What was wrong with him? Was he really such a guy that feeling Beatrice pressed against him one time in a closet had him thinking about her like this? Or was it the fact that he'd struggled to find her annoying yesterday? She'd helped him clean and come up with a plan. He'd actually enjoyed her company.

But that made it one time out of five million.

Oliver definitely blamed their time in the Chapel for the dream. He flung himself out of bed, flicked on the dim overhead bulb, and wandered toward the sink. He tossed water on his face and recoiled at the cold.

But it was the shock he needed.

Beatrice is Albert's annoying little sister. I have my own family to worry about.

There was an old rag beside the sink, but Oliver would sooner let the water freeze on his nose than put that on his skin. Instead, he went to the apartment's single drawer, where his clothes were folded. He grabbed a shirt and wiped his face.

It was only when he went to put it back down that Oliver noticed something missing.

16

BEATRICE

Beatrice leaned against the smooth white wall in the alley outside of Very Good Food. The winter wind whipped from the East, but the buildings acted as a shield, making her unseasonably warm. She'd unclasped the buttons on her red winter jacket and pushed her hair to one side, letting it fall over one shoulder. Bean's head peeped out the pocket of her coat, watching for Oliver's arrival.

"You won't be able to see him," Beatrice reminded the familiar, scratching his head with a red gloved finger before returning her attention to the latest copy of *Witch Whisper*. It was full of rumors about the Blackwells, which was nothing unusual. The gossip magazine loved to invent stories about the wealthy coven.

What was new, however, was Beatrice being mentioned.

She read and re-read the passage, smile growing larger each time, she returned to the beginning: *According to some sources, this murder mystery might actually be a romance.*

*That's right readers, Mr. Wyrmwood's motive was actually love
for none other than coven outsider Beatrice Blackwell.*

The magazine offered a thrilling description of an illicit,
forbidden love affair between Beatrice and Oliver, which
Tabitha had discovered. The warlock had murdered the
Matriarch either because she refused to allow them to wed,
or because she was going to banish him from the city, or—
the most titillating—because she intended to have Oliver
killed to put an end to the romance for good.

It was all complete nonsense, of course. But that didn't
make Beatrice delight in the story any less.

Bean squeaked, and Beatrice looked up from the
magazine.

Oliver stalked toward them in an oversized tan trench
coat that fell past his knees. With his shadow of a beard and
intense gaze, he reminded her of a sexy detective from a cop
movie.

But why can I see him?

"Why aren't you invisible?" Beatrice rolled the magazine up and shoved it into her jacket. "Where's your scarf?
Is it in your pocket? Why aren't you wearing it?"

Oliver watched her lips while she spoke. He blinked,
shook his head, and stepped backward, leaning against the
opposite wall as if trying to maximize the distance between
them. "Amos confiscated it. He left a note. I think he overheard
us planning this yesterday and thought this would stop us."

"It does," Beatrice said, pulling her phone out and
checking the time. "The delivery truck is going to leave here
in ten minutes. We can't sneak on if we're not invisible."

"You don't have a backup plan? What happened to all
your magical prowess? Even I'd have thought to bring a
forgetting potion."

That was one of the Wyrmwood coven's specialties. Although the Castor's Government provided official amnesiac powder for its citizens to use on Grovers who accidentally witnessed an act of magic, the substance was taxed and heavily monitored. To purchase more, Castors had to file reports explaining what happened to their previous supply. There was a branch of law enforcement dedicated to investigating the powder's misuse.

The Wyrmwoods' forgetting potions had no such checks and balances, which made them popular with a certain sort. However, they were also more volatile and difficult to control. A sip could erase more than intended.

Beatrice couldn't believe that Oliver would even suggest it. "We can't use magic on someone without their consent."

"Except when it presents a direct threat. I'm familiar with the rule. Still, didn't stop your grandmother from bombing me with a sleeping spell."

Before Beatrice could defend Gigi, the warlock sighed and leaned his head back. The dark circles stood out underneath his red-rimmed eyes.

Has he been getting any sleep?

"Look, you're right. I'm not saying we attack a human. But there has to be a way to get into the Blackwell Estate. Proving my innocence is a matter of life and death."

Beatrice cast her eyes down to her boots. *How could I judge him for being willing to use illegal magic when my coven is attacking his?*

"You're right. I'm sorry," she said. "I should've come more prepared."

Oliver's tired eyes grew alert. He stared at Beatrice, expression unreadable.

"But I can fix it," she said quickly, just in case he was about to admonish her. "I have an idea."

It wasn't a lie. She really did. Beatrice just didn't like it.

———

The Very Good Food van was undoubtedly breaking a number of city regulations. It was parked around the back of the building beside a large black garbage bin. The missing mirror on its passenger side suggested that it hadn't been quite narrow enough to fit through the alley.

"Maybe we should just threaten to alert the police if they don't help us," Beatrice suggested, peeping out from behind the corner to study the van.

"You catch more flies with honey," Oliver said. "Relax. Your original idea is good. How do I look?"

Beatrice turned to study the warlock.

He'd unbuttoned his coat and pulled the baggy sweater beneath tighter by tucking it into his pants. If that didn't make his muscles obvious, the rolled-up sleeves revealing his forearms left no doubt.

Beatrice's body grew warm staring at the warlock. She pulled her eyes up to his face and smiled, trying to act more relaxed than she felt. "Good."

"And you're sure she seemed interested the other day?" Oliver sounded far too pleased by the idea. "Oh, she's here. Wish me luck."

Beatrice scowled. She would do no such thing.

As Oliver walked toward the van, Beatrice hid behind the corner

Their waitress from before, Kenya, had stepped outside. She had her curls pulled back in a short ponytail again, but she'd taken off the Very Good Food apron. Even her thick winter pants couldn't hide a sculpted pair of legs. She smiled at Oliver as he approached, and her teeth looked extra bright and perfect against her dark skin.

If she falls for him, I'll have no one to blame but myself.

But Beatrice couldn't save every girl from Oliver. She'd tried her best while he was at Dashmoor, but he'd still broken more hearts than he realized. Warlocks were notorious for short-term flings. Given the frequency of arranged marriages in covens, the behavior typically got a pass. They weren't expected to find anything serious on their own. But human girls didn't know that. Beatrice had hated watching Oliver flirt and charm their classmates, but it had been even worse when they'd broken up. She'd lost count of how many of his exes—though some barely qualified given the length of the relationship—had come sobbing to her after.

Oliver leaned against the van with the bottom of his boot against the door. His hand combed through his curls, and he lowered his head in a gesture that seemed shy until you saw his smile—wicked and confident. It hinted at all the things he could do to a girl.

That smile—disarming and alluring and oh so suggestive—had haunted Beatrice far too many nights when she lay in bed. But she only knew it because Oliver had used the same move on over half the girls in their high school.

The waitress appeared equally susceptible to its effect. Kenya twirled the pencil behind her ear, pulled it out, and brought it to her lips.

Oh, please don't tell me she's going to start sucking it!

The waitress froze, eraser poised at the corner of her mouth. Her eyes locked onto Beatrice.

Crap!

Kenya's demeanor changed at once. She stepped away

from Oliver, extended her arm, and pointed her pencil at Beatrice.

The warlock reached forward, trying to reassure the waitress. But it was too late. Kenya pushed his arm away and opened the driver's door.

Forget Oliver flirting their way into the delivery van. They needed a new strategy.

"Wait," Beatrice shouted, running out from behind the corner. She threw herself at the open door, blocking the waitress' path with outstretched arms.

"What are you doing?" Kenya tried and failed to step around Beatrice. "Look, if this is a robbery, there's cash inside the restaurant. That'll be a much easier target than those rich people's mansion. Trust me, they're creepy. Especially those twins." She shuddered and pressed her hand to her forehead.

The waitress must have meant Debby and Libby. The two looked similar enough that they were often mistaken as twins, and they were certainly petty enough to scare a Grover. But Beatrice didn't have time to worry about what her cousins had done to upset Kenya.

"No, we're not thieves," Beatrice said, lifting Bean up and holding him before the waitress. "I'm a Blackwell, remember. That's my family."

The familiar gave a squeak of support.

Kenya's expression softened at the sight of the bilby. She took Bean and scratched under his chin, but her eyes narrowed at Beatrice. "If that's true, then why is your friend trying to convince me to smuggle him inside?"

Beatrice met Oliver's gaze over the waitress' shoulder. He opened his mouth and waved his hand for a few seconds, eyes growing more anxious. Clearly, inventing a believable excuse was up to her.

"Because we're in love," Beatrice said, stealing the idea from *Witch Whisper*. "My family don't approve of him, so they kicked me out. But all my stuff is still in there. We just need to go back to retrieve it."

Kenya raised an eyebrow. She crossed her arms and stepped back, turning her head to consider Oliver, then Beatrice. "You're telling me that you two are a couple? When he was just flirting with me? Yeah, sorry, not buying it."

"It's true," Oliver said, stepping forward suddenly. "She asked me to do that so we could get into the manor, but the truth is that we're together, and we're madly in love. Right, B?"

To Beatrice's surprise, he rested his hand on her chin and lifted her face toward his.

She stared up into his dark eyes, unable to respond.

What is he—?

The answer came before she could finish the thought. Oliver's lips crashed into hers.

Beatrice's body trembled; her mind grew giddy. All thoughts of the waitress, or the Blackwells, or the card in her sleeve vanished. Oliver consumed her senses.

He'd had coffee that morning. The taste lingered on his tongue as it flitted hesitantly into her mouth before growing bold. He smelled lightly of sweat, salty and earthy, and oddly delicious. His hand tangled in her hair, and his beard prickled her cheeks, sending shivers of excitement shooting through her skin and into her chest. She wrapped her arms around his shoulders, running her fingers over the strong, hard muscles and pressing her chest closer to his.

Then Oliver took control. One hand still tangled in her hair, he slipped the other beneath Beatrice's jacket, grabbed her waist, and pushed her against the van. Heat coursed through her as he deepened their kiss. Her tongue copied his movements. Oliver's fingers pressed against her hip, then his palm slid over her stomach and higher toward—

"Okay, okay, I believe you," Kenya said. "No need to start having sex against my van."

Oliver pulled away taking his hands with him. Beatrice could only stare. Her entire body felt hot. Her chest rose and fell in slow, heavy breaths. Her mind struggled to process what had happened.

Oliver Wyrmwood just kissed me.

True, it had only been to convince Kenya that they were dating. But he couldn't have faked that passion. He must have felt something.

Unless Beatrice's imagination was running wild again and her own desires were clouding her judgment.

"You two are lucky that I'm a sucker for a good romance," the waitress said.

"Wait. Does that mean—?" Beatrice's mind finally started to function. She straightened and turned to Kenya.

"This job is boring as hell. Might as well do something spontaneous." The waitress opened the back of the van. "So hurry and get in before I change my mind."

17

OLIVER

Beatrice's idea worked. The guards barely glanced in the back of the van and failed to notice the two stowaways, hiding in opposite corners beneath grease-stained tablecloths. Kenya drove through the gate and followed a long twisting road through the trees.

Oliver had intended to head straight to the manor, sneak through the servant entrance he'd used before, and search Tabitha's office for the agenda. Once he knew the identity of the killer, it would be easier to find evidence to condemn the guilty party and prove his own innocence.

However, Beatrice asked Kenya to let them out in the middle of the woods.

Oliver considered objecting. He saw no benefit to trekking through the mud. But given the past few days, he trusted Beatrice.

She might be almost as clever as she thinks.

Oliver glanced at the witch, a few paces ahead. There were no paths in the Blackwell woods, but she marched through the evergreens with a clear sense of direction. The wind flicked at the ends of her hair, the back of which was a tangled mess that he found strangely attractive.

Because I tangled it when I kissed her.

Oliver's stomach did an odd flip. His ears felt unusually hot considering the wind. The entire ride to the Blackwell Estate, he'd made a point not to think about the kiss.

He'd had to do it. The pretend romance had been Beatrice's idea. How else would they have convinced the waitress?

But did I have to enjoy it?

Beatrice's lips tasted like berries, no doubt the result of a flavored gloss. But that didn't explain why the rest of her mouth tasted sweet. She'd pressed her body closer to his, and Oliver had lost it. He'd wanted to feel all of her. Then her tongue had slipped into his mouth and his hands took on a life of their own. He'd forgotten that this wasn't just some girl who'd gotten him excited. It was Beatrice.

Albert is going to kill me.

Oliver had felt guilty enough realizing he'd had a dream about kissing his friend's sister. Now, he'd made it a hundred times worse by acting on it. And the memory wouldn't go away.

The breeze carried the scent of vanilla toward Oliver. Beatrice's hair had felt so soft between his fingers. He wanted to see how tangled it would be after—

Oliver forced his eyes toward the ground. He tried counting roots to distract himself until Beatrice's voice forced him to pay attention to her again.

"Here we are. The Blackwell Greenhouse," Beatrice announced, stopping before an opening in the trees and holding out her hand toward a large glass building full of greenery.

She was stating the obvious. But Oliver was too grateful for the distraction from his own thoughts to be annoyed.

"There's a wealth of ingredients in here and an assortment of other things," Beatrice explained as she went toward the door. "I doubt I'll have time to make a potion, but we can gather a few things to defend ourselves. I know, I should've packed beforehand, but there'll be more here than what Gigi has anyway."

The witch pricked her palm on a spike on the side of the wall, winced, then allowed her blood to drip onto the handle of the door. Somehow, she managed to talk through the entire ordeal, listing the many plants that Oliver could expect to encounter within.

He recognized almost none of the names.

The door swung open, and they entered, abandoning a wintery forest for a tropical jungle.

Heat engulfed Oliver, and the scents of a hundred different blooms overwhelmed him, making the air feel heavy and dangerous. He coughed and covered his mouth with a black-gloved hand. The other unzipped the heavy jacket.

Vines crept along the walls, leaves fell from the ceiling, and mosses glistened on the ground. Long rows of tables displayed pots full of wild shrubbery, bright flowers, and small trees full of curious multi-colored fruit. Amid the greenery were hints of iron and brass. Metal figurines, antique tools, and burnished plaques added to the décor.

"I also thought," Beatrice continued. "That given the array of items stored here, it might not be a bad place to hide—"

"A murder weapon," Oliver finished the sentence for her.

That is clever. If I find the weapon, I might actually have to give her a compliment.

They shed their extra layers of winter clothing and began hunting amid the plants. Bean scoured the back of the room, while Oliver and Beatrice searched near the front, him for the dagger and her for ingredients. The witch was by far the more successful. There didn't seem to be a single plant species in the greenhouse that didn't fascinate her.

"Look! This must be where Elle got the seawave root to make Gigi's sleeping potion." Beatrice plucked a deep blue leaf from the shrub before them. She rolled it between her thumb and forefinger, grinding it to dust. "You know, in nature, it can only be found underwater? It grows on reefs in the Caribbean. I always planned to travel there to see it if I... well, not that it matters."

Had Beatrice just stopped herself from talking?

Oliver looked up from a miniature replica of a silver spinning wheel he'd been examining. The sharp point of the spindle had drawn his eye, and he'd initially mistaken it for a weapon. "If you what?"

Beatrice pressed her lips together, cheeks pinker than normal. "Nothing. It's just this idea I had about going to different areas and doing magical outreach while seeing the world, or something."

I didn't know she wanted to travel.

Oliver's mouth opened as he searched for the correct response. The witch was constantly speaking. She must have hinted at this desire before. How could he not have known?

Because I normally make a point of not listening.

"I know, it's silly," the witch said, tucking a strand of hair behind her ear and turning back to the plants. "Don't worry. I've abandoned the idea."

She'd completely misinterpreted his silence.

Oliver hurried to reassure her as he rested the statue back on the table. "No, I don't think—"

"Stop!" Beatrice reached out and grabbed his hand, taking the spinning wheel from him. She pointed toward the table where he'd been about to rest it, right in the center of a tray of black mushrooms. "Those are deathcap. It would probably be fine just to touch, but why take the risk?"

"Right." Oliver glanced at the fungi, noticing the way the flesh rippled and bubbled, like there was something oozing under the surface. Beatrice's fear and the name were enough to let him know it was poison. Maybe he'd been too quick to remove his gloves.

But Beatrice's hands were bare. She inspected the plants without concern. It was annoyingly impressive. Oliver felt like a child, ignorant and out of his depth, beside the witch.

She's kind of incredible.

Oliver shook his head and slipped his gloves back on. He should not be thinking good things about Beatrice Blackwell. Oliver refocused his efforts on hunting for a dagger. A few steps later, his eyes landed on something else along the path. A plant he actually recognized.

"That's shadowmoss," Oliver said, stepping forward to identify it before Beatrice could. He tapped the deep green mass with the tip of his boot. "It grows deep beneath the city."

"And is a key ingredient in Wyrmwood invisibility spells."

Oliver's eyes widened, and his mouth dropped open as he stared at the witch. "How could you possibly know that?"

It didn't seem fair. The only reason Oliver himself knew was because he'd accidentally walked into his mother's potions den as a child and seen her adding it. Lucille had been careful to ensure that her son was never around when she crafted her family's most powerful spell thereafter.

"So I am right." Beatrice giggled and clapped her hands. "It was just a hunch. Don't worry, no need to tell me. I already know I'm brilliant."

Oliver's jaw tightened. But he appreciated Beatrice reminding him how conceited she was. He was worried he'd been starting to like her.

"It's amazing your ego can fit inside with all the plants," Oliver said, rolling his eyes and turning away.

"Oh, it's definitely a squeeze." Beatrice walked alongside Oliver and nudged him with her shoulder. "Come on, is it so bad to be aware of how awesome you are?"

"It is if you go around giving yourself compliments."

"Well, I wouldn't get any if I waited for other people."

The comment caught Oliver by surprise. He stopped a few feet before the greenhouse door and turned to the witch just in time to see a small, sad smile vanish from her face.

"Don't you ever compliment yourself?" Beatrice asked, facing him with her arms crossed beneath her chest. With her winter layers removed, she'd been left with only the white bell-sleeve shirt that Oliver had run his hand over earlier. It featured another distractingly low neckline.

Oliver's ears burned. He turned away, making an effort to roll his eyes. "Oh, all the time. I wake up every morning, stare in the mirror, and say, *Oliver you magnificent beast, the women of Castor's Grove are so lucky you're here.*"

Oliver was being sarcastic. He thought this was quite obvious.

But Beatrice didn't laugh.

"Well, you are ridiculously handsome," she said, shaking her head. "But you've got better qualities to compliment. You're brave and compassionate, and you help people when they need you. That's more impressive."

Oliver waited for Beatrice to burst out laughing. He was selfish and a coward. His first plan when things had gone wrong had been to run, abandon his family, and travel the world. And the thought of helping people with magical outreach as he went hadn't crossed his mind. The only thing he'd considered was how he'd save his own ass.

But Beatrice's expression remained serious and sincere.

"You're describing someone else," Oliver said. "That's not me."

The sad smile flickered over the witch's face again. "Hopefully, one day you'll stop telling yourself that."

The softness of her words hit harder than a scream. Oliver stared down at the plants by their feet, unable to meet her gaze. He'd always considered Beatrice's crush a nuisance, but suddenly, he felt unworthy of her interest.

I want to be, though.

Before Oliver could process what that thought meant, a shout came from near the door.

"Step away, miss!" One of the Blackwell guards, dressed in a crimson uniform with a cauldron stamped on the pocket, stormed into the greenhouse. "That's the murderer. He's back!"

In an instant, the man transformed into a leopard and leaped at Oliver.

18

BEATRICE

Beatrice had been worried something like this might happen. Most of the Blackwell guards were shifters who patrolled near the buildings. This one must have spotted them moving among the plants and come to investigate. Luckily, he didn't seem able to distinguish her from the rest of the coven.

Otherwise, he might have realized it was two against one and approached more cautiously.

Beatrice reached into the pockets of her sleeve and found the spindle she'd plucked from the spinning wheel. It was already coated with seawave dust. She closed her eyes, willing the enchantment into a makeshift weapon, and stepped in front of Oliver.

The leopard was already in midair, too late to stop, but he retracted his claws to avoid scratching a Blackwell.

Beatrice whipped the spindle out and stabbed between his eyes.

The shifter dropped to the ground, leopard skin retracting to reveal the human form of the guard. His chest rose and fell in the heavy rhythm of sleep.

"Maiden, mother, and crone." Oliver's hands made the shapes of the Three Moon Goddess. "How did you manage that? I thought you didn't have a sleeping potion."

"A very fast enchantment." Beatrice showed him the spindle. "We're lucky you found that spinning wheel. Now, strip."

The warlock's eyebrows rose. "Pardon?"

"Oh." Beatrice's face grew hot. It seemed so obvious to her that she'd forgotten to explain, but without the details, her comment might sound very different. "The guard. His clothes. You can put them on and sneak into the mansion, but first, you'll need to, you know."

A smile tugged on the corner of Oliver's lips. "Take mine off?"

"Albert's sweatshirt would look a bit bulky under the uniform."

"True." The warlock grabbed the bottom and pulled the fabric up. The bottom of his abdomen appeared, full of firm, chiseled muscles. His bronze skin glistened with sweat from the heat of the greenhouse. He paused, shirt halfway up. "Are you going to watch me?"

Oh crap! Beatrice was staring.

She closed her mouth and gave him her most innocent smile. "Of course not. Jeez, now who has an ego?"

He laughed as she turned to face the plants.

"Hey, can I ask you something?" Oliver's voice was muffled for a moment. Then, he tossed the gray sweatshirt onto the grass within Beatrice's line of sight. "I get the seawave root, but how did you think to grab the spindle?"

Is he joking?

Beatrice almost turned her head to look at the warlock to see, but she caught herself in time.

"She pricked the spindle and fell into an enchanted

sleep?" Beatrice pressed the back of her hand against her forehead and pretended to drop. "It's a fairly crucial part of Sleeping Beauty."

"So you got the idea from a fairytale." Oliver scoffed.

"Yes." Beatrice grated her teeth, annoyed with the casual dismissal. "They're foundational texts for anyone who wants to be half decent at enchantments. The stories have been molded over the centuries. They contain the archetypes that inform the essence of every act, of every object. They're nothing to scoff at."

She was exaggerating a bit, but Beatrice was too annoyed to care. Without thinking, she spun so that she could lecture Oliver properly.

The sight of the warlock made the words vanish from her mind.

Oliver crouched among the plants, wearing nothing but a pair of dark green boxers. His muscles shone and glinted in pockets of enchanted sunlight that streamed through the roof. He looked so perfect; he could've been mistaken as part of the greenhouse's décor if he'd stayed still. However, his fingers unbuttoned the guard's shirt.

"Relax," he said, turning his gaze up to Beatrice. "I was scoffing at myself for being an idiot. Fairytales are incredible. And I've been blind to it for a really long time." He smiled and cast his eyes away, looking almost embarrassed. "Now turn back around and give this guard some privacy while I steal his clothes."

———

Beatrice considered using an impression on Oliver once he was disguised. Providing he agreed, it would have been possible, not to truly alter his appearance, but to mask it with magic. However, impressions on people tended to be finnicky. Even in the guard's uniform, someone perceptive would notice the illusion and grow more suspicious. It would be too risky, so Beatrice dismissed the idea.

Instead, they restrained the guard and left the greenhouse, hurrying through the woods toward the manor while Bean scouted the surrounding area. Beatrice had doused the shifter with as much enchanted seawave root dust as could be risked, but it was only a matter of time before he awoke and broke free of the vines holding him. Oliver needed to be off the estate before that happened. And Beatrice...

Either I bond with the grimoire, or I'll have to flee too.

Wilburn might have her arrested for trespassing otherwise.

"You know," Oliver said, voice was soft, and more nervous than usual. "I was thinking once I clear my name, I'd like to enjoy some guilt-free travel. Maybe, South America to start, then Europe. I could stop in the Caribbean. Is that something that would interest you?"

Is he inviting me to travel with him?

Beatrice stumbled over a protruding tree root into a rare pocket of sunlight, catching herself just in time to avoid falling on her knees. She turned to the warlock, who'd stopped beside her. He rested his hand on his curls, tucked his chin, and smiled—his signature move for hitting on a girl.

And he was using it on Beatrice.

Her heart stopped. She'd wasted more time than she should have fantasizing about a moment where Oliver finally noticed her as something more than Albert's sister. Of course, his offer interested her! What could be more enticing than traveling the world with the boy she'd spent almost eight years dreaming about? Especially when his smile teased the many ways they could pass the time.

You can't abandon the coven if you're the Matriarch, Gigi's voice scolded her before she could respond.

Beatrice's answer died on her lips. The subconscious manifestation of her grandmother was right. Any trips the Blackwell Matriarch made would be short and purposeful. There would be no year of exploration. And probably no Oliver either.

Without Beatrice to warn them away, the warlock would leave a trail of sobbing, heartbroken women in his wake. When he returned to Castor's Grove, he'd likely still be single. But any fleeting interest Oliver had in Beatrice would have vanished.

Would it last if I did go with him?

Most likely not. Oliver would get her, lose interest, and run off with some gorgeous foreigner. And Beatrice would've missed her one chance at gaining the incredible power, wealth, and prestige that came with the title of Matriarch.

The answer was obvious. She couldn't entertain the thought of traveling with the warlock. Just as she went to answer, however, something caught her eye near the edge of the sunlit earth: a white lily.

It wasn't an impossible discovery. The Blackwell Forest was enchanted so that every tree, herb, and shrub was sustained through the winter. Yet, like a sign from the universe.

Beatrice bent down, plucked it, and impressed the petals with her will so that they turned a perfect black. Satisfied and feeling more than a little clever, she offered it to Oliver as they resumed their walk toward the manor.

"I'm not much of a botanist," he admitted, accepting

the flower with a shy smile. "But I must admit, I've always had a fondness for black lilies."

Beatrice's heart pounded. "They're my favorite too."

And had been since her first day of middle school when Oliver had given her one.

The lily's presence, right at the spot where he'd invited her to travel with him, had to mean something. Maybe if she said yes, the warlock's feelings wouldn't fade. Maybe they were supposed to be together.

"I wish I could make them," Oliver said, holding the flower back for Beatrice to take.

There was no root to trip her this time, or she might have fallen flat on her face. "What are you talking about? Of course, you can."

"I know everything with magic comes easily to you, but some of us aren't so lucky. Truth is I can't enchant a damn thing when it comes to plants." He patted his curls again and turned his head away. "Pathetic, right? My mum was teaching me just before I started seventh grade. It seemed like I was getting close, but I never mastered it. Think my brain is just broken when it comes to botany."

He gave an odd, nervous laugh, and glanced at Beatrice once more.

She stared back with wide-eyed disbelief. "You gave me a black lily the day I first started at Dashmoor Middle. Don't you remember?"

From the way Oliver's eyebrows rose, it was obvious he didn't. He shrugged. "Maybe I painted the petals as a trick?"

He really doesn't remember.

Beatrice's chest tightened. She wrapped her jacket tighter and turned away. The pivotal moment in their relationship, which she'd replayed over a thousand times, engraving every moment into her memory, had meant so little to Oliver that he couldn't even recall changing the color of a flower.

The lily was a sign. Just not the one Beatrice wanted.

Just as the manor came into view, something jumped onto her leg and scurried to her shoulder.

Beatrice turned to find a small, pointed face staring at her. Bean had returned, and not without reason.

He squeaked, long ears twitching. His tail pointed back into the woods.

Beatrice translated the familiar's message for Oliver's benefit. "We need to hide. My cousins are coming."

19
OLIVER

O liver climbed the nearest tree and hid among its branches. There was no time to help Beatrice up. She stayed on the ground, back pressed flat against the large trunk.

From his vantage, Oliver was able to spot the trio. Rett marched at the front, tall, thin, and pale, like a skeleton draped in a black winter coat. Gabriel, never too far from his brother, stomped behind, red-faced and extra round in a navy puff jacket. And then there was the newest addition to their crew, the one who'd replaced Oliver and Albert. Elle was dressed all in crimson. Her fair hair streamed behind her as she struggled to keep pace with their fearless leader.

"Trust me, it's in the North-West tower." Rett's voice drifted into the trees as the trio approached. "Wilburn increased the guards and laid traps, but I have a plan." He tapped his pocket. "You guys don't need to worry."

Typical Rett. Thinks he's Caesar ordering his soldiers around. Why share his plans? Oliver couldn't believe how much he'd once idolized the older warlock.

"It's not getting there that's the issue," Gabriel said, his voice unusually annoyed. "What happens when we do?"

"Isn't it obvious? Elle presents the card, and hey-presto!"

"But that isn't fair, and she knows it. Don't you?" Gabriel stopped, turning toward the girl in crimson.

Elle slowed. "Obviously, if Rett wants, I'll—"

"No," Rett interrupted, his voice firm. "I would only end up failing the coven. It's a role for a witch."

Now that was a change. Oliver remembered Rett with an ego twice the size of Beatrice's own. He'd boasted that he could cast spells as powerful as any witch and never thought anyone more capable than himself.

Unless they were talking about a gender-exclusive position.

Did Tabitha choose Elle to be the next Matriarch?

Oliver had given the uncertainty surrounding the Black-well succession only passing thought over the past few days. His own problems felt more pressing than worrying about internal strife among the wealthy coven. But rumors in Castor's Grove claimed that Elle had been blessed with the incredible, innate power occasionally seen among the Blackwells. It was possible that she was even stronger than Beatrice. Talent like that would explain Rett's brief flicker of humility, and why he'd been suddenly drawn to his cousin when he started high school.

Oliver climbed down the tree, jumped from the lowest branch, and landed in a crouch amid the grass. He stood and dusted any stray leaves from the stolen uniform.

Beatrice stepped out from behind the tree, her lips pulled in a tight line. "Come on, we need to hurry."

Her voice was anxious.

"Don't you think we should wait for them to go a bit

further?" Oliver whispered, glancing in the direction the trio had vanished. The last thing they needed was to run into people who would recognize them within the manor.

"I—" For once, Beatrice seemed at a loss for words. "Of course. You're right."

That's it? No argument?

Oliver's eyebrows rose. Tempting as it was to bask in hearing *you're right* from Beatrice Blackwell, he felt too anxious to enjoy it. She was acting odd.

Was it because he'd invited her to travel with him? She hadn't said yes. Did she not want to?

No, that can't be it. She's liked me for years. Maybe I just caught her off guard.

"Sounds like Elle is about to be the next Matriarch," Oliver said, running his hand over his curls as he searched for a topic of conversation. "Think maybe she killed Tabitha to seize power?"

Beatrice glared at him from the corner of her eye. "Elle would need to buy an invisibility spell. She's not clever enough to make one."

"I don't know. You guessed one of the ingredients pretty fast, and isn't she supposed to be one of the best of our generation?"

"No, she isn't." The witch scoffed, and then her eyes widened. She turned, increasing her speed, as she weaved between the trees.

Oliver stared after her for a second. *Is she jealous because I called Elle talented?*

His legs were almost twice as long. He caught up to Beatrice within a few steps. "B, you know, you're also—"

"Once you're inside, don't bother going back to Tabitha's office," Beatrice said, cutting him off. She stared straight ahead, green eyes blazing. Oliver wondered if she'd even been aware that he was speaking. "Wilburn will have already cleared it out. Anything important will be in his possession."

Like the agenda.

"Got it." Oliver appreciated the advice, but his stomach tightened as the dark walls of the manor appeared between the trees. "You don't have a disguise. What's the plan if your family recognize you?"

"Depends. I might need them to."

That didn't make sense. Her coven might not physically maim Beatrice, but there would be definite repercussions for her intrusion. Plus, they might look more closely at the guard accompanying her.

The two teens left the safety of the woods and stepped onto the flat lawn that surrounded the manor. There was no sign of anyone else nearby, and Oliver led her toward the hidden door at the base of one of the towers.

It opened as easily as it had on the night of Tabitha's murder.

"Meet me back here in an hour," Beatrice said. "I had a plan to get us out, but I'm not sure anymore. We might have to improvise. Take this, just in case you need it."

She shoved her makeshift weapon into his hand. The door swung shut. It was only then Oliver realized that Beatrice wasn't coming with him.

He was completely on his own in the Blackwell manor, just like last time. Only now, everyone inside wanted him dead. And Oliver and his family were going to be in a lot of trouble if he couldn't find Tabitha's agenda and uncover the identity of the real killer.

20

BEATRICE

Beatrice ran across the field toward the North-West tower where her cousins had gone. Her chest felt tight. She kept glancing over her shoulder, in the direction she'd last seen Oliver. Sending him into the manor alone was a risky move. But the warlock was disguised and most of the Blackwells barely looked at their servants. He would be fine. And Beatrice couldn't let Elle reach the grimoire before her.

Still, she looked at the familiar peeping out of her pocket. "Keep an eye on Oliver for me again? Just in case."

Bean squeaked, jumped out, and hurried off, leaving Beatrice on her own.

The Queen of Spades rattled in the pocket of her sleeve, slapping against her palm.

Elle has a card too.

It made no sense.

Only, of course, it did. Tabitha had chosen multiple replacements. Because nothing in the Blackwell coven was ever given freely. Everything was a test.

And Beatrice intended to win.

I'm stronger than Elle. And twice as talented. I know I am.

Beatrice reached the base of the tower and found the door missing. Instead, a blue daze floated down from the stairs.

She covered her mouth, creating a pocket of air within her jacket. The remnants of the spell drifted over her, making her eyes feel heavy. She steeled herself against the magic, which begged her to lie down, and charged up the stairs.

Loud snores echoed through the passage. Beatrice counted over a dozen guards sleeping with their heads against the wall.

The air cleared as she climbed higher. Whoever crafted the sleeping spell had designed the magic to sink to the bottom.

Clever trick.

No way Elle had made it.

Beatrice reached the top of the seventh flight of stairs, lungs burning. Fighting the urge to collapse to her knees, she gasped for air. The muscles in her legs objected to so much running especially while holding her breath.

But there was no time to waste. Elle might be seconds away from claiming the grimoire. Beatrice couldn't lose focus. She turned the corner at the top of the stairs and came face-to-face with two of her cousins.

"Beatrice?" Gabriel was faster to react than usual. He blinked his round green eyes. "What are you doing here?"

Rett looked significantly less pleased by Beatrice's sudden appearance. His jaw clenched, pulling his skin tighter over his long, narrow face. "Didn't Wilburn ban you from the manor?"

It certainly sounded like something the executor would do, but he was the last of Beatrice's concerns now. "Is the grimoire in there? Is Elle claiming it? She's not the strong-est. She shouldn't be the next Matriarch. You have to let me in."

"Gladly," Gabriel said.

He started to step aside, but Rett grabbed his brother's elbow and held him in place.

"Sorry, B," Rett said, shrugging his shoulder. "But Tabitha chose Elle. She's our most powerful witch."

"Except she's not the most powerful member of our coven," Gabriel snapped at his brother in an uncharacter-istic display of annoyance. "And we both know it because—"

Before he could finish, a shriek came from behind the door.

Both boys turned.

Beatrice used their distraction to her advantage. She barreled past them, pushed the door open, and charged in.

It was the same room Beatrice had seen when she'd scried Linda through the mirror. Clusters of cobwebs descended from the high roof and stretched across the walls. A thick layer of dust coated the wooden floor, and the only small, window near the top was covered with a black curtain.

In the center of the room, the grimoire sat on a tall, black stone pedestal, surrounded by a sheen of glowing red. It cast the room in a dark red glow and spread a fiery heat. Before it, stood Elle.

She had removed her winter jacket to reveal a matching crimson shirt beneath. The bell sleeves dropped as Elle raised her arms to stare at her palms. Fire blazed over the skin, running up the lengths of her fingers. With a pop, it flashed out at the tips, leaving her hands red and bloody.

Tears pooled in Elle's eyes, and her voice was a dry, hoarse whisper. "It didn't work."

She tried to get the grimoire and failed.

A smile spread across Beatrice's face.

"How is that possible?" Rett ran forward and reached for Elle's hands. He studied the damage, brushing her palms.

Elle winced, choked out a sob, and turned her head to find Beatrice grinning at her.

Oops. Beatrice tried to get her expression under control. But it wasn't like her cousin had ever shown her much empathy. Why did she need to be the one to care?

Beatrice's eyes flicked to the grimoire, still on its pedestal. It was hers to claim.

So why wasn't she rushing to do so?

"Perhaps in death, Tabitha knows the truth," Gabriel suggested, sounding smug as he crossed his arms.

"The truth about what?" Beatrice asked, turning away from the grimoire and toward her wild-eyed cousin.

"Why is she here?" Elle asked, addressing her question to Rett.

But Gabriel answered Beatrice, "The truth about the poison."

"Enough, Gabe." Rett dropped Elle's hands and went to his brother. He pushed the shorter, plumper boy behind him, and placed himself before Beatrice. "A few days before she died, Tabitha was poisoned, and so was Bean. She asked Elle for a cure. We figured it was a test. Everyone knew our former Matriarch wasn't fond of leaving her legacy to Linda."

"And after I gave her the cure, she gave me this." Elle winced as she slipped her burned fingers into her pocket and pulled out a piece of black and crimson card with the

Blackwell cauldron near the top. Tabitha's signature shone in liquid gold cursive near the center. "Proof. She chose me to succeed her."

But if that was all true, then why was Gabriel so annoyed?

Her cousins were lying about something.

Beatrice thought back to the cemetery when she'd spied on Elle struggling to perform an enchantment that would bring leaves back to a winter tree, even for a few seconds.

"You didn't create the potion that saved her, did you?"

Elle's cheeks turned pink. Her lower lip trembled. "Of course, I did. I just—"

"Needed Rett's help," Gabriel said, stepping out from behind his brother to cut her off. "Because he's the talented one."

Elle burst into tears, and Rett hurried to comfort her, wrapping an arm over her shoulder.

Beatrice didn't blame her cousin for crying. She might as well if a warlock had more talent than she did.

Although both genders were capable of magic, knowledge of spellcraft passed from mother to daughter. No one would risk training a warlock, who left their covens when they wed, in anything but the basics.

"Is that why you left the silverbloom in Tabitha's coffin?" Beatrice asked, studying Elle and trying to solve another mystery that had been confounding her. "Because it was the main ingredient in the cure?"

Judging from the expressions on both boys' faces, they hadn't been aware of Elle's offering.

The fair-haired girl sniffed. "I thought that maybe there was still some poison left in her system that made her slow. I mean how else to explain how Tabitha was murdered? She was so powerful! Obviously, the antidote didn't work properly."

Rett's arm lowered. He cast his eyes toward the floor.

Elle noticed at once. "No, I didn't mean that it was your fault or anything. Tabitha probably let Bean drink too much of the silver tea and didn't take enough herself. He was the only creature she ever doted on. But maybe if you'd made more, she—"

"Stop trying to blame him," Gabriel rushed to his brother's defense. "Rett has more talent in his little finger than the rest of the coven put together."

Beatrice frowned waiting for him to add *present company excluded.*

He did not, and as his rant continued, her eyes returned to the grimoire. If she stepped forward and claimed it, that would shut her cousins up. They'd stop debating who was strongest and realize that the answer was in front of them the entire time. Just because she was a barely-Blackwell didn't mean she wasn't powerful.

Beatrice reached for the card in her pocket and stepped closer to the red light that surrounded the grimoire.

She couldn't bring herself to cross it.

Why? Because Oliver invited me to go traveling with him? I can't throw everything away for a boy who probably doesn't even like me in that way!

Becoming Matriarch meant power, wealth, and prestige. It meant her coven bowing to her, following her every command, and eagerly trying to please her whims.

And that was what Beatrice truly wanted. Wasn't it?

A loud, sharp caw, like fifty ravens shouting in tandem, blasted through the tower.

"The alarm," Elle said, looking up. "Wilburn is onto us.

Damn it. Here, Rett, you take the card. Try if you want, it probably should be you who leads us. Warlock or not."

There was a glimmer of desire in his long, gaunt face. Rett's hand flinched toward the card, but he didn't take it.

Beatrice's head swiveled between the grimoire and the door. Either she had to claim it, or she had to run, but she couldn't stand still, or the guards would catch her.

This was ridiculous. Beatrice was a lot of things, but indecisive wasn't one of them. She was just going to—

The door swung open and something small and gray ran into the room.

Bean stopped before her feet, jumping and squeaking. The wooden spindle was wrapped in his tail.

Beatrice understood at once. The alarm wasn't about them.

Something had happened to Oliver.

21

OLIVER

Oliver had gone barely a few steps into the manor before he was spotted.

"Oy!" A short man in a guard's uniform marched forward, arms swinging at his sides. He stared at Oliver with a pair of close-set, orange eyes.

Another shifter.

Oliver tightened his grip on the spindle. He'd been hoping that he wouldn't have to use it.

"You don't look familiar," the guard said. He chewed the side of his cheek as he considered the warlock before him. "New hire? What've you got there?" He pointed to the spindle.

An idea occurred to Oliver. "It's some sort of magical artifact. I'm supposed to deliver it to Mr. Wilburn's office, but I don't know the way."

"You want to be on the fourth floor. Second door on the East Wing. I'll show you. Name's Grizz." He stuck out his hand.

"Claw," Oliver made up an alias as they shook. It was the last name of a shifter his mother had once hired.

"Well, stick with me. I'll show you the ropes." Despite being half a foot shorter, Grizz managed to throw his arm over Oliver's shoulders.

The guard guided him through the long passageways of the Blackwell Manor, past ancient oil portraits, gold chalices, and many other servants. Oliver kept his head down, afraid someone might recognize him. Grizz didn't make it easy to keep a low profile. He exchanged pleasantries with everyone they passed until they finally reached a dark mahogany door with the Blackwell cauldron engraved above the handle of the door. The artist had added a stack of books beneath.

"Here we are. Let's see if the boss is in, eh?" Grizz rapped his knuckles on the frame and put his ear to the door.

Oliver's breath caught. He hadn't considered that Wilburn might be in his study.

"Out and about for the moment." The guard shrugged and turned the handle.

The door swung soundlessly on its hinges to reveal mountains of paperwork.

Stacks of loose pages tottered and swayed. Some rose so high that they threatened to touch the beams of the dark ceiling. The piles swayed despite the lack of wind. Somewhere among them was Tabitha's agenda.

"Bit of a balancing act, eh?" Grizz said, stepping into the room, and turning his head. "Suppose we can drop the thingie on the table and scamper off."

Had Oliver not followed the guard's gaze, he might never have noticed the small black desk hiding in the corner. A twisting narrow path carved through the stacks of paper toward it.

But Oliver had other plans.

"I think I'd best wait here until he returns," Oliver said, searching for a suitable excuse. "Ms. Linda said to deliver it in person."

It seemed an innocuous statement, but Grizz's orange eyes narrowed. "You mean Ms. *Be*linda. We don't use nicknames for the bosses."

"Right. Of course." Oliver could have slapped himself. He knew Linda's full name, of course, but he'd grown up listening to Albert and Beatrice and picked up the habit of referring to the Blackwell coven in the same casual manner. Their guards would be more formal.

"Who'd you say hired you again?" Grizz said, rubbing his jaw and narrowing his orange eyes.

Oliver had no idea who oversaw the Manor's staff. His chances of guessing correctly were slim to none.

The time for subterfuge had ended.

Oliver pushed his will into the spindle and stabbed the guard's arm.

Grizz swayed on his feet, eyes blinking. "Who...? Who...?" His mouth opened in a yawn.

"Damn it." Oliver didn't have Beatrice's raw power. He couldn't work with only an old spindle and a dusting of some sleep-flower. "Sorry about this, Grizz."

Oliver dropped the spindle and punched the shifter square between his orange eyes.

The guard collapsed, stumbling backward into a stack of paper and sending loose pages flying. He wouldn't stay asleep for long.

Oliver needed to find the agenda and get out. Fast. He searched hints of black among the white and cream paper and found several. It would take ages to go through all of them.

What the hell kind of lawyer keeps their office so disorganized?

The last of the disturbed pages landed on Oliver's shoulder. He grabbed it, ready to toss it aside, before he noticed one of the lines: *I see a beautiful city and a brilliant people rising from the abyss.*

It was from *A Tale of Two Cities* by Charles Dickens. He scanned the rest of the paper before grabbing two more. All contained excerpts from novels.

These aren't anything. They're just a distraction.

Of course! Oliver felt like a fool for not realizing. Anyone could walk into the office. Wilburn wouldn't keep important documents lying in stacks. They must have been somewhere safe, likely behind lock and key.

The falling paperwork had buried the path to the desk, but Oliver climbed over the notes to reach it.

Just as he suspected, there were several drawers. All locked.

"Ugh," Oliver grunted as he tugged on one of the handles. He doubted strength alone would help him here. The drawers would be enchanted. "Why couldn't Beatrice have made a key?"

It was a silly thing to blame on the witch. She couldn't be expected to think of everything.

"Squeak, squeak!"

Oliver looked around the room. Was that Bean?

The drawer he'd been fighting with suddenly opened. The familiar twitched his ears and squeaked at Oliver from within.

"Holy shit, Beatrice does think of everything," Oliver whispered, grinning at the marsupial. "Bean, you're amazing. Next drawer."

The bilby's ears wiggled in delight at the compliment

before he vanished to repeat whatever special brand of magic allowed him to bypass the magical enchantments.

Something in the first drawer caught Oliver's attention: a wooden box with the Wyrmwood snake engraved on the top.

This is what my mom dropped off for Wilburn the morning Tabitha was killed.

Bean squeaked and bounced onto the desk. He'd finished his task and now wanted Oliver to hurry. The familiar wanted to return to his witch.

"I get that," Oliver admitted. He'd prefer to have Beatrice with them too. But he couldn't get distracted thinking about whatever that kiss had done to force him to acknowledge that he enjoyed the witch's presence.

Oliver found the agenda in the last drawer. Its silver letters sparkled against the black. He fumbled through the pages as he searched for the most recent entries.

"The killer must have met with her right before I did. My guess is—"

He was going to say *Wilburn*. However, it was a different Blackwell whose name had been looped in the Matriarch's cursive.

"Gabriel?"

According to the agenda, he'd met with Tabitha that morning as well. But the old Matriarch had left a cushion of ten minutes between appointments. Gabriel's meeting would have needed to run late for him to have killed her. But it hadn't. Oliver had seen Gabriel in his house when the murderer had occurred.

If anything, his meeting must've ended early.

Otherwise, Oliver would've met Gabriel walking through the woods. But what did that mean? Had Gabriel's meeting been interrupted by the murderer? Or could he have seen something suspicious when he left?

Oliver recalled the strange look in Gabriel's eyes that night. He'd looked bewitched. Could someone have used magic on him?

Bean tapped his tail on the desk, pointed his nose toward the door.

"Give me a minute," Oliver apologized. "I just need to check—"

He pulled open the first drawer with the Wyrmwood box and opened the lid. Five spherical glass bottles nestled between dark-green satin. White liquid smoked within, sending pale gray wisps licking at the corks.

Illegal forgetting potions.

That couldn't be a coincidence. There was a clue here. Something that would prove Oliver's innocence. Something he could give to Amos, and have the sergeant use to solve the case. There had to be.

"I ordered nothing to my office," Wilburn's voice came through the wall, muffled and softened by the stacks of paper. "Search the premises. I'm telling you, we have an intruder."

The sound of ravens cawing filled the room. Some strange sort of alarm.

Shit.

Oliver searched for a place to hide. Maybe if he buried himself in pages, Wilburn wouldn't notice him in here. It wasn't the worst idea.

Before he could move, however, a loud growl rumbled from a few feet away. Oliver turned to see a massive grizzly rising from the notes. It charged toward him.

Instinct took over.

Oliver ran toward the door.

And straight into Wilburn.

22

BEATRICE

"Attention, Blackwells."

Wilburn's voice, amplified by magic, echoed across the estate, reverberating in the small room of the North-West tower. "The man who murdered our beloved Matriarch has been apprehended on the premises. We believe the treacherous Mr. Wyrmwood was plotting to kill again. Now, we have him in our custody, and we seek vengeance. The moment the sun is at its peak, the killer burns!"

Cheers, though Beatrice had no idea whose, followed the announcement.

She stood in the tower with her three cousins. They exchanged anxious looks before all broke the silence at once.

"Did they say burn?" Beatrice asked.

At the same time, Elle inquired, "Who do you all think Oliver was planning to kill?"

"How did he get here?" Gabriel asked, deep creases forming in his brow.

"I think I'm going to be sick." Rett clutched his stomach,

catching all of them off guard. He scowled as their eyes turned to him. "They're going to burn him at the stake. That image doesn't make you all feel ill?"

A chill crept through Beatrice.

"Will they really do that?" Gabriel pressed his hand to his chest. He started to wheeze as the reality of the situation kicked in.

"No, we won't let that happen." Beatrice ran to one of the small windows, pulled the black sheet down, and stared into the sky. Her chest tightened. It was closer to midday than she'd realized. The sun would reach its peak in twenty, maybe thirty, minutes. But that still gave them time. "If we work together, we can rescue Oliver. We just need to—"

"Absolutely not," Elle cut her off. The fair-haired girl stood with one burned palm hovering an inch shy of her hip. "He killed our Matriarch. His death is justice. We should burn the familiar with him one time." She pointed to Bean with her chin.

"What the hell is wrong with you?" Beatrice shouted, grabbing the bilby from the floor and shielding him protectively in her hands. "We can't go around killing people because you decide they're guilty! That's not how the law works!"

"You're right," Rett said, stepping forward and grabbing Beatrice by her shoulders. He stared straight at her, thin face unnaturally pale. "But it doesn't matter. There isn't time to make a plan, and the four of us—"

"Three of you," Elle muttered, crossing her arms and turning away.

"—can't take out all the guards and our entire coven on our own. I'm sorry, but there's no scenario in which Oliver doesn't end up dead. The question is if you want to join him."

"What if we had the power of the grimoire?" Gabriel asked, creeping up behind his brother.

Rett turned on him. "Enough, Gabe. Now isn't the time."

But it was.

Beatrice stared at the grimoire. Its dark leather turned blood red in the glow of the magic that protected it. The ruby twinkled in the center.

The grimoire had the power needed to control the coven.

Beatrice couldn't keep procrastinating.

"Hey, stop! What're you—?" Rett's voice cut off as Beatrice collided with the spell.

A wave of heat washed over her as she collided with the red glow. The room spun. Bean vanished from her hands. Her cousins disappeared.

It was just Beatrice and the grimoire. Her hand stretched toward the ruby, but something invisible blocked her.

"I was wondering when you'd show up."

That voice.

Deep. Confident. Brash.

Beatrice turned and came face-to-face with a ghost.

Tabitha leaned against her cane, surveying her descendant over the top of her half-moon spectacles. Red garnets glistened on the sleeves and waistline of her gown. She smiled with a pair of crimson-painted lips.

"How long did I last before they offed me?"

Beatrice blinked at her former Matriarch, trying to process the question. "You know you were murdered. Do you know who did it?"

"I'm a memory, not a ghost." Tabitha raised a hand from her cane and waved it, revealing the gold rings and dark gems that adorned her fingers. "When the banshee warned me of my impending demise, I made my preparations. Tell me, did we have a chance to talk?"

Beatrice shook her head.

"I'd been watching you for many years, you know. There was a reason I allowed your family to remain Blackwells. Your grandmother was a gifted witch though unfortunately insubordinate. After her tragic mistake, I hoped some of that talent had passed to her descendants. You exceeded my expectations."

It was precisely the kind of praise that Beatrice had been longing to hear her entire life. A smile spread across her face, but she couldn't quite enjoy it.

"I'm sorry, if you're a memory, made when the Banshee first shrieked, then how do you know you were murdered?"

Tabitha snorted. It was loud and uncouth, a noise too great for her small frame. "An easy guess. Once everyone knew that I intended to pass the title to the most powerful Blackwell, things were bound to get..." She paused, thin lips disappearing into her mouth as she searched for the right word. "... messy. I'm just pleased to see you weren't the one murdered instead. Last time I suggested returning to traditional succession laws, all my favorites were picked off one-by-one, or they eliminated themselves from the running. But I learned my lesson. Have you got the card?"

In the shock of seeing the Matriarch, Beatrice had forgotten about it. She searched the pocket of her sleeve, found the queen still within, and produced it.

"Pity. You can toss it in the trash."

"Sorry?" Beatrice didn't understand. Was this not the right card?

"It's useless. A gimmick. I hoped anyone in the coven with Matriarchal ambitions would attempt to steal the card instead of murdering you. Figured they'd use it to try get the grimoire, and I'd be able to confront my killer. Terribly clever idea, isn't it? Except the only two to show were Linda and that damned little brat. Neither have the talent or brains to have killed me."

Beatrice suspected that the memory's response would've been the same no matter who appeared. Tabitha's hubris blinded her to others' capabilities. The memory of the former Matriarch would be no help in solving her murder.

And there wasn't time to puzzle through clues now anyway.

"I'd love to stay and chat, but I need to bond with the grimoire. Otherwise, the coven is going to burn Oliver alive." Beatrice turned away from her great-great-grand-mother and back toward the spellbook.

Suddenly, Tabitha blocked her path. A scowl accentuated the wrinkles on her face. "You mean that Wyrmwood boy that you and your brother insisted on befriending?" Her voice was a growl. "He's still in the picture? Did I die before I could buy him off?"

Beatrice frowned. She had no idea what the former Matriarch meant.

"I want you to succeed me, girl," Tabitha said, resting a thin, bejeweled hand on the grimoire and rapping her fingers against the metal corner. "But there is a stipulation. I will not allow the Blackwell name to be tainted by having a Matriarch engaged in any way with a coven that only continues to exist through one lucky invention and half-baked contraband."

"Their invisibility spells are more than just—" Beatrice

tried to defend Oliver's family, but Tabitha's scowl grew deeper.

The former Matriarch slammed her cane on the floor, making the room shake. "When the time comes, you may join with someone from an acceptable coven. A Hallow or a Cherith. Even a Malice might suffice. But never a Wyrm-wood. You will make a blood oath and swear this on your life right now."

"And if I don't?"

Fury flashed in Tabitha's bright green eyes. "You forsake the title of Matriarch and lose the chance to gain the power of the grimoire. Forever."

23

OLIVER

The light shone into the open courtyard. An architect, with foresight and a cruel sense of humor, had built a white marble sundial in the center.

Oliver watched the shadow creep along the gold-plated numerals. In a few minutes, the twelve would be in shadow.

And I'll be burned to death.

Oliver turned to one of the guards and made a desperate attempt. "Please, I didn't kill Tabitha. It was—" He hesitated. Oliver had assumed Wilburn had purchased an invisibility spell from his mother that morning. But he'd found forgetting potions instead. Still, maybe the lawyer had purchased both. "Wilburn is hiding something. He's fooling everyone."

The guard, a broad-shouldered shifter near seven feet in height, swung his fist and sank it into Oliver's side.

So much for pleading his case..

Oliver's stomach heaved. His back tried to curl inward, but another two guards yanked him upright. Their fingers curled tight above his elbows. They forced him to stare straight ahead toward where a crowd of Blackwells had amassed before a wooden platform with a large stake in the center.

Did they build that just for me or are they insane enough to keep one at the ready?

Round faces with angry eyes yelled curses and spat in Oliver's direction. A row of guards held them at bay for now, but a few of the more talented witches raised their fingers and sent sparks flying. One caught the edge of Oliver's eyebrow, heat licking at his skin before it sizzled out.

"Are you two blind?" Debby Blackwell pushed through the guards, pointing at the sky. She'd fashioned her hair into a dark braided crown on her head and adorned with dark orange flowers that matched her dress. Festive for the occasion. "Look at the position of the sun. It's not going to get any higher."

Her younger sister, Libby, hurried behind her. "It's not time yet. Look at the sundial."

Debby glared at her. "The sundial is probably slow."

Libby let out a nervous sound that was half-laugh, half-snort. She fell silent when she realized that her sister wasn't joking and started to fiddle with the long sleeves of her inappropriately cheery yellow dress. Her eyes flicked to Oliver for a second before falling to her feet.

She doesn't seem as eager to watch me die.

He recalled the whispered conversation he'd overheard the night of Tabitha's murder.

What had the two sisters said? *Wilburn will put a stop to it, no matter the cost.*

They'd been talking about the Matriarchal succession.

"You don't think I did it," Oliver said, heart pounding

with a momentary flutter of hope as he stared at Libby. "Wilburn promised your mother that he wouldn't let her be disinherited. If you think it was him who murdered Tabitha, you have to say something. You can't let your coven—"

Another punch knocked the words from Oliver.

"Don't fill my sister's head with garbage." Debby stepped forward. She pulled a white glove from her hand and shoved it in his mouth.

Oliver gagged at the taste of her sweat.

Is she silencing me because she knows I'm right?

He tried to get Libby's attention again, but it was too late.

Wilburn's voice echoed from the base of the wooden platform, "It is time."

The guards parted, forming a path from the sundial to the stake. One of them pushed Oliver forward, forcing him to march.

Blackwells hissed at him from either side. A tomato slammed against his head and exploded, dripping juice into his eye. Next came a head of cabbage, ricocheting off his arm. Then came an eclectic onslaught of items, some more creative than others: a baseball that was luckily aimed too high, a pin that almost took out Oliver's eye, a globe that collided with his hip before cracking like an egg and falling in halves on the ground.

Oliver stumbled over the Northern Hemisphere.

So much for seeing the world.

Adventures that he'd never have flashed through Oliver's mind: exploring the ruins of ancient castles, searching foreign fields for magical plants, star gazing on a tropical beach. In every instance, he imagined Beatrice with him. She chattered at him about history, explained the purpose of every flower, whispered a fairytale about the origin of the constellations.

Oliver blinked tomato juice out of his eyes, barely aware of the sting.

I'm about to die. Beatrice should be the last thing on my mind.

Instead, as Oliver climbed the steps of the platform and the guards bound him to the stake, memories of the past few days with her filled his mind: Beatrice brewing a memory expulsion, appearing at his safehouse, kissing him in the alley, saving him from a leopard, identifying every plant in the greenhouse.

Since Tabitha's murder, Oliver's family had gone into hiding without him. His best friend had advised he keep his distance for both their safety. But Beatrice had helped him with every request he'd made, and even the ones he didn't.

I'll never have the chance to tell her how incredible I think she is.

Why hadn't he before? Because he'd been too stubborn to accept that he was attracted to her? Because he'd know that once he started to listen to Beatrice—to actually pay attention to her—then he'd—

Pain cut off Oliver's thoughts as the guards bound him to the stake with an iron string that bit into his wrists and neck. His eyes watered, blurring the angry crowd before him into a sea of dark hair, angry eyes, and pale faces that glowed in the full light of the sun.

"My fellow Blackwells," Wilburn's voice boomed from the base of the platform. "Our beloved Matriarch, Tabitha, honored this lowly Wyrmwood with a meeting, and what did he do? Murder her in cold blood! Slit her throat and run like a coward! We will not stand for such insolence! He shall know the wrath of our coven!"

His voice shook with genuine fury. The crowd shrieked in frenzied agreement. Fireballs crackled over witches' palms.

It was really happening. They were going to burn him to death.

In novels, heroes gained a sudden clarity in these moments or relived the most significant moments of their lives. Oliver felt nothing but a rising panic and desperate desire to live. He struggled against the iron strings until blood dripped from his wrists.

"Burn him!" Wilburn commanded, leaping from the platform with surprising dexterity.

Fireballs launched. The flames caught the wooden stake. A massive blaze roared to life and surrounding Oliver.

"Stop!"

That voice.

It was difficult to see beyond the rising smoke, but Oliver knew it was Beatrice.

She's trying to save me.

But powerful as the witch was, she couldn't face the might of her coven.

"You!" Wilburn's voice trembled with fury. Through the flames, he raised his hand to point at Beatrice's approaching figure. "Did you help this murderer return to our estate? You should be tossed in the flames with him!"

"Yes!" Linda's voice came from the crowd high and panicked. "Burn her too! She's not one of us. She's barely a Blackwell."

Smoke filled Oliver's lungs. Sweat dripped into his eyes. The heat made his head spin. What happened next was a feverish dream.

"I won't ask again. Oliver is innocent. Put out the

flames!" Beatrice's voice trembled with an authority that made the flames bow.

Wilburn shouted at their coven to arrest her. Half of them obeyed, rushing the witch. But before they reached her, Beatrice slammed her palm against the ground. The Blackwells fell like dominoes.

Spots swam in Oliver's vision. He blinked, and the flames were gone. Blinked again, and Beatrice appeared before him.

Sunlight fell from the sky, surrounding the witch in a nimbus of light. A pink flush colored her cheeks like an illustration from a fairytale. And her hair. Oliver had never seen anything so radiant. Every strand glowed, a hundred shades of deep, rich browns.

Beatrice pulled the glove from his mouth.

Delirious, lungs full of smoke, and staring at the witch before him, Oliver said the first thing that came to his mind.

"I think I love you."

Then something cut the wires binding him, he fell to the ash-covered platform, and the world went black.

24

BEATRICE

B eatrice turned before the mirror, examining one of the dresses Gigi had brought for her to try on. It fit well-enough, but why did it have to be so dark? The Blackwell's official colors felt unnecessarily depressing.

The large mirror displayed the dark, rich carpets, and massive four poster bed of Beatrice's new room. The expensive mattress and pillows should have ensured the best sleep of her life. Instead, she'd spent the past day feeling like a prisoner and worrying about Oliver.

His last words haunted her sleep: *I think I love you.*

"What did he—? Why did he—? Ugh!" Beatrice groaned, unable to complete the questions as she unbuttoned the dark gray dress.

Bean offered a sympathetic sigh. As her familiar, he understood her frustration better than most.

After Beatrice commanded her coven to release Oliver, he'd passed out. She'd been on the verge of doing the same. The grimoire's well of magic was deep, not inexhaustible. Beatrice had compelled her family to obey through sheer force of will. The effort had sapped her strength.

Luckily, she'd drained her coven too much to take advantage of her momentary weakness, and the guards had shifted their allegiance to her at once. They followed her orders, summoning an ambulance, the police, and Gigi.

Oliver had been taken to Castor's Care Hospital. Amos had arrested Wilburn and Linda, who'd been a witting accomplice in rousing the witches, for attempted murder. But Beatrice felt certain they'd be found guilty of achieving one too. After all, who else could have killed Tabitha?

Wilburn had the means—money and a known connection with the Wyrmwoods; Linda the motive—she wanted to be the next Matriarch. They must have teamed up and tried to act before the will could be changed. Only they'd miscalculated, and Beatrice had claimed the grimoire anyway.

Though not without paying a considerable price. She'd sworn a blood-oath to Tabitha's memory. Beatrice would never be with Oliver Wyrmwood. If she broke that promise, she'd die.

"And then he has the audacity to tell me—"

"Tell you what?" A cheerful, familiar voice asked.

Beatrice spun, dress half undone in the back, to find Eva, smiling in the doorway. The angel, in her white feather dress, had never looked more out of place. Gothic spires twisted around the doorway. Black stained the walls. Blood red blankets drowned the bed. The only other white came from the candles in a macabre chandelier overhead.

"You shouldn't be here!"

Eva's face fell. "I thought you'd be happy to see me. I brought the notes you missed today." She held up her backpack.

"I am," Beatrice assured her. "But do you have any idea what my coven would do to get their hands on your feathers? It's not safe for you on the Blackwell Estate. How'd you even get in?"

"Albert talked to the guards at the gate and snuck me inside through a servant's entrance."

Beatrice snorted. Of course her brother had. Eva had a boyfriend, but Albert still considered the angel too pretty not to help. But wait a minute— "Al is on the estate?"

"He said he stayed in a guest room last night," Eva said. "I think he was worried about you. They're saying that you seized control and then immediately got sick. I wanted to check on you too."

Beatrice groaned and collapsed onto the four-poster bed. The *they* Eva referred to must have been reporters. All her life Beatrice had wished to appear in tabloids and newspapers like her more elite relatives. But they'd have nothing good to say about her now.

The Blackwell Matriarch had a hundred magical duties, all of which Beatrice had needed to postpone while she recovered, much to the distress of the Castor's Government officials clamoring for her attention.

"You don't have a fever." Eva pressed her hand to Beatrice's forehead.

"No, but I have a headache," Beatrice complained, not sitting up. "Do you know how much paperwork running a coven requires? And there was a huge backlog. Gigi confiscated my phone and refused to let me go to school today because she said I needed to finish it. Then she sent me in here to try on dresses."

"You love dresses," Eva said.

"Not this one. I look like I'm going to a funeral." At the thought of death, Beatrice sat up again. "Do you know how Oliver is? Gigi won't tell me anything other than that he's alive."

"He's in a magically-induced coma so they can heal his burns and undo the damage the smoke did to his lungs. I figured you'd ask, so I called and checked." Eva unzipped her bag and pulled out a folder with a unicorn sticker. "I'm sorry, you probably have bigger concerns than missed notes. I wish I could help you."

"The best thing you can do for me is leave," Beatrice admitted. "My coven are dangerous, and I can't keep compelling them to obey if it drains me this much. Gigi's had to guard the door and check my food. She's afraid someone might try to poison my meal so that they can free the grimoire again and choose a new Matriarch. And I wish that was farfetched, but Tabitha was a hundred times more popular—" Beatrice paused, nose wrinkling as she considered that statement. "—at least, everyone feared her too much to want to replace her. But Wilburn and Linda still killed her."

"You found evidence?"

"No, but I will. The murder weapon will be enough for the police to catch the killer. Finding it's on my to-do list. Somewhere between school, paperwork, and managing the city's magical barriers." A footstep on the stairway outside made Beatrice jolt out of bed. Bean squeaked and leaped to her shoulder in attention.

It was only a guard. He knocked on the door and informed Beatrice that Gigi had *requested* she return to her study so that they could go over her movements for tomorrow. Eva really needed to leave.

"I'm sorry, I promise, I'll come see you as soon as I find a way to slip free," Beatrice said, as they exited the manor and stepped into the courtyard. She'd insisted on watching Eva leave the compound safely. Gigi could wait for a few minutes. It would do her good. After all, Beatrice was supposed to be in charge!

Eva hid behind the guards escorting them as a pair of nearby Blackwell witches gave them suspicious glares. But she offered Beatrice an amused look. "I think we both know I'm not the person you're desperate to see."

25
OLIVER

Oliver awoke in a memory.

"You're being childish," his mother objected, swishing her long green skirt and turning away.

Oliver knew his lines. He followed his mother into the narrow dining area of their cramped upstairs living space. "I just don't see why Beatrice has to come too. Albert is my friend."

"I like Beatrice," Sophie piped up. She skipped around the table, setting the plates. Cartoon snakes dangled from her ears. She'd insisted on wearing them for months after she'd turned eleven. "She's really talented."

"Don't tell her that," Oliver muttered.

"Beatrice is talented," Lucille said, turning on Oliver. "And she's also the entire reason that I sent you to that human school. Albert's a nice enough boy, but what do I care if you have a former Blackwell warlock for a friend?"

"What are you saying?" Oliver asked, but he knew.

"You're too old to act like you can't understand how these things work. Do you know how beneficial an alliance with the Blackwell coven could be for us? Beatrice is a catch."

Oliver glanced at the mirror on the far wall, saw the reflection of his fifteen-year-old self, thinner and with longer curls. He shook his head. Oliver loved his mother, but loathed her scheming. To think of his friendship with Albert as a way to Beatrice was sick.

"I will never be with Beatrice. Ever! I don't like her!" Oliver insisted.

His mother waved her hands and muttered something about the romanticism of youth.

Sophie stopped skipping around the table to rearrange a fork. "That's too bad. Beatrice looks really pretty now that her braces are gone." She straightened as though struck by a horrible thought. "I don't have to get any, do I?"

Before Lucille could respond, the world faded like smoke.

———

Beatrice curled against Oliver. Her head rested on his shoulder, and Bean slept in her lap. An open field, scattered with trees, stretched before them toward a storm-filled night. Lightning cracked in the distance.

This wasn't a memory.

Oliver turned his head. A large tent behind them remained bone-dry despite the rain and wind whipping a nearby tree. Beatrice must have shielded them from the weather with an enchantment.

Thunder grumbled.

"When shall we three meet again?" Beatrice asked, in a dramatic croaky voice. Then she started to laugh.

A smile spread across Oliver's face at the sound. He turned back to Beatrice, and his breath caught.

Another flash of lightning brought out the green in her eyes. Her hair blew, loose and wild around her head. She smiled at him, and the effect was striking.

Oliver had never seen anything more beautiful.

He leaned closer. His fingers tangled in her hair as he pulled her lips to his, and—

———

Oliver was fifteen again, sitting at his family's dining table.

Beatrice dominated the conversation. Sophie watched with genuine awe, nodding and grinning at everything the older witch said.

Oliver tried not to look. Beatrice didn't need more attention.

She'd gotten her braces removed over the summer, and her hair had grown longer. It fell in loose brown waves over her shoulder and toward her chest. Beatrice had started filling her shirts in a very flattering way.

But Oliver didn't want to notice that!

At least Beatrice remained obnoxious. She could find a thousand ways to say absolutely nothing. Oliver clutched that belief like a lifeline. Every time Beatrice moved toward a topic that interested him, he made an effort to zone out. Because if Oliver ever started enjoying her company then—

———

A new vision formed. Oliver sat in an unfamiliar café with a book open on the table before him. A nearby window showed rolling green hills dotted with sheep. This was not Castor's Grove.

"—Eva and Nathan will only have a week. Do you think we should tell them to meet us in—" Beatrice started listing European cities. Her face grew animated as she talked. Excitement made her expunge on the benefits of each.

It remained annoying. But also a bit endearing.

Oliver held up his book. "I'm trying to read, B. And you're planning like six months ahead."

Beatrice's lips closed in a guilty pout. Then, she flashed a smile that was so suggestive it sent a fire shooting through Oliver's blood. "Well, you know what you could do to get me to shut up?"

Oliver slapped a twenty-pound note on the table, stood, and grabbed her hand. He pulled her toward a flight of stairs in the back.

———

Eleven-year-old Beatrice, smaller but still round, rushed into the living room where Oliver and Albert played cards.

"I wanted to give this to you," she said, holding out her hand. Her voice had always been deep, even as a child, but not in this instance. Now she sounded squeaky. "As a thank you. For yesterday. Because I really appreciated it. So, you know. Thanks."

Oliver had no idea what was happening. He'd been friends with Albert for over a year. Beatrice played with them sometimes if they needed a third, but otherwise, she studied magic in the basement with her grandmother. He'd never seen her get giggly and nervous. Her entire face turned pink as she gave Oliver a card. She'd drawn a black flower on the front.

"Uh... you're welcome?" he said.

Beatrice's cheeks grew brighter. Instead of talking, she ran off.

Oliver turned to Albert. "What was that about?"

"I have no idea." Albert studied his cards. "B is weird."

So she'd given him a thank you card with a heart drawn inside? Oliver studied the flower on the front. It seemed safer than the heart, until—

Oliver stood before a massive white wall. It curved, sealing away something beyond. He touched the wall. A sharp pain exploded through his mind. He tumbled back.

————

Beatrice lay on her dining room table. Her arms rested at her sides; her eyes closed. Pink flushed her cheeks and her dark brown hair streamed around her head. She'd chosen a red dress with a laced bodice and too flattering a fit.

Oliver stood over her. His heart pounded. The old crown on his head meant he was a prince. She expected him to kiss her.

A desire to do just that swept over Oliver. The strength of it terrified him. He leaned closer, then froze, petrified by a sudden realization.

————

Her lips met his in a sweet, yet salty kiss. Oliver recognized the feeling of Beatrice wrapped in his arms. She pulled away too soon.

Oliver's eyes opened and discovered a beach. Aquamarine waters glistened below a setting sun. He wriggled his toes and felt the sand.

"I can't believe you found it!" Beatrice squealed. She held something in her hands. He'd given it to her a moment ago. It was—

But Oliver didn't get to see. He slipped into another vision, drifting between memories and fantasies. He ranted and complained about Beatrice Blackwell over a hundred times, and over a hundred times, he kissed her.

26

BEATRICE

Beatrice stepped through the large glass doors of Castor's Care Hospital and was immediately stopped by the receptionist, a large, middle-aged elf with graying temples.

"Name and purpose of visit?"

Beatrice hesitated. The lobby was surrounded by small stores that had made their home on the hospital's ground floor. People shopped for balloons, teddy bears, and candy hearts behind the glass. They had larger concerns than eavesdropping on the receptionist's conversations.

"It's Beatrice Blackwell."

Forty-eight hours ago, the receptionist would have nodded politely at the name. Now, her thin, over-plucked eyebrows twitched in immediate recognition. Her polite smile remained, but her eyes scanned Beatrice with a new curiosity and more than a hint of judgment.

Tabitha would never have left the house in jeans and a pink sweatshirt.

Beatrice shifted her schoolbag, raised her chin, and attempted to copy the former Matriarch's ever-present sneer. "I'm here to assess the protective barrier on the hospital."

It was a lie. But the Blackwell Matriarch couldn't admit that she'd come to visit an insignificant Wyrmwood warlock. It would stir unsavory rumors. And Gigi had forbidden it.

The receptionist gave Beatrice a card. "Complete access. Wherever you need to go in the hospital. Should I refresh the server just in case? The rush of magic always takes us offline for a while."

"If you think it best," Beatrice said, shrugging before crossing to the elevators on the opposite side of the lobby. She felt a bit guilty wasting the receptionist's time with the task. Even if the magical barrier protecting Castor's Care Hospital from accidental human discovery had been fading, Beatrice hadn't regained enough strength to replenish it. She'd had to beg Gigi to let her attend school today.

Her grandmother had only relented after incessant complaints, and she'd still seemed suspicious.

She wasn't wrong to be. I always planned on getting the guard to drive me here afterward.

"But Gigi doesn't understand," Beatrice whispered to her familiar as she pressed the number seven. The elevator doors closed. "I need to talk to Oliver and get some closure. Otherwise, I'm going to be distracted for the rest of eternity."

Bean poked his nose and front paws out of the bag. His whiskers twitched doubtfully. He closed his eyes and stiffened in an attempt to mimic Oliver's current condition.

"It's better if he can't respond," Beatrice assured the familiar, scratching between Bean's ears. "Then he can't interrupt me."

Or hear me.

Which was also ideal because despite having three days to form an eloquent, measured rejection of Oliver's invitation to travel, Beatrice's mind kept latching on to what he'd said, just before fainting.

He told me he loved me.

Correction. He'd said, "*I think* I love you."

What did that even mean? Did he need to mull it over for a few days and then get back to her? Had the coma given him the required time? Would he awake with sudden certainty and declare *yes, actually, it was love,* or instead inform her *nope, turns out it was just indigestion?*

But it didn't matter.

Whether Oliver's mind had been addled from the smoke— quite likely— or he'd actually had an epiphany and fallen head over heels for her— definite wishful thinking— it made no difference.

Beatrice could never be with a Wyrmwood. Not unless she was willing to die.

———

Her pink sweatshirt and backpack felt like a disguise. The healers in their pale blue uniforms smiled politely, but none recognized Beatrice as anything but a regular teenage girl.

Lucille would know better.

Oliver's mother walked down the windowless corridor, away from her son's room. The rich fabric of her emerald dress swished above the white tile floor, following the motion of her hips. Sophie followed a few paces behind, still in the dark green skirt and tie that identified her as a Wyrmwood witching student. Her neck bent forward ninety degrees, and her fingers flashed against her phone screen.

Oh no.

Beatrice turned her head, searching for somewhere to hide. There had to be a conveniently located supply closet somewhere.

"My word! What an honor," Lucille's voice dripped like honey from a spoon. Yet a bitterness hid behind the sweet. "The Blackwell Matriarch visiting my son."

To Beatrice's horror, Lucille's knees bent in a curtsy.

Further down the corridor, a pair of healers pushing a tray of folded sheets, stopped and turned to watch the display.

So much for keeping this visit a secret.

Lucille coughed and elbowed her daughter. Sophie's head finally snapped up from her phone.

"Oh, hi Bea—"A sharp *ahem* from her mother alerted the fifteen-year-old that she was to curtsy as well. Sophie did so in a quick, awkward movement, flinging her hands too wide and knocking her wrist against her mother's side.

Lucille glared at her daughter from the corner of her eye as they both straightened.

"That really isn't necessary," Beatrice said, trying to hide her discomfort behind a smile.

Curious. She'd always imagined basking in the praise and exaltation that came with being the Blackwell Matriarch. But healers pretending they needed to stop and refold sheets so they could glance at her and whisper wasn't the kind of attention she'd envisioned.

"And I'm actually here on official business," Beatrice added, raising her voice purposefully so that the healers could hear.

Not that it would do much good. Once Gigi heard that Beatrice had visited the hospital, she'd know that her granddaughter had disobeyed her orders.

"Still," Lucille said, flashing a smile that showed far too many teeth. "Your first act as Blackwell Matriarch was to save the life of a lowly Wyrmwood." Her dark red lips curled in a barely concealed snarl around the word *lowly*.

It added a sour note to the compliment that Beatrice didn't understand. She'd always thought Lucille liked her.

But perhaps Oliver's mother had a right to be annoyed. Her son had almost died because Beatrice snuck him onto the Blackwell Estate. Saving him was the least she could have done.

But Lucille wasn't blameless herself by that logic. She'd sold Wilburn the invisibility spell that he'd used to kill Tabitha. And that was what set everything off.

Did she know what he was going to do with it?

Beatrice couldn't openly question Oliver's mother in the middle of the hospital corridor. She needed to be subtle.

Not my strong suit.

"I'm afraid Wilburn incited my coven to violence," Beatrice said, making a point of mentioning the executor's name. "I apologize on their behalf."

"Indeed." Lucille's lips curled into the faintest hint of a sneer. "But I have to wonder if there wasn't some overarching plan guiding the whole ordeal."

"Oh wow!" Sophie interrupted the conversation with a sudden gasp. She pointed to Bean, whose front paws, long snout, and large ears hung over the side of the bag. "Is that your new familiar? He's so cute! Do you think I could take a photo with him?"

Bean wiggled his ears and squeaked in delight.

Beatrice smiled as her familiar hopped from the bag and onto Sophie's outstretched hand.

At least he's getting some positive attention.

Beatrice watched for a moment as the fifteen-year-old

looked around for the best place to pose in the poorly lit corridor. But she was less concerned with Sophie's selfies and more confused by Lucille's comment.

"Are you implying my coven had a long-term plan to trap Oliver and burn him?"

"I'm certain my son is beneath such effort. But I do find it curious that Oliver was invited to speak with Tabitha the very day that she was murdered, and we still have no idea what purpose this meeting would have served."

You're the one who's so friendly with Wilburn, you tell me.

Beatrice drew herself up to her full height. She was still half a foot shorter than Lucille, but it was the best she could manage. If Oliver's mother wished to speak to the Blackwell Matriarch, then that's the role Beatrice would play.

She did her best to channel Tabitha. "What I find curious, is a Wyrmwood selling an invisibility spell to a Blackwell warlock without reporting it to the Matriarch."

The fake smile slid from Lucille's face. "How do you know that? It wasn't in your ledgers."

Of course not! Wilburn wouldn't borrow money from the Blackwell account and alert Tabitha to his plan to murder her.

Beatrice bit her tongue.

Aloof. Dignified. Fewer words. That's how a Matriarch should behave.

"Oliver saw you. He mentioned it."

Lucille's eyes grew wide with an apprehension Beatrice had never seen the older woman display. She pressed her hand to her chest. The emerald rings shone against her dark skin. "I didn't think he'd remember. Given everything."

There was an edge of anxiety to her voice, possibly even guilt.

Why am I pressing the issue?

Lucille could be cold and calculating, but she was still

Oliver's mother. She wouldn't have set him up to take the blame for a murder. And it was clear she regretted her transaction with Wilburn.

"Gigi is sorting through Tabitha's files as we speak," Beatrice assured Lucille, changing the topic as tactfully as she could. "If the meeting was a trap, and someone else summoned Oliver, I'm certain we'll find out."

It wasn't likely. A formal request from a Matriarch would have been a difficult thing to fake. But a seed of hope sprung within Beatrice.

A calculated plan to frame Oliver would be much better than her current leading theory: a marriage proposal.

Tabitha had wanted to ensure a Wyrmwood never married the future Blackwell Matriarch. What if she'd offered to wed Oliver to one of her less powerful descendants instead?

The thought of Debby or Libby giggling with their arms around him made Beatrice feel sick.

"Your grandmother is assisting you," Lucille said, tapping a finger against her cheek. "I suppose she's a valuable resource given that she was slated to be Matriarch herself once."

From a few feet away, Sophie cooed over a photo and showed Bean, who perched on her shoulder.

"You're mistaken," Beatrice corrected Lucille. "Gigi was never in line to be the Matriarch. She's descended from a second daughter."

"And you from the male line." Lucille's voice took a sharper tone. Then, there was a twitch of guilt in her eyes, and her expression softened. "It is kind of you to come, even if only on *official* business."

Lucille inclined her head before continuing down the corridor.

Sophie noticed a few seconds later. She grinned at Beatrice before running after her mother, and Bean leaped from the fifteen-year-old's shoulder back to the bag.

Beatrice scratched between his ears absentmindedly as she walked toward Oliver's room. "Gigi's never said that she was supposed to be the Matriarch. She would've told me something like that, wouldn't she?"

Bean's upper legs did their best attempt at a shrug.

Beatrice pushed the matter from her mind. She needed to stop mulling over every peculiarity she encountered. The murder was solved. Only the missing murder weapon stopped the case from being officially closed.

Perhaps Gigi will find it hidden in Wilburn's things, and I can finally stop worrying about it.

27

BEATRICE

The hospital room was as windowless as the corridor beyond, but the walls had been painted to resemble the sky. White fluffy clouds bounced near the ceiling, and a yellow sun spread from one corner. Beatrice couldn't decide if the design was sweet or sadistic. Two pieces of furniture were all that fit within the small room: a metal side table and a bed with white sheets.

Oliver lay in the center,. Beatrice resisted the urge to look for as long as she was able, but inevitably, her eyes found their way to him.

A lump rose in her throat.

Oliver's bronze skin was two shades darker on his arms, a remnant of his burns. Two pale scars wrapped around his wrists from where the iron ties had sliced him. No sign of a beard remained on his chin or lips, and his eyebrows had been singed.

It should've robbed him of his usual good looks. But it didn't. Even burned and scarred, Oliver remained handsome. His bare chest showed beneath the sheet revealing a shallow dip between his pectoral muscles. Beatrice recalled the feeling of them pressed against her when he'd kissed her against the van.

At least I got that.

Beatrice closed her eyes and summoned the memory, trying to savor it: the tickle of his stubble on her chin, the firmness of his muscles beneath her hand, the tug of his fingers as they tangled with her hair. She couldn't be with Oliver, but him kissing her was already more than she'd ever expected.

And he invited me to go traveling.

Oliver would have rescinded the offer in a few days. His attention always wavered once he got whichever girl he'd decided to pursue. At least Beatrice could reject him first and not have to watch him lose interest.

It's better like this.

So why did Beatrice keep toying with the dream of freeing herself from the vow she'd sworn to Tabitha's memory? Blood oath or not, there had to be some way to break it without forfeiting her life.

The grimoire offered nothing to help. Beatrice had checked during a brief moment of respite yesterday when Gigi had gone downstairs to discuss room reassignments with Debby and Libby.

Without a recipe for guidance, undoing Tabitha's spell would be a dangerous undertaking, and it could take years. By then, Oliver would be back to thinking of her only as Albert's little sister.

Beatrice needed to stop dreaming about escaping her oath and accept her fate. Even if it was proving more difficult to rid herself of her childhood crush than it logically should.

"It's because you're so stupidly handsome," Beatrice said, addressing the comatose warlock as she stepped into the room. She pulled her bag in front of her, removed three books, and stacked them in a neat pile on the table beside him. Her eyes kept stealing glances at Oliver. "You should look ridiculous. Your eyebrows are barely there, you know? But with your muscles and curls and jawline, you've managed to step out of a fire and stay just as hot."

Unfortunately, it wasn't only Oliver's looks that kept him at the forefront of Beatrice's mind. Handsome warlocks abounded in Castor's Grove. But was there another who could talk about the craft of a poem for an hour, who panicked over the slightest speck of dirt in his room, who dreamed of exploring the world, or who protected the people he loved with a fierceness he couldn't even recognize?

Does that include me? He can't even remember when he saved me.

Oliver's hand grabbed Beatrice's wrist.

She squeaked and jumped, almost knocking over the books she'd just arranged.

Oliver's eyes fluttered open, a deep, rich brown that focused on Beatrice. A hint of a smile tugged on the corner of his lips.

"I survive a fire, and you greet me with a pun?" he asked, his voice hoarse and dry.

At the sound, Bean leaped from Beatrice's bag and onto Oliver's chest. The wounded warlock smiled and wrapped a hand around the bilby in a sort of hug, scratching between his ears.

And is there another warlock who'll cuddle with a familiar?

Seeing Oliver with Bean was just about the cutest thing that Beatrice could imagine. Which somehow made this entire situation even worse.

"You weren't supposed to wake up." Beatrice's mouth spoke before her brain realized it.

Oliver stopped scratching Bean, and his smile faltered. He glanced around the room, perhaps only now realizing that he was in the Castor's Care Hospital and not still outside on the dais.

"Now, I mean, from your coma," Beatrice tried to explain, pulling her hand away. There was a water bottle on the bedside table along with her books. A healer must have left it, expecting the warlock to return to consciousness soon. Beatrice tapped a finger against the top, trying to find a way to make this encounter less awkward. "Obviously, you were supposed to wake up eventually. Just not while I was talking."

She'd had a whole plan. She was going to confess all her feelings as a way to put them to rest. It would've been therapeutic, like writing a letter that you never bothered to mail. The first step to casting aside her childhood crush and embracing her new life as the Blackwell Matriarch.

But telling Oliver everything when he was awake and could hear and respond was an entirely different matter.

"I could close my eyes and pretend to be asleep again if you want to keep complimenting me," Oliver suggested. He lifted his hand, likely to run it through his curls, then paused and stared at the darkened skin.

Bean gave a sympathetic whine and retreated to the foot of the bed, giving the warlock space to come to terms with what had happened.

Oliver brought his fingers to the white scars on his wrists, then up to his forehead. "Do I really not have eyebrows?"

"There's still some hair," Beatrice assured him, "But what does it matter? You already heard me admit that you don't need them." She unscrewed the cover from the water bottle and passed it to him.

Oliver's hand trembled as he brought it to his lips. He took a long gulp before resting it down on the table once again. His eyes landed on the books.

"You brought these for me." Oliver's voice was still a bit hoarse, but there was a sweetness to it now. He reached out and touched the spine of the topmost book: an old atlas with metallic blue waters and soft, textured greens.

It had once belonged to Beatrice's grandfather, who'd passed away long ago, around the time of Gigi's accident. He'd been a warlock from a minor coven who'd been hired by Tabitha to search for ingredients. The atlas still had some of his original notes scribbled in the margins.

"For us to plan our future travels?" Oliver guessed, a hint of his usual confidence returning as he turned his gaze toward Beatrice.

A lump rose in her throat.

She couldn't wait for Oliver to fall asleep to make her speech. And it would be ridiculous to run now and send a letter.

Beatrice would need to tell him the truth.

At least some of it.

"I can't go traveling the world, Oliver. With you, or with anyone," Beatrice said. "My place is here in Castor's Grove."

She took a deep breath and forced a smile onto her face.

What I'm about to say next is good news.

"I'm the new Blackwell Matriarch."

28

OLIVER

Beatrice was halfway through her story when a thin fairy with graying temples entered the room. She wore a healer's uniform. A pair of green dragonfly wings folded behind her.

"No visitors for Mr. Wyrmwood now," the healer said in a sharp, no-nonsense voice that made Oliver think of a French teacher he'd had at Dashmoor. The fairy's thin lips closed into a sudden frown as she squinted at Beatrice. "You're the new Blackwell Matriarch. I thought you'd come to inspect the barrier."

Beatrice hesitated for a moment. "I have. This room is a weak spot."

"Mr. Wyrmwood has just awoken from a coma. He needs rest," the healer said walking toward the bed. She shooed Bean off the mattress, patted Oliver's leg, and gave him a smile. "Don't mind her title. I'll kick even a Matriarch out if she's bothering one of my patients."

"No, I'd rather she stay," Oliver found his voice. "I'd hate to be the reason a protective spell failed."

The healer snorted at the continued lie, but she didn't force the issue further. She flicked the tips of her wings and a light appeared on the tip of one of her right index fingers. With her left hand, she took Oliver's chin and tilted it back, so she could examine his eyes.

Beatrice peered over the healer's shoulder, watching what was happening.

Oliver tried to focus on her, but the fairy's light filled his vision. His mind grew fuzzy; his body relaxed.

"Any dreams while you were in the coma?" the healer asked, squinting her eyes.

"Yes," Oliver said, the answer slipping from him before his brain had even registered the question.

"You remember them? Some witches claim they had prophetic dreams while in magically induced comas." The healer snorted. "Mind you, it's probably wishful thinking on their part. Only the oracle can see the future."

"Actually, there have been accounts—" Beatrice began detailing a long list of historic examples to the healer.

Oliver didn't listen. Impressions of his dreams flickered in his mind. They all shared one thing in common: Beatrice.

Could they have been prophetic? A sign of things to come? Adventures he and Beatrice would share.

No.

As the healer moved her light from his eyes, the fuzziness lifted from his mind, and reality set in for Oliver once more.

His dreams had been the result of guilt and wishful thinking. Memories reminded him of all the moments he'd ignored Beatrice. The rest must have been inspired by the fantasies that had filled his mind when Wilburn had marched him to the pyre. They couldn't be glimpses into the future. Because Beatrice could never go traveling the world.

The Blackwell Matriarch was vital not just to her coven, but to all the Castors in the city. It seemed unlikely the title came with much vacation time.

Oliver sat with that thought as the healer examined the rest of his injuries.

"Burns are healing nicely. Might take a few days to get your hair back, and these scars on your wrist are stubborn. But I'd say you'll be ready to leave within the week."

But what would Oliver do then?

I can see the world, or I can pursue Beatrice.

But not both.

"I'll go see about some food for you, Mr. Wyrmwood. You ought to eat something," the healer said, flicking her wings again and diminishing the light on her finger. She gave Beatrice an annoyed look. "I'll be back in five minutes. I trust you'll have finished conducting your investigation by then?"

The healer's tone made it clear that no time would be allotted thereafter.

Beatrice raised her thumb in reassurance.

Once they were alone in the room again, the witch rushed to the end of her tale. "You passed out from the flames, I called the police, and here we are." She spread her arms, gesturing to the small, oddly painted room.

"That's it? I didn't say anything to you?" Oliver asked. Beatrice hadn't mentioned him confessing that he loved her before fainting. It seemed like something she'd have held over his head. Had it been another dream?

If I told her I love her, I can't take it back and go travel the world. I'll have to stay. And if I didn't tell her...

Well, he could go traveling for a bit, couldn't he? Just

like he'd always planned. Beatrice would still be in the city when he returned.

That was it. Heads or tails. The witch's answer would determine Oliver's course of action when he left the hospital.

"No. Don't think so," Beatrice said.

"Oh."

Oliver slumped back onto his pillow. He'd gotten his answer. And if anything, it was the one he should've wanted.

So why was he filled with this sudden disappointment?

"Listen, these are only for you to borrow while you're in here," Beatrice said, resting her hand on the trio of books beside Oliver's bed. "They're my favorites. So give them back to Al when you finish."

"Wow, I nearly die, and I don't even get something for keeps?" Oliver smiled as he sat up to read the titles.

The sight of the atlas made his stomach grow tight. He looked to the one below: a thin copy of *Macbeth*.

"I didn't know you were a Shakespeare fan."

"Are you kidding? It revolves around witches. They're responsible for the entire story."

Beatrice's lips pressed against his. Thunder rolled in the background. They ignored the storm. He'd never felt so deliriously happy.

Oliver shook his head, pulling himself from the memory before he lost himself in it.

It wasn't real. It's not possible. Forget about the dreams.

Oliver turned his attention to the book at the very bottom of Beatrice's stack.

"Finally, the one I expected! You always said this was your favorite." He forced a grin and pulled the text free. It was a hardback copy of *Snow White* wrapped in a red velvet cover with illustrations inside. He opened it and caught a glimpse of the fairytale princess: dark hair, pink cheeks, green eyes.

She looks like Beatrice.

Another flash of a dream came to Oliver. But this one had been real, not a fantasy. He clung to it, trying to recenter himself. "Do you remember that time you convinced us to act it out as a play? You were Snow White, Al was the queen, and I was the prince."

Beatrice crossed her arms and leaned against the wall, a pout appearing on her face. "How could I forget? You jerks changed the ending."

It had been the summer just before Oliver's junior year. They were teenagers, too old for dressing up and putting on fake performances. But an early storm had knocked down the city's powerlines. They'd been stuck indoors with no electricity, and Beatrice had recalled the game she'd been begging them to play with her since middle school.

They'd only agreed to mess with her.

The play, mostly improvised, was still supposed to follow the general story of Snow White. But when the time came for Oliver to kiss Beatrice, Albert jumped out from behind the wall and threw a bucket of water on his sister instead.

Beatrice had sat up in shock, and Oliver decried her as a cruel witch who'd only pretended to be dead to steal a prince's kiss for her potion ingredients. He flew off on his broomstick alone to great applause from Albert and Beatrice's parents, who assumed their daughter had agreed to the change.

"Albert made fun of me for the next year for actually thinking you were going to kiss me," Beatrice muttered, twisting a lock of hair around one of her fingers.

Oliver glanced down at the storybook in his hand, guilt tightening his stomach. He remembered that too. He also remembered laughing and agreeing with Albert, all the while denying the truth.

"I almost did."

He couldn't bring himself to look at Beatrice as he admitted it, so he stared at the clouds on the ceiling instead. It was the first time Oliver had admitted it out loud. He'd tried very hard to forget and bury the memory for years, but the coma dream had forced him to remember

There was a moment, just before Albert threw the water, when Oliver had stood above Beatrice, lying on her parents' dining table, eyes closed, hands to her chest, and he'd seen her. Maybe for the first time.

She wasn't just Albert's annoying little sister. She was a girl, a beautiful one, with dark hair and flushed cheeks and curves. A girl who could bewitch an apple to hover in midair, memorize long stanzas from storybooks, and steal the attention of an entire room.

And Oliver wanted to kiss her.

But then I chickened out and tried to forget I'd ever had the desire.

He'd spent the next few years insisting that Beatrice Blackwell was an annoying pain in the ass, and he'd sooner wash a thousand dishes by hand than be in her presence.

But it was all a lie. Just a wall he'd built to hide from the truth. Because deep down, he'd known that once he fell for her, there would be no going back.

Beatrice was it for him.

Oliver pulled his eyes from the painted clouds, met her gaze, and found her eyes burning with all the emotion and brilliance that lived within the witch. His heart stumbled in his chest, two quick, desperate beats.

It was exactly as he'd always feared. The wall was gone, and Oliver was a mess. His dreams lay crumpled at his feet. He *could* travel without Beatrice, but it would be an exercise in suffering. Every new place Oliver visited, he would feel her absence. His mind would forever haunt him with the false memories of how much better his journey could have been if only Beatrice had been at his side.

There's no adventure worth having without her.

He needed to tell her.

But he couldn't just say it like that. It would have been unbelievably sappy.

What's a sensible, rational way to inform someone that you've decided you can't travel the world after all because you'd miss them too much?

Oliver didn't have time to formulate the correct phrase before an alarm sounded in Beatrice's bag.

Bean's head appeared. He held the witch's phone balanced between his ears.

"You set a five-minute alarm?" Oliver guessed.

"No, it's a message from Gigi. She found something in Wilburn's files" A panicked look went over Beatrice's face.

"What is it? The murder weapon?" Oliver asked. But it struck him as wrong almost at once. He'd been operating on the assumption that Wilburn had murdered Tabitha. But that was before the pyre, before Oliver saw the fury and hatred in Wilburn's eyes.

Why would he have been so willing to kill me if he knew I was innocent?

The healer returned before Oliver could voice his thoughts. A tray of food hovered in the air behind her. She frowned at Beatrice. "I'm afraid I really must insist, Miss Blackwell. It's for Mr. Wyrmwood's own good."

"I understand. I'm finished in here now anyway. And

your patient should be resting." Beatrice leaned over to take the copy of *Snow White* from Oliver and return it to the table. As she did, she brought her lips close to his ear and whispered, "I think I'm about to find out why Tabitha summoned you that morning."

29
BEATRICE

The Sunday after her not-so-secret visit to Castor's Care, the new Blackwell Matriarch finally found time in her schedule for a visit to the police station.

"And Linda is excited to meet with me?" Beatrice clarified as she followed Amos down a dark corridor. It gave the path to the prisons an unnecessarily eerie vibe. The police needed better lightning. Maybe the Blackwell coven should donate the money.

The sergeant shrugged his broad shoulders, then glanced back. "She maintains her innocence. Given Oliver's recovery and Wilburn's skill with the law, I expect a jury will agree. Unless you've got that search warrant for me?"

Guilt rose in Beatrice's chest. Amos had protected Oliver and rushed to the Blackwell Estate when she called. The sergeant had every right to come onto the property and perform a thorough investigation.

But her coven disagreed.

"*You know witches don't always operate above the law.*" Gigi had explained. "*There are many in our family with items of questionable origin. And a few things it would be best the King never learned that we have in our possession."*

According to her grandmother, the Matriarch couldn't have Blackwells arrested, nor could she have them return their illegally purchased goods or order them to stop acting unlawfully in the future. To make such outlandish demands risked revolt and internal uprising. And Beatrice hadn't forgotten about the banshee's shriek at the graveyard.

Another Blackwell was going to die.

But not me, or I'd know.

A shriek was enough warning for the average witch, but a Matriarch deserved better. Custom dictated the banshee would visit her personally in her dreams prior to her death.

Which was partly why Beatrice had spent so little time sleeping since taking the title.

"I assure you that we're conducting a thorough investigation on our own," Beatrice lied. The coven had declared that a search of their rooms or private quarters constituted a violation of privacy.

"Yeah. That's what the Captain said." The sergeant grunted, stopping before a large door. He pulled a key from a chain at his hip, then turned his deep-set eyes on Beatrice with an admonishing gaze. "Don't know why I thought it would be any different with you in charge. Suppose you're still paying half the station under the table."

"I'm quite certain I don't know what you mean, Sergeant." Beatrice fluttered her hands again, trying to ignore the tightness in her chest.

Bribing the Castor's Police was a necessary evil. Beatrice had little respect for the officers on her payroll, including the station's Captain. But if their Matriarch abruptly cut their funding, the Blackwells' unscrupulous allies would soon become enemies. The last thing the coven needed was dishonest cops inventing reasons to arrest them.

"Any way, evidence or not, you have the guilty party," Beatrice reminded him. "We just need a confession." She fluttered her hands in what she hoped was a conciliatory gesture. Her bell sleeves fell artfully to the side, heavy with a variety of magical artifacts.

The new dress had been custom-made three days ago. Beatrice had compromised her preferred pink for a deep red that remained morbidly blood-colored. However, gold embroidery cinched her waist and lined the hem and collar. A pair of matching rubies sparkled in her ears. Gigi said that a proper outfit was crucial if Beatrice was to represent her coven and conduct business with the important members of Castor's Grove.

But the dress didn't appear to be impressing Amos.

He grunted again, unlocked the door, and simply muttered, "We'll see."

———

"Oh thank goodness!" Linda rushed to her cell's bars. Without the make-up and finery, she appeared like any large, middle-aged woman. Wisps of gray curled in her dark hair, and a brown jumpsuit accentuated her girth. "I was wondering when you'd come to release me."

Beatrice stepped back before Linda could grab her hand. The older witch's exuberant approach might've been a ploy to steal magic from Beatrice's sleeves.

"The food in here is ghastly," Linda said, giving Amos a withering look as though the sergeant cooked the meals himself. "And there isn't even lotion. Feel how dry my skin is." She stretched out her arm.

Beatrice wasn't falling for it. "You're being held in the jail until your trial."

Linda's face dropped. She retracted her hand and gave a mournful, almost childlike sob. "But I thought you were the new Matriarch."

"I am." Didn't Beatrice's dress make that clear?

"Then why won't you pay to have me released? That's your job. You're supposed to protect the coven."

"You killed someone," Beatrice reminded her.

Linda waved her hands in dismissal. "Only a Wyrm-wood. Anyway, I thought he didn't die."

Beatrice's stomach clenched at the way the older witch had dismissed Oliver. "I meant Tabitha. We know you and Wilburn conspired to kill her so you could be installed as Matriarch."

Linda's thick eyebrows rose. "You think I—?" She laughed. "Oh, no, no, no. Wilburn's the one who's obsessed with primogeniture and inheritance. I liked being Tabitha's heir. I certainly didn't want her job. I'd have been quite happy if she'd outlived me. But I didn't want Debby and Libby to lose their status in the coven. You haven't made them change rooms have you? They really don't deserve—"

Beatrice listened to her distant aunt prattle on about all the luxuries that she and her daughters should still be entitled to enjoy with a sense of awe.

People think I talk a lot?

Amos watched Beatrice throughout the exchange. The sergeant's face was easy to read.

"You don't think she's guilty," Beatrice accused as they left the women's section of the police jail.

"She's a spoiled child, not a conniving killer."

Beatrice pursed her lips. "Maybe Wilburn did it on his own."

"Maybe." Amos guided her toward another locked door. The male prisoners' cells would be beyond. "I visited Oliver yesterday. He didn't seem to share your confidence about Wilburn. Have you spoken to him recently?"

"Of course, I have," Beatrice lied, ignoring the panicked increase in her heart at the mention of Oliver. She'd hadn't seen him since her last visit when she'd told him that she was the new Blackwell Matriarch. "And he agrees it was Wilburn. Perhaps you misunderstood."

"Sure." Amos' voice took on a gentle, almost paternalistic quality that made Beatrice suddenly certain of two things. The sergeant had children, and he knew how to spot a lie. "You tell him about the money yet?"

And there it was. The reason she'd been avoiding Oliver.

Among Wilburn's documents, Gigi had discovered Tabitha's will and an enclosed letter to Oliver Wyrmwood. The former Matriarch had bequeathed him a rather generous sum. But the gift was conditional. Oliver would need to leave Castor's Grove and forsake all communication with the Blackwell coven.

He would take the money, of course. Only his friendship with Albert might give him pause. But few warlocks remained permanent members of their covens. Albert would marry in a few years. Oliver could resume their friendship then, and the money would be enough to give him everything he wanted.

And then I'll never see him again.

Beatrice's cheeks quivered from the effort of forcing a smile. She didn't want to cry in front of the sergeant. "I suppose you knew the whole time. It would've been in the files Wilburn originally gave you."

Amos nodded. "That's why we were curious about your relationship. It might look suspicious now if you allow him to take the money and still stay in the city. Not that you couldn't pay my superiors to look the other way." He muttered the last part.

"That won't be necessary," Beatrice reassured him. She could bribe the police, but not her coven. They wouldn't be happy if she altered Tabitha's offer. "It will be given how it is."

"Oh." Amos frowned. "Well, good then." He didn't sound certain. "I'm sure he won't take it. He'd be a fool if he did." Amos offered another fatherly smile, then he unlocked the door.

————

"You." Wilburn glared at Beatrice as he crept forward. His lips twisted in a snarl. Imprisonment had done little to change the old warlock. He'd already been thin and graying.

At least he's clever enough to know that I haven't come to free him.

"You won't get away with this," Wilburn said, whisper trembling with barely suppressed rage as he approached the bars. "I won't let you."

Beatrice crossed her arms. She assumed this performance was for Amos' benefit. "You're the one who's guilty. Not me."

"Did you think I wouldn't figure it out? Tabitha would never have chosen an undeserving, barely-Blackwell like yourself to be Matriarch." Wilburn spat through the bars onto Beatrice's new dress. His eyes grew wild with fury, and he pushed himself closer.

Cold crept across Beatrice's skin. She fought the urge to

run. Wilburn appeared so thin that he might squeeze between the bars and attack her like a wraith.

"I know you manipulated her, you devil," the old man hissed. "You stole my forgetting potion from my private stash and used it on her somehow, and once I find proof, I'll —" His hands lashed out toward Beatrice.

Amos appeared before her in an instant, blocking the old man's claws. "Are you confessing to having illegal forgetting potions in your possessions, Mr. Blackwell?"

Wilburn lowered his arms. The fury dissipated into a cold, calculating smile. "A private conversation between a coven member and their Matriarch is inadmissible in court. The illegality of anything I mention is of none of your concern."

The old warlock might have been right on a technicality. But a stolen forgetting potion concerned Beatrice greatly.

Not because such a thing was illegal. But because it was a Wyrmwood specialty.

No more procrastinating and worrying about Tabitha's offer. Beatrice needed to talk to Oliver.

30
OLIVER

Oliver stood before the mirror, inspecting his jaw. No evidence of burns darkened his chin and cheeks. His skin had returned to an even brown. But his beard was still growing in patchy.

He flicked the razor over the pockets of stubble, wiped his jaw, and patted his curls into position. Then, he practiced a smile in the mirror.

Oliver was being released today. But that wasn't what had him nervous.

Since her visit on Wednesday, he had been waiting for Beatrice.

Why had her great-great-grandmother wanted to speak with him? Had she found the murder weapon? Would she want to maybe grab dinner somewhere and then discuss Shakespeare while they watched a thunderstorm?

Oliver slipped his arms through a dark green shirt and did up the buttons. He considered himself in the mirror once more, and then undid the top two, playing with the positioning of the collar.

What am I doing?

He'd spent the past twenty minutes staring at his own reflection, worrying about how he looked. Beatrice had liked him for years. Did he really think that if he showed up with a wrinkled shirt, she'd reject him?

Maybe?

She hadn't visited him again. That couldn't be a good sign.

Or she's just busy now that she's the Blackwell Matriarch.

Oliver left the rather large hospital bathroom to return to his much smaller, sky-painted room. The healers had been nice, but he wouldn't miss the hospital.

To his surprise, Albert sat on the edge of the bed, wrapped in a stretched-out gray hoodie. He looked up from his phone as Oliver entered and flicked his gaze over his friend.

"You look a bit nice for Four-Point-O."

Oh crap. Four-Point-O was a café and bar near the university that was popular with the students.

Oliver had forgotten that he'd agreed to go there with his friend to celebrate his release from the hospital. They'd made the plan yesterday before the message from Beatrice arrived.

"Sorry, dude," he said, shoving his toothbrush and razor into the packed bag beside his bed. "Can we go tomorrow instead? Something came up." Oliver pulled out a small container of cologne, shook it, and sprayed it near his neck.

Albert raised his eyebrows, a slight smile on his lips. "Are you ditching me to go on a date with one of the healers?"

"No, it's not a date." Oliver gave an awkward laugh and shoved the cologne away. "I'm meeting your sister."

Any hint of amusement vanished from Albert's face. "Why?"

"I don't know. One of your servants showed up today and said she wanted to meet with me this evening."

A healer arrived to discharge Oliver. She signed the chart at the end of the bed, handed him a prescription for a specialty skin ointment, and gave him the all-clear to leave.

Albert got up from the bed, slipped his phone into his pocket, and helped gather the last of Oliver's belongings. "I'll come to the manor with you. We can go to Four-Point-O after."

Absolutely not.

Oliver wanted to speak to Beatrice in private. How could he say what he really wanted to if her brother was there?

"I don't think that's a good idea," Oliver said, searching for an excuse as he grabbed his gray winter jacket from the hook on the door. "Would be disrespectful to bring a guest to a meeting with the new Matriarch."

Albert's eyes narrowed at him. "We're talking about Beatrice. I'm her brother."

Exactly.

"You think she wants to speak with you in an official capacity?" Albert asked. "Maybe about why Tabitha summoned you in the first place? Your mother was hoping for a marriage proposal, but obviously, you don't have any interest in that. You want to travel the world still, don't you?"

"Oh, I mean. I don't know." How could Oliver explain that the idea of traversing the globe alone didn't seem as tempting now since he'd dreamed how much better it would be with Beatrice. "Traveling the world was always a bit far-fetched."

"Is it your mother?" Albert guessed as they stepped onto the elevator. He pressed the button to the ground floor. The doors closed and he turned to his friend, expression serious. "She's pressuring you to pursue Beatrice now that she's the Matriarch, isn't she?"

Oliver paused. His mother had soured a bit on the Blackwells since they'd attempted to murder him. But no doubt she'd warm to them again in a few months when her memories of their attacks on the Wyrmwoods faded. Lucille would likely resume her efforts to marry her son to Beatrice.

Am I still going to fight with her about it?

"Maybe." Oliver's stomach flipped. He couldn't meet his friend's eyes as he continued. "I mean, would it be so terrible if I did?"

The elevator stopped. There was a ding as the doors opened.

Albert stepped forward, blocking the exit. "You're serious."

Oliver tried and failed to step around him. "Dude, what's the problem? I'm not saying I will. I just don't see what the big deal would be if I did. You've always said your sister had a thing for me."

"Because she has, and you've known it for almost eight years and had less than no interest. You'd rather die than be with Beatrice, isn't that what you said?"

Had he really? "That sounds a bit extreme. Your sister's nice."

The numbers rose on the display above the door as the elevator carried them back up.

Albert shook his head, mouth twisting into a scowl. "I can't believe it. Gigi was right the whole time. You're a piece of shit social climber. Just like your mother."

"What did you say?" Oliver's voice rose. He dropped his

bag and raised his fist, but he stopped himself shy of hitting his friend.

Albert stared at the hand hovering a few inches shy of his head, a clear threat.

Ding! They stopped on the fifteenth floor before a confused couple, holding a newborn baby.

Embarrassed, Oliver lowered his hand and stepped back. He'd never fought with Albert before. But his friend had never been such an asshole either.

Does he really think I'd take advantage of Beatrice like that?

Oliver didn't have the opportunity to ask. His friend stepped off the elevator and into the maternity ward. The couple took his space, huddling in a corner as far from Oliver as they could get.

"Stay away from my sister," Albert warned. "And my coven."

Then the doors closed, sending Oliver back down.

31
BEATRICE

Beatrice climbed the stairs to the Matriarch's study. Although it was her office now, it didn't feel like it. The space was still full of Tabitha's things: the black desk, the shelves stacked with gothic literature, the stuffed raven with his mouth open in a silent, never-ending caw. The large black armchair was new, but only because Tabitha's blood had dripped onto the old one.

Gigi was waiting for her when she opened the door.

"You're late," her grandmother said. She floated in the center of the study, one hand clutching the gleaming mahogany of her new broomstick, which seemed to have permanently replaced her wheelchair. "No more unnecessary trips to the hospital, I trust?"

Beatrice sighed and shook her head as she walked to the armchair behind the desk. Her plan to keep her visit with Oliver secret had been a spectacular failure. By the time she'd returned home that evening, whispers were already flying among the coven. Sophie had posted one of the pictures she'd taken with Bean onto some social media account, and the younger Blackwells had seen it within seconds and shown their parents.

Gigi spun in the air, eyes following her granddaughter. The moment Beatrice was seated, the old woman unfurled a long list, holding the paper at arm's length. Her eyes widened as she attempted to read the small writing without her glasses.

"Mabel wants an increase to her family's monthly allowance, Elder Bethany and Younger Bethany are squabbling over a patch of Lycan's root that's sprouted between their houses..."

Beatrice wasn't listening. Since her visit with Amos that morning, she'd spent the entire day in meetings, pretending to care about stock investments, magical contracts, and political matchmaking. Now she was too tired to keep up the pretense.

There was only one appointment today that she cared about.

And it definitely wasn't Gigi's daily run-down on coven affairs.

"... and Basil's mother has decided that he's ready to wed. There's a list of witches from suitable families for you to peruse. It should be in one of Tabitha's binders." The old woman flew toward one of the bookshelves, examining a row near the top. She plucked a silver spiral-bound booklet and brought it to her granddaughter.

"Put it with everything else." Beatrice pointed to a growing pile of notes on the edge of the desk. Her unfinished math homework, almost a week late, threatened to fall from the top.

Gigi frowned. "That is hardly the right attitude. These are matters of serious importance. It would be best not to push them aside."

"I don't think shackling some poor witch to bad-breath-Basil should really be that high of a priority," Beatrice said, taking a seat behind the desk. "We haven't officially solved Tabitha's murder."

And Oliver is going to be here soon.

But she knew better than to admit that she was nervous about seeing him.

"Wilburn and Linda are guilty." Gigi flicked her hand, dismissing the issue. She shook the booklet at her granddaughter. "I must say, I'm very disappointed with how you're handling your responsibilities. You've been given an opportunity that every witch dreams of, yet this entire week, you've been sullen and mopey. And why? The whole coven is finally recognizing how powerful you are. You've gotten new dresses, a new bedroom and office, servants at your beck and call."

"And no freedom to do anything I want." The response slipped from Beatrice before she could stop it.

"You're upset with me for guiding you?" Gigi's thin gray eyebrows rose to the center of her forehead. "Child, you might be Matriarch, but you do have neither the love nor the fear of the coven. You cannot rule them the way Tabitha did. In time, you will earn their respect, but you complicate matters when you abandon your duties to visit a Wyrm-wood in the hospital. Do you have any idea the damage control I had to do so that they wouldn't think you frivolous and immature, or worry about—"

Beatrice stopped listening again, staring at the stack of books and files on her desk. They made her think of the three that she'd lent to Oliver, full of inspiration for adventure, and magic, and romance.

Gigi had misunderstood her comment. As frustrating as

it was having so little agency within the coven, Beatrice was mourning the loss of her freedom to leave.

But crying wouldn't fix things.

Beatrice's eyes flicked to the dark wooden lectern beside her desk. The Blackwells' leather-bound spellbook rested atop. Her blood swirled in its ruby eye. She'd bound her soul to the grimoire, an even more binding covenant than her oath to Tabitha. Beatrice would be the Matriarch until her death.

"You're right, Gigi," Beatrice interrupted her grandmother's tirade and forced a smile. "Let's take a look at Basil's eligible bachelorettes."

———

Her grandmother had barely left before a cautious tap sounded on the door.

Beatrice looked up from the first sum of her math assignment, heart pounding in her chest. Oliver was early.

The handle turned. Gabriel's head peeped around the door, his eyes wide and unfocused.

Beatrice could've slapped herself.

How the hell did I forget?

All week, she'd been trying to find a moment to talk to her cousin, but she had so many meetings. She'd eventually gotten frustrated and penciled Gabriel in for the end of today.

"Sorry, I'm a bit early, but I saw Gigi leave," he addressed his apology to the stuffed raven. "I can come back in a few minutes."

"No, that's fine take a—" Beatrice cut herself off. There were no other chairs in the office besides her own. Tabitha's idea. Apparently, it intimidated visitors.

"It's okay." Gabriel managed to make eye contact long enough to shrug. "I stood last time as well."

Beatrice's eyebrows rose. Her cousin had unwittingly gotten straight to the point. "So you did meet with Tabitha the morning she died. Because your brother insisted that you missed the appointment."

She'd spoken to Rett a few days ago while doing an inspection of the greenhouse. He'd gotten annoyed by her questions and kept glancing toward Elle.

"I lied to him," Gabriel admitted, staring at his feet.

Beatrice almost didn't know what to say. She'd had a hunch something strange was going on, but she hadn't expected her cousin to just come right out and say it. Did he understand the implications of what he was telling her?

"That means you were the last person to see Tabitha alive," Beatrice said, standing up from her seat.

Gabriel blinked, seeming surprised by her sudden movement. Slowly, his eyes focused on her. "I think that would've been the killer."

Exactly. Beatrice didn't want to spook her cousin by spelling that out for him. "Why did you lie to Rett?"

"Because when I told him about the meeting, he ordered me to cancel it." Gabriel fiddled with his fingers, almost as though he were twisting imaginary rings. "But I didn't listen to him. He kept trying to protect Elle. I don't understand why. He's the talented one. He deserved credit."

Beatrice tapped her fingers against her chin, trying to understand. "You told Tabitha the truth about who cured her from the poison?"

Gabriel nodded. "It was a very short meeting. I told her that she'd given the card to the wrong person and that Elle had been passing off Rett's magic as her own for years. I thought she'd leave with me and fix her mistake at once, but she didn't get out of her chair. Just told me to return home and let her think on things. Whole thing lasted barely five minutes."

Which explained why he'd been standing in his house when Oliver entered the compound several minutes prior to the murder. This line of investigation felt like a dead end.

"You didn't see anything strange when you left, did you?" Beatrice asked. She was grasping at straws. She already knew the murderer had been invisible.

"Not really. I mean, I did run into Elle when I was leaving, and she was pretty curious about what I was doing in the manor. I was terrified that she'd piece everything together and tell Rett, but then, the next day, it was like she'd forgotten the whole thing."

Beatrice hadn't quite processed the implications of what Gabriel had said when another knock came and the door opened again.

Oliver stepped inside, looking like the cover of a romance novel. He held his gray winter jacket over his shoulder, and his dark green shirt opened enough to highlight the firm muscles of his chest.

"Sorry I'm so early. It was nerve-wracking coming in here again. Glad to see you alive and standing." Oliver smiled, and Beatrice's heart melted into a puddle.

She'd spent the past five days imagining what she would say to him when she finally worked up the nerve to meet. Nowhere in her imagination had Beatrice conjured that Gabriel would be present.

What was she supposed to say in this situation?

I think I love you too, but it doesn't matter because I made a deal with the memory of a dead woman and now we can never be together, but I can give you a rather large sum of money and you can travel the world without me and probably fall in love with some gorgeous blonde, and I'll see pictures of the two of you all over social media because I'll still be stalking your life from a distance even though you'll have gone back to forgetting that I exist.

Beatrice's lips moved, soundless for a moment before she finally convinced her mouth to form a word. "Sorry."

"For what?" Oliver rested his hand on his curls and bent his head, shooting her a sweet, almost shy gaze that made Beatrice's heart race a hundred times faster than his confident smile ever had. "Saving my life? Stopping your coven from attacking mine? Looking great in that dress?"

Beatrice's heart grew louder. If she'd been struggling to speak before, he'd just made it a hundred times worse.

He complimented me. He never compliments me.

Oliver smiled. "Isn't this the part where you say, *I know* and do a spin?"

"Excuse me," Gabriel said, looking away from the raven that he'd become fascinated by since Oliver's arrival. "Should I leave?"

Beatrice hesitated. The only thing more awkward than having her cousin hovering nearby would be being alone with Oliver. At least Gabriel gave her an excuse to keep quiet about Tabitha's will, which meant Beatrice could enjoy a few more hours before she said goodbye to Oliver for good.

"Um, no, it's good you're here." It was ten times easier to find her voice when addressing Gabriel. "You were telling me that Elle saw you the morning that Tabitha was murdered but didn't remember later. Wilburn has illegal forgetting potions. What if she saw him do something incriminating, so he used one on Elle?

"I don't think so," Oliver said, stepping into Beatrice's line of vision. "Wilburn wanted to burn me alive because he thought I was guilty. I doubt he'd have been so enraged if he was the real killer. Plus, I saw the vials of forgetting potion when I was in his office. They were all still full."

"Well, he claimed someone stole some," Beatrice said. She wasn't sure how much stock they ought to put in Wilburn's deranged accusations, but she was relieved to have managed to string together a full sentence.

Oliver's brow furrowed. His mind seemed to be piecing something together, but before he could say what it was, they were interrupted by yet another knock.

"What?" Beatrice shouted, turning toward the door. She was a hundred percent certain that there were no other meetings that she'd forgotten about. This had to be Gigi, interrupting her with some tedious task that she'd insist was essential.

Libby Blackwell, round cheeks flushed and short hair a wild mess around her face, stumbled into the office. She still had on a pair of solid-white winter boots and a matching coat.

Beatrice didn't understand. "Has Debby sent you to kill me?"

She was joking. Mostly.

Oliver at least laughed.

Libby didn't. She pressed her hand to her chest, took a few quick, ragged breaths, and finally said, "The banshee is here. I just saw her leaving the greenhouse."

32
OLIVER

Moonlight shone through the glass roof into the center of the building, illuminating a body on a stone slab like it was the star of a play: fair hair loose around a pretty face, big brown eyes staring, unblinking at its audience. There was no twitch of her toes, no flutter of her eyes, no rise and fall of her chest.

It was the second time in a month that Oliver had discovered a dead body.

I have to stop attending meetings with Blackwell Matriarchs.

At least he wasn't alone this time.

"Elle," Beatrice whispered her cousin's name before rushing toward the body.

Beside Oliver, Libby gasped, clutching her chest. Her breath came in ragged, anxious, half-strangled sobs. Gabriel was more composed. His head tilted to the side, and he studied the body with his wide, unfocused gaze.

"Is she—?" He started to ask, but the answer must have become obvious to him. "What should we do?"

Oliver had no idea. Run? That was his response last time, and it had probably saved his life.

"Take Libby and call the police," Beatrice said. "We have to report her death."

Gabriel gave a wobbly salute. His shock appeared to be wearing off, and he looked like he might've started crying as well. But he managed to grab Libby and pull her out of the greenhouse before any tears shed.

Oliver remained standing in the midst of the foliage, sweat pooling on his temples and dripping toward his eyes. He'd known Elle only as a casual acquaintance. She'd been too proud to associate with a Wyrmwood. Still, seeing her lifeless on a stone slab made him feel as though there were worms crawling over his skin.

He didn't know how Beatrice was so collected. The witch stood behind the body, lips pursed, head tilted down as she studied her dead cousin. Had something caught her eye?

Oliver took a deep breath. The scent of death hadn't entered the greenhouse yet. Instead, his nostrils filled with the thick, heavy scent of the multitude of plants. He didn't inhale again as he slunk nearer to the body, not until he stopped opposite Beatrice.

When he spoke, his voice came out in an anxious rush of breath. "Do you think it was the same person who killed Tabitha?"

Beatrice looked up from the body. "Linda and Wilburn have been imprisoned. They couldn't have done this."

"Agreed."

Beatrice's lips pressed together. She understood the implication of what Oliver was saying, but she shook her head. "There's nothing similar about the two deaths. We can't assume Elle was murdered."

"I don't think a healthy twenty-two-year-old just happened to lie down on a stone table and die."

"I know." Beatrice's voice grew soft. She twirled a strand of hair around her finger, eyes flitting away from both Oliver and the body. "But what if Elle did this herself?"

"What? Like some sort of ritual suicide?"

"Maybe. Elle wanted to be chosen as the Matriarch. She might've been more upset than anyone realized. Not that she should've been."

Oliver couldn't help but notice the way her tone turned bitter with that last sentence. "You're not enjoying being the Matriarch."

The witch gave him a small rueful smile, looking guilty for mentioning it. "It's no fairytale adventure."

We could have one though. Oliver thought he'd abandoned the dream, but it rushed back to him in a second. They could run off and explore the world, just like they'd discussed. Surely, another witch could perform the protective spells the city required. Beatrice would just need to abandon her viper's nest of a coven.

"What if it wasn't jealousy, but guilt?" Beatrice continued, unaware of the direction Oliver's thoughts had wandered. "Gabriel saw Elle that night. After his meeting with Tabitha." Beatrice's hands grew animated, bell sleeves swishing as she talked. "What if Elle figured out that Gabe had gone to tell Tabitha the truth about who had really made the potion that healed her? Elle thought she had the card that would allow her to become Matriarch. She might've wanted to kill Tabitha before the offer could be rescinded."

Oliver didn't know anything about Gabriel's meeting or a healing potion. But Elle couldn't have killed Tabitha.

"The killer was invisible. If Elle isn't that good at magic, how could she have figured out my family's recipe?"

"Good point. She'd need to have purchased a spell. But Tabitha would never have paid for it, and Elle didn't have access to private funds." Beatrice pursed her lips as she twirled her hair. "You're a pretty good detective."

She smiled at him. The moonlight illuminated the rich browns of her hair, making them glow with an aura of light. Oliver's breath caught.

How did it take me so long to realize how beautiful she is?

He licked his lips. It didn't seem the right time to make such a comment, given the corpse between them. Instead, Oliver settled for, "We make a good team."

Beatrice's smile grew broader before it vanished.

"Look!" She pointed at Elle's wrist.

Oliver leaned closer.

A black mass moved through Elle's veins. It pressed against her skin, making it bubble as it crept toward her palm. The sight made Oliver's stomach twist.

Beatrice wrapped her hand in the long fabric of her sleeve and grabbed her cousin's wrist. She turned to Oliver. "Get me a syringe. There should be some in the cupboard."

She had a way of issuing a command.

Oliver didn't hesitate. He raced to the supply closet beside the entrance, found the packaged syringes, and grabbed one.

"We use them for extracting fluid from the plants, but it should work on a person. I want to get a sample of whatever this stuff is." Beatrice seemed unable to resist explaining as she tore the wrapping open with her teeth. One-handed, she constructed the needle and syringe.

Oliver debated offering assistance. "You're tampering with a crime scene. Isn't that illegal?"

"I knew you had a moral compass." Beatrice smiled as she stuck the needle into her cousin's wrist.

"Ha. Ha." Oliver winced as the black fluid rose into the syringe. It made a strange hissing noise as it left Elle's veins. "I just don't think we're making Amos' life any easier by interfering. And I kind of owe him. He went to a lot of trouble to keep me out of prison."

"I know." Beatrice sighed as she withdrew the needle. "But if there is a killer on the loose among my coven, then I need to study this." She flipped the syringe upside down and held it up to the moonlight. The black liquid seemed to have solidified into a bubbling mass that crept along the glass.

"Is it—?"

"Poison," Beatrice answered before he'd finished the question. "And a nasty one by the look of it. If this wasn't suicide, if someone did this to Elle, they might strike again, and we're going to need an antidote."

33
BEATRICE

The Blackwells arrived before the police did. Old aunts, distant cousins, and curious servants slunk through the woods and down the path, trying to peer through the glass and the foliage to catch a glimpse of the body. A group of guards created a perimeter around the entrance, holding them at bay. But the coven shouted to Beatrice as she stepped out of the greenhouse, the poison hidden up her sleeve.

"Is it true? Is Brielle dead?" one called.

"Was she murdered?" another asked.

"Is that Oliver Wyrmwood in there with you?"

"Is he the killer?"

A cry of anguish broke through among the shouts. Beatrice turned to see her Aunt Sybil, Elle's mother, sobbing into Rett's shoulder. He looked up at Beatrice with a steady, unflinching gaze.

What did it say about him that his closest cousin had been announced dead, and he hadn't shed a tear?

Is it strength? Shock? Apathy?

Beatrice wasn't crying either. She was afraid to consider what that said about her.

Gigi bypassed the guards, swooping down behind their ranks. She stopped her broomstick just in front of Beatrice. "Poor timing for your appointment with Mr. Wyrmwood."

Beatrice glanced through the glass to where Oliver waited. She could just make out his curls through the leaves. "This isn't his fault. He was with me when she died. Libby saw the banshee. Gabe can confirm—"

"He already has," Gigi said. "Luckily for you, Gabriel and Libby were wise enough to come to me before rushing to call the police as you advised. I trust you're certain that Brielle is dead?" There was the slightest tremor in her voice as she asked. Elle had been Gigi's granddaughter too.

"Yes." The word felt heavy and unpleasant on Beatrice's tongue, and the syringe of poison grew cold and clammy where it pressed against the fabric of her sleeve.

Gigi's eyes closed for a moment. Then she became steel once more. "We'll need to move the body before the police arrive. We can't have them snooping around the greenhouse. You speak to the coven. I'll take both Elle and Mr. Wyrmwood out the back. It will give me the chance to relay Tabitha's offer and send him on his way."

"No!" Beatrice's voice was a fraction too loud.

Any attention that had drifted elsewhere returned to the new Matriarch once more. The Blackwells drew closer, shouting questions, objections, and general frustrations. Anguish, fear, malice, and strange mixtures of the three laced their tones.

Beatrice stepped closer to her grandmother, trying to ignore her coven. Her initial concern had been Oliver, but the Blackwells were more than she wanted to handle now.

"I'll take the body. You talk to everyone. Please, they'll only twist anything I say."

The old woman's eyes narrowed, and she tapped her fingers on the mahogany broom. "Fine—but just this once. You'll have to face the more difficult aspects of being Matriarch eventually."

Have I been dealing with the fun ones?

Gigi flicked the wrist of her right hand, and her fingers disappeared into a deep red sleeve. They emerged with a flat white balloon, squeezed between her thumb and palm. "Take this, attach it to Elle's body, and then guide her to the courtyard. That's where I told the police she was discovered." Gigi placed the balloon in Beatrice's outstretched hand, but hesitated to release it. "Make sure you talk to Mr. Wyrmwood when you're finished. The faster he's out of our lives, the better. Unless you wish to be reunited with your cousin sooner than expected." Gigi muttered the last part like an afterthought.

Beatrice's fist clenched around the balloon. She focused on the grave look in her grandmother's eye. Gigi knew that Oliver wasn't a murderer. So why the ominous warning? Beatrice could think of only one reason.

"You know about the promise I swore to become Matriarch. How? I never told you." Beatrice hadn't told anyone. She'd assumed the only ones alive who knew were herself and Bean.

"It was my suggestion. Tabitha would never have allowed you to become Matriarch if it provided a chance for the Wyrmwoods to enter our coven."

Beatrice's shoulders trembled. How could Gigi have encouraged something so cruel and admit to it now in such a crisp, matter-of-fact tone? There wasn't even a hint of regret.

This wasn't the time to discuss the issue. The coven spied from behind the wall of guards. Elle's body was still warm. The police would arrive soon.

But Beatrice's anger hissed from her, low and erratic. "How could you do that to me? You know how I've always felt about Oliver. If Tabitha cared so much, she never needed to pass her title to me. I was never even supposed to be Matriarch."

Gigi's right hand flashed forward. She grabbed Beatrice's cheeks and squashed her lips shut. "The moment I ceased to be an option, this title was yours. Tabitha would've made certain Oliver wasn't an issue. Be grateful my alternative gives you both everything you want, and focus on performing your duty."

The old witch turned Beatrice's head toward the greenhouse door and pushed her away.

Beatrice felt strangely numb as she returned to the warm air, floral scents, and pale corpse within.

What did Gigi mean that she wasn't an option anymore? Was she in line once herself? Like Lucille said?

"B, what's happening? Are the police on their way?" Oliver stepped out from amid the foliage near the entrance. His eyes were wide and nervous, staring at her with a relief that almost burned.

"I think so." Beatrice ran her fingers through her hair, took a deep breath, and avoided looking at the warlock. She needed to keep it together. "There's another door in the back behind some vines. We'll go out that way and wait in the courtyard."

She retrieved the balloon from her pocket. It contained a levitation spell, a specialty of the Cheriths. Not long ago, Beatrice would've been mad to study it and attempt to create her own version. But a coven Matriarch couldn't take those chances.

Beatrice brought the balloon to her lips, closed her eyes, and willed an enchantment into her breath. A single exhale was all it took to trigger the spell.

The balloon expanded in a bright white circle, like a second moon born amidst the foliage. A thin silver string unfurled from beneath.

Beatrice affixed the string to a button in the center of her cousin's dress. A moment later, Elle's body rose, levitated by the spell.

"You're not moving her, are you?" Oliver stepped closer, as though he might attempt to stop her, but he paused a foot shy.

Beatrice didn't answer. She rested one hand on her cousin's shoulder and guided the hovering corpse before her, moving through the long rows of flowers and shrubs, careful not to let her cousin's frozen limbs bump against any thorned bush or perfumed petals.

Oliver followed, his footsteps loud against the cobblestone path. "B, you can't. How is Amos supposed to solve the case if he doesn't even have the correct location for where we found her?"

"It doesn't help him if we leave her here either," Beatrice said. She pushed aside a waterfall of vines to reveal the hidden exit. There was a spike in the center of the door.

She clenched her jaw and pressed her left palm against it, feeling a prick of pain as it broke her skin. Two drops of blood sufficed to release the lock, and the door swung open to reveal the woods beyond.

Beatrice swore she heard the poison hiss in her sleeve. Almost as though it could smell her blood. She swapped the syringe to one of the pockets on her right.

I'm probably just being paranoid.

Beatrice stepped into the night, took a deep breath, and continued to explain the situation to Oliver, "No one but Blackwells are allowed in the greenhouse. You're an accidental exception. Coven's orders."

She picked her way through the trees, maneuvering the floating corpse as gracefully as she could.

I'm so sorry, Elle. This wasn't how any of this ought to have happened.

"You're the Matriarch," Oliver objected. His boots traded the sharp taps of stone for the soft squelch of mud as they progressed through the woods. "You're supposed to give the orders. You're really okay tampering even more with a crime scene?"

"Of course not!" Beatrice snapped.

They were a safe enough distance that she could no longer hear the cries of her coven. She lifted her hand from Elle, leaving her suspended in the air, and spun toward Oliver.

He stared at her with that burning intensity. She couldn't help but read an accusation in his eyes. Amos had helped them, they owed him, and instead, she was destroying the Sergeant's investigation before he had a chance to start.

But Oliver didn't understand.

"This title doesn't work the way you think it does, okay? It's not my decision. None of this is my decision!"

Beatrice waited for him to argue, to tell her to fight harder, or be more assertive, or find a clever way to deceive her entire coven. They were all suggestions that she'd made to herself this past week.

But Oliver remained silent. Instead, eyes trained on

hers, he stepped forward, spread his arms, and enveloped her in a hug.

Beatrice felt his arms, strong and secure, pull her toward him. Her forehead dropped onto the firm muscles of his chest. His cheek brushed the top of her head. She closed her eyes and took in his scent, fresh and woodsy at the same time. She heard his heart, beating beneath her ear, a steady rhythm that reassured her that she wasn't alone.

And for one peaceful moment, Beatrice could imagine that everything was fine.

34
OLIVER

Oliver breathed in the light vanilla scent of Beatrice's hair as his fingers brushed the loose waves falling down her back. The softness amazed him.

She must use incredible shampoo.

He shouldn't have been thinking about that now, but feeling Beatrice's body, warm against his as she curled onto his chest, made it difficult not to lose himself in the moment.

A flash of silver at the corner of his eye forced Oliver's attention elsewhere. He looked up, over Beatrice's head, to Elle's body. Her corpse remained rigid, suspended by a gradually deflating balloon.

Did that light come from her?

Beatrice wriggled free of Oliver's arms, stealing his focus once more. She stared up at him, eyes sad but dry, a hint of their usual fire rekindled in the green. "Thank you for understanding."

She offered him a solemn nod, smoothed the skirt of her long red gown, and turned back toward Elle's body. Beatrice took hold of her cousin's shoulder once again and continued leading them through the woods.

Calm, practical, determined.

The trees stretched before them. The night filled with horror and awe. The silence grew heavy.

But Matriarch or not, Beatrice was still Beatrice. Silence could only survive so long in her presence.

"Obviously, I feel guilty hindering Amos' investigation," she said, waving her free hand as she spoke. "But my coven will barely allow him on the premises. I think they'd riot if I tried to let him into any of the buildings. Of course, I could use the grimoire's power to force them to obey. I did when I saved you, but that left me weak and vulnerable for days. And any sign of weakness, they'll strike. Believe me."

They stopped at the edge of the trees. The Manor's courtyard loomed, a vast sea of darkness before them. The sundial rose from the shadows like a shark's fin.

Beatrice took a deep breath. "I have to solve this case and protect my coven on my own. That's what it means to be Matriarch." She stepped forward, guiding her cousin's body to the sundial.

Oliver's chest tightened. He'd almost died in this courtyard.

Then Beatrice had appeared—glowing with a wild, brilliant power. She'd been the most incredible thing he'd ever seen.

She still was.

How does she remain so in control in the midst of chaos?

Oliver had arrived at the Blackwell Estate with every intention of telling Beatrice how he felt. But watching her now, the words stuck in his throat.

She was too impressive, the night too full of tragedy and

terror, and Oliver too unaccustomed to elaborate confessions.

I've read hundreds of sonnets and romantic verses. That has to have counted for something.

Oliver approached just as Beatrice snapped the string that bound the balloon to her cousin's body. He cupped his palms— left, together, right— forming the three moons of the Goddess over Elle, and recited a common prayer for the deceased.

Beatrice remained crouched beside her cousin, leaning against the sundial as she folded the balloon and vanished it up her sleeve.

"You don't have to be on your own, B." Oliver coughed and extended his arm.

Beatrice didn't look up to notice. She pushed herself to her feet, then offered him a small, rueful smile. "You don't have to worry about solving the murders, Oliver. You're not under suspicion anymore. I can't do much as Matriarch, but I can at least assure you of that."

She doesn't understand. I'm not just talking about solving Tabitha's murder.

Oliver ran his fingers through his curls, staring at the base of the sundial as he collected his thoughts.

"Do you know the scariest part of tonight for me?" He glanced up and found her head tilted in curiosity, eyes focused on him. It made him feel embarrassed, like he was saying too much. But he'd already started, and something about Elle's unexpected death compelled Oliver to speak. He needed to tell Beatrice how he felt now. While he had the chance. "I realized that if there is a killer still on the loose, you could be a target."

Oliver paused, trying to summon the courage to say the

rest. It came in a sudden rush, barely audible over the sounds of sirens, approaching the estate.

"You've been around for almost as long as I can remember, and I took that for granted, but the thought of losing you makes me feel physically ill. I couldn't bare it."

She stared at him, mouth open as if waiting for words that refused to come.

Was he still not being clear? Maybe not. Oliver might've said something similar to his own sister or even Albert. But he wouldn't miss them in the same way. Beatrice had to realize that, didn't she?

Oliver drew closer. He rested his hand on her cheek.

Beatrice closed her eyes and nestled against it.

He brought his lips closer to hers, desperate to show her how he felt.

Beatrice pulled away, stepping backward into the shadows as the purple lights from the Castor's Police flashed up the long, sloped driveway to the manor.

"I can't. I swore. There's money—" It was difficult to hear Beatrice, but the words he made out sounded like gibberish.

"I'm so sorry." Oliver slapped his palm to his head. How could he have tried to kiss her when her cousin's body lay only a few feet away? "That was so stupid. I wasn't thinking. This whole night has been enough to send me mad."

A police car pulled into the massive courtyard and slammed to a stop.

"Now you're apologizing?" Beatrice raised her hands, fingers clenching into fists for a moment before she began pulling at her hair. "Can you stop doing things that make everything more difficult? I just want..."

She trailed off, turning toward the police car just as its door opened.

Amos marched toward them, his prominent brow furrowed, eyes flicking from witch to warlock to the corpse by their feet. "We got a call from a Bridgette Blackwell. What happened here?"

Beatrice launched into her version of events.

Oliver nodded in agreement when necessary. But his mind kept turning, trying to figure out what she'd been about to say before Amos arrived. What did Beatrice Blackwell want?

Given everything that had happened, and all that she'd said, Oliver could think of only one thing.

She wanted to solve the murders of both Tabitha and Elle.

In that case, Oliver would help her do it.

35
BEATRICE

There was no trace of poison in Elle's body when Amos examined it.

Beatrice didn't understand. She'd extracted only a small amount. The substance should still have been hissing and bubbling beneath her cousin's skin.

Yet another clue Beatrice had stolen from the sergeant.

After the police left, carrying the body with them to perform a complete autopsy at the morgue, Beatrice found herself truly alone with Oliver—no cousins, no corpses, no cops. She needed to tell him the truth. Then Oliver could take the money, leave, and sever his connection with the Blackwells for good.

But Beatrice didn't have the capacity to deal with Oliver now. She needed to focus on the poison.

Had it vanished from the syringe like it had Elle's veins? Was it the same toxin that had been used on Tabitha? Or just a strange coincidence?

Beatrice pulled the syringe from her sleeve. The poison remained within, oozing and pulsing as though it were trying to break free. Beatrice had never seen anything like it.

"I have to study this," she informed Oliver, hoping he'd take it as his cue to say goodbye.

Instead, he turned with her, following toward the side door that led to the Matriarch's tower. "Agreed. It might be the clue we need to solve the case."

Beatrice stopped before the door and turned to him, eyebrows raised.

He must have sensed the looming objection. "You said yourself that I'm a good detective. It'll be easier to figure out the truth with both of us working on it together."

Gigi won't like that.

But Beatrice considered it. Having an extra mind on the case could be beneficial. And, as Matriarch, she needed to prioritize her coven's protection. That meant catching the killer. Accepting Oliver's help would be for the good of the Blackwells. She was morally obligated to agree.

Or Beatrice wanted another excuse to procrastinate Oliver's inevitable farewell.

But this would be the last one! Once they solved the murders, Beatrice would tell him the truth, give him the money, and then never see him again.

———

Beatrice stood in the corner of the study where the grimoire lived on a large wooden lectern, which had been painted black so as not to clash with the gothic décor. She flipped through the pages in the desperate hope that Tabitha might have written something about the poison before she died.

"You're sure you never saw anything like it?" Beatrice asked for the fifth time, turning to her familiar.

Bean balanced on his hind legs near the corner of the desk. Oliver stood nearby. They'd placed the poison in a covered petri dish to study its movements.

The familiar turned to Beatrice. He shook his head and twitched his whiskers in a slightly exasperated manner that meant *it's still no, and the answer isn't going to change.*

All Bean remembered of his alleged poisoning was an upset stomach, a smoky black burp, and sharing a silver drink with Tabitha.

"I know. I know. I'm sorry." Beatrice rubbed her temples and looked back at the grimoire. "It's just that you're the only one still alive who was poisoned. But if you never saw it bubbling in your veins, then the toxin that killed Elle—"

"Must be a different one," Oliver finished, glancing away from the black liquid long enough to meet her gaze.

Beatrice turned back to the grimoire quickly. When Oliver grew focused, his jaw tightened, and he rubbed his chin with a thumb. His eyes gained a sudden intensity that made her heart quicken. He looked even more appealing— gorgeous and clever. What more could a witch want?

But her attraction to Oliver was the last thing Beatrice needed to be aware of right now.

"It's also possible that it's the same poison, but someone modified it to work in a different manner," Beatrice said, resuming her search through the grimoire. Even if Tabitha hadn't bothered to make a note of the poison, there had to be something useful within. "Or maybe its appearance changes as it matures. The poison could have been in Elle's system for longer than it was in Tabitha and Bean." Beatrice continued to turn the leathery old pages. "But if it is the same poison, why didn't Elle go to Rett for a cure? She knew he made an antidote for Tabitha. So either she didn't know she'd been infected, or it's a different poison, or it was modified to act more quickly, or Rett didn't help her, or—" There were too many options, and Beatrice wasn't finding a clear sign to help narrow them down. "Why isn't there anything about toxins in our grimoire? No wonder Tabitha needed help finding a cure!"

Beatrice groaned and attempted to slam the spellbook.

The enchanted cover refused to give her the satisfaction. It swung shut gently on its silver hinges and winked up at her with its large, ruby eye. Her own blood swirled within the depths of the stone.

Beatrice glared back at it, feeling like the grimoire was taunting her with the evidence of their bond, the thing that made her Matriarch, forced her to stay in Castor's Grove, and refused to let her ever be with Oliver.

If I could just pull it free...

But she couldn't. Prying the ruby from the grimoire would break Beatrice as well. And even if she could sever the connection, it would make no difference in regard to Oliver.

He thought he *might, maybe, possibly* love her, which meant nothing. She was just the most recent girl to capture his attention. It wouldn't last.

Oliver's attention was fleeting when it came to any kind of romance. He couldn't even remember saving her and giving her the black lily when they were kids.

Beatrice kept that thought in the back of her head as she turned to him, using it to anchor her heart.

"You need to know exactly what's in a poison to create an antidote, correct? Is there any way of figuring out the ingredients?" Oliver asked.

Beatrice stepped away from the lectern to join him and Bean by the desk. She stopped far enough from the warlock to be certain their skin wouldn't accidentally brush, but close enough that she could examine the toxin as well.

The black poison bubbled and hissed in the glass petri dish, coalescing into a large glob in the center. As a mass, it moved toward the edge attempted to squeeze through a slight space between the cover and its base.

Oliver picked up the syringe and tapped the needle against the side. At the touch of the metal, the toxic glob melted and spread into its liquid state, only to resume its cycle once again.

Whatever ingredients had been used to create it were dangerous and potent. Given enough time, Beatrice might be able to identify a few. But all?

She sighed. "Maybe if I knew more about combining poisonous plants."

Unfortunately, her grandmother had glossed over that topic.

"Guess I'm not as talented as I think, huh?" Beatrice leaned against the velvet wall, crossing her arms as she watched the poison coalesce once more. "Go on. I bet you're dying to rub it in."

She was hoping for a snide, cruel comment. It might make it easier to let Oliver go when the time came.

Not that his insults had ever done much to quell her crush before.

"You're just as talented as you think," Oliver said, catching her off guard. "Maybe even more so. Which makes me wonder how Rett could have created an antidote for a poison that's stumping you."

"It might not be the same one. You said so yourself."

Oliver opened his mouth, but before he could speak, someone hammered on the door. They exchanged a look. Who would be coming to the study at this hour?

Surely no one with good intentions.

Bean bounded onto her shoulder, back arching and tail standing straight up into the air.

Beatrice searched her sleeve as she crept toward the door. She'd wanted to copy Rett's sleeping bombs, but she'd been too weak and her Matriarch schedule left little time for brewing or crafting anyway. The best she'd been able to manage had been a more permanent spell on the spindle.

It worked well enough before.

Beatrice gripped the handle, ready to attack the moment she pulled the door open.

"Finally!"

The sight of her brother, standing before her in a pair of loose black pajama pants with a too-short red bathrobe tied around him made Beatrice freeze.

"Why are you here? I thought you went back to your dorm!"

Albert's heavy eyebrows lowered as he frowned. "Only to get my things. I'm done rooming with Oliver. The servants already have a room ready for me here, but Gigi said that if I want it permanently, then I need your permission." He stuck his tongue out as though the idea disgusted him.

Beatrice snorted. Her brother clearly had no concept of how to ask for a favor. Normally, she'd have enjoyed making him grovel. But given the petri dish of poison and the recent murder, it was low on her priority list.

"Consider whatever room you've been staying in officially yours," she said. "But I don't know why you'd move in here. It's not safe."

"Yeah, I heard about Elle. That's why—" Albert's voice caught. He blinked a few times. His eyes were red. "I thought it might be better for me to stay close. You know?"

Albert's eyes shifted from Beatrice to something in the room behind her. His nervous expression shifted into a dark scowl. "What is he still doing here?"

"Al, I'm sorry, I just—" Oliver started to speak from behind Beatrice.

But Albert didn't let his friend finish. "Excuse us. Private conversation. Blackwells only. No Wyrmwoods."

He pulled Beatrice out of the study and into the narrow stairway. The door swung closed.

"What the hell is he still doing here? Gigi told me about Tabitha's offer. I thought he'd take it and run!" Albert's voice was a low angry hiss. He muttered a few choice curses toward the high beams of the tower ceiling.

Beatrice brushed her hair behind her ear, uncertain how to admit that she had yet to tell Oliver about the money or the conditions left for him in Tabitha's will. "Are you two fighting?"

"Tell me you're too smart to fall for his shit." Albert grabbed her shoulders and pulled her close. His voice softened, but his eyes remained furious. "Oliver said he would rather die than be with you. Now, you're Matriarch, and he's suddenly interested? There's no way! He's using you. And he probably used me to get to you. This whole time, he's been lying about what he really wants."

Albert kept going, accusing Oliver of being a power-hungry schemer. Beatrice barely heard. Her chest felt tight, her skin numb. Albert could be over dramatic, but he wasn't a liar.

Did Oliver really say he'd rather die than be with me? Was that before or after he thought he loved me?

"Come on, we're kicking his ass out of here." Albert turned back toward the door.

"Wait!" Beatrice tried to stop him, but it proved as effective as an attempt to change the course of a raging bull.

Albert barged into the study. Oliver stood behind the desk, examining the poison again. He held the petri dish in the air before him.

"You're done making moves on my sister," Albert said, stomping toward his friend. "Take your money and get out. We never want to see you again."

"Dude, I'm not—" Oliver started to defend himself, then his brow furrowed. "What money?" He wiped his forehead, the petri dish of poison pinched between his fingers, dangerously close.

"Stop," Beatrice warned him, gesturing to the poison.

However, neither boy paid her any attention. They were too busy glaring at each other.

"The money Tabitha left to make sure you'd disappear from our lives," Albert said, voice cold. He flicked his eyes over his friend with such disdain that Oliver suddenly seemed the smaller of the two. "She obviously knew exactly who you were. A pathetic, money-grubbing Wyrmwood who's desperate to be part of our coven."

"Really?" Oliver waved the petri dish before him. "Because this pathetic Wyrmwood is the one trying to help your sister solve Tabitha's murder while the rest of your amazing coven are too focused on their own shallow, vacuous lives to give a shit."

"Please, be careful." Beatrice hurried forward, reaching for the poison. The black glob pressed against the line where the cover clicked onto the dish. It looked like it might seep out the side.

"What are you talking about? It was Wilburn and Linda. They're slime balls. And what is this thing that you keep waving in my face?" Before Beatrice could reach them,

Albert grabbed the dish from Oliver. He tapped his finger against the edge.

Each time Oliver had done so with the needle, the glob had broken up and fled.

But not now.

As if the poison could sense the difference between metal and flesh, it pushed against the glass. A crack formed, and the black fluid slipped through, sinking beneath Albert's fingernail.

"What the hell!" He dropped the glass onto the floor.

The dish shattered. No hint of poison coated the shards. Instead, the black mass bubbled in Albert's vein.

36
OLIVER

"I don't like this," Oliver muttered. He stood at the same window where he'd seen Gabriel the morning of Tabitha's murder. The woods stretched before him, but beyond the first row of dim trees, he could see only darkness.

After Beatrice's attempts to remove the poison from her brother had failed, they'd had no choice but to try Rett.

The three of them had thrown their winter jackets on, descended from the tower, and hurried through the woods. Albert's objections to Oliver's presence dulled the higher the black mass crept along his arm. It was moving faster than they'd anticipated. How had Bean, so much smaller than any human, survived the poison?

You aggravated it. Those were the first words out of Rett's mouth when they'd arrived. Oliver, Beatrice, and Albert had found the older warlock already outside. Rett lay on the grass, limbs exposed to the cold as he gazed at the stars. His feet stuck up, like two pale sticks in the mud. Beatrice spotted them first and shouted to him.

Rett had been slow to react, unusually lethargic and

dumb. He sat up and blinked in silence until his gaze landed on Albert's hand. Rett's eyes pale green eyes grew hauntingly wide, and he'd finally spoken. *"You aggravated it!"*

Which meant that, even in the dark, Rett had recognized the poison.

He'd rushed them inside.

Oliver remembered the layout of the house from when he'd visited as a child. It wasn't large, though the furnishings cost as much as a large apartment in the heart of downtown. The bedrooms were upstairs. One for each of the boys and a third that now belonged only to their mother. Rett took Albert to his, claiming to have the ingredients for the antidote within. But the space was cramped. He insisted Oliver and Beatrice stay downstairs and keep quiet so as not to wake anyone.

And, like always with Rett's commands, they'd obeyed. Now Oliver and Beatrice waited in the small living area with its massive television on the far wall, cream sofas, crimson cushions, and matching rug.

And Albert is upstairs with someone who's very likely a murderer.

"How did he recognize the poison so quickly?" Oliver whispered, hand clenched into a fist against the wall. "Or know that we'd aggravated it?"

"Because it was obvious." Beatrice's voice was so soft Oliver barely heard. She perched near the edge of a loveseat, clutching a cushion against her chest. Bean peeped up at her with wide, concerned eyes from the pocket of her red winter jacket, which she'd been too distracted to remove. "I did aggravate it. I almost killed my brother."

Oliver stared at her, frozen for a moment. He'd never seen Beatrice look so small or sound so broken. She curled herself around the pillow as though attempting to disappear into it.

"B, that's not— You were trying to save him."

When Beatrice had seen the poison enter Albert, she'd sprung to action. There was another syringe in the office. She'd grabbed it and plunged it into his vein, trying to extract the toxin. Instead, the black semi-liquid had hissed and bubbled and shot from his finger and up to his wrist with alarming speed, leaving a trail of tainted blood behind it.

"I rushed without thinking. It worked with Elle, but she was dead. I should've known the poison might react differently when inside a living body." Beatrice hugged the cushion tighter. Her brown hair fell like a heavy curtain before her face. "But you're right. I have a massive ego, and I just assume that I'm brilliant, and I'll figure things out. But I'm not that clever. Rett found a cure for something that I couldn't even begin to guess the nature of."

Exactly! How can she not see it?

Oliver left the window to sit on the loveseat beside Beatrice. He leaned forward, not daring to speak the next words too loud lest the wrong person overheard. "How do you know that Rett didn't purchase both the poison and the antidote?"

In her pocket, Bean's large ears twitched. He understood what Oliver was suggesting.

Beatrice shook her head, and her veil of hair trembled. "Because I— I don't know. And I don't care right now once he saves Albert." She pressed her hand to her forehead, pushing aside her hair. "Tabitha wanted me to be the next Matriarch because she thought I was the most powerful Blackwell, but I'm not. I'm a fool, and so was she."

Oliver thought he'd been bothered by Beatrice's self-praise, but hearing her put herself down was a thousand times worse. He pried her hands from the pillow, pulled her toward him, and forced her body to pivot.

Beatrice stared at him, the usual spark in her green eyes diminished by a curious mix of fear and uncertainty.

"B, you are the most powerful witch possibly in the entire city. Tabitha didn't make a mistake."

The hint of a smile fluttered on her lips, but Beatrice's eyes remained fireless. "Then I did. I hate being Matriarch. I know I'm not supposed to feel that way because it's a position every witch dreams of, but I do. My coven are cruel and demanding. One of them is probably a murderer! But I'm stuck spending the rest of my life working to benefit them? And even worse, I—" Her voice broke.

Oliver waited for her to continue. But when she did, the conversation took an unexpected turn.

"You shouldn't have been in the study with me when Albert came up. You two shouldn't have fought, and he shouldn't have ended up poisoned. If I'd just been honest —" Beatrice broke off. She pulled her hands free, tucked her hair behind her ears, and took a deep breath. "Tabitha left money for you in her will. Enough for you to travel for much longer than a year if you want. It's yours on the condition that you cut ties with the Blackwells for good."

Oliver leaned against the back of the seat as the information sank in, aware of both the witch and the familiar watching him.

So that's what Tabitha wanted to meet with me about. She wanted to make a deal to get me to leave.

And his mother had thought it was a marriage proposal.

Maiden, Mother, and Crone bless Lucille Wyrmwood for her optimism.

The offer was an insult, a message that Tabitha wanted

him nowhere near her coven, and a sign that she assumed he valued money more than his relationships. Oliver should be offended. He should turn it down without hesitation.

Beatrice had finished with her self-pity. Though she still clung to the cushion, her back and neck were straight. The fire was slowly returning to her eyes, quivering in the light as she stared out the window.

An image of Beatrice curled against him outside a tent and laughing at a storm flashed through Oliver's mind.

With it came a new, better idea.

He sprang from the couch too nervous, too excited, to remain seated. Oliver turned to Beatrice and three words rushed from his lips. "Come with me."

Her head snapped toward him. "What?"

"We'll take the money and leave," Oliver said. The words came faster than he was accustomed, and his tongue tripped over them. "You and me. Bean, of course. Maybe Albert too if he gets over himself." He couldn't bring himself to sit again, but it felt strange talking down to Beatrice, so he knelt on the floor before her, grabbing her hands once more. "We can go everywhere, explore magical ruins, find new plants and species, become a traveling witch and warlock, just like you dreamed, right? No murderer on the loose, just us. It'll be perfect. So come on, B, what do you say?"

37

BEATRICE

B eatrice stared at Oliver, kneeling on the crimson rug and holding her hand in a strange perversion of a proposal.

Her heart pounded in her chest, a million responses rushing through her head.

She could burst into tears. *My brother is upstairs, possibly dying, and he chooses to do this now? This is even worse than trying to kiss me while we were by Elle's body.*

She could laugh. *The idea of the Blackwell Matriarch abandoning her coven and the city is ludicrous. Who's going to oversee the protective barriers?*

Or she could shout *yes* and wrap her arms around him. *Because that's what I want to do.*

And likely how she would've responded if he'd asked a month ago. But now, it was too late. Beatrice had bound her soul to the grimoire and sworn a blood-oath to a memory. She could never be a traveling witch. She could never explore the world. She could never be with Oliver.

Beatrice cleared her throat, trying to rid her brain of any romantic notions. "Let me get this straight. You want me to abandon my family and run off with you because you *think* you love me?"

Oliver frowned, then his eyes grew wide. "So that did happen." He stood, running his hand over his head and shooting her a shy look that managed to be just as charming despite the darkness. "Why didn't you say something sooner?"

"Are you joking?" Beatrice's voice rose. She covered her mouth with her hand and took a deep breath before standing from the couch, trying to gather her composure. But it was difficult. If anyone had a right to complain about timing here, it was her. "You know I've liked you for ages. Why didn't you make this grand gesture before I became Matriarch? Or even better, back when we were in high school together and no one had been murdered?"

"Hey, I did invite you before you became Matriarch," Oliver said, tone turning defensive. He held up his hands. "And seriously, when I was in high school? I was an idiot! I didn't want to fall for you, so I never paid attention to you. I just decided you were annoying and talked too much, and didn't listen to what you were actually saying." He lowered his hands and turned his gaze to the rug for a moment before his eyes rose to meet hers. "If I had, I would've realized that you're brilliant, and kind, and smart, and not just with magic stuff. I mean it. You talk a lot, but I like listening, and B, I want to hear everything you have to say because it's fascinating hearing how your mind works."

It was everything that Beatrice had spent the past seven and a half years daydreaming about Oliver saying to her. Each word sent a shudder of excitement pumping through her chest, but they made her heart ache even worse.

When she'd sworn on the grimoire, she'd assumed there was no chance of a real relationship with Oliver. Now, it was like he was taunting her with the idea, holding it before him like an apple and begging her to bite.

But it's not just the vow that would keep us apart.

Beatrice's mind flicked through the many girls Oliver had dated— never for longer than a month. She recalled Albert's warning: *He said he'd rather die than be with you;* the tepid confession: *I think I love you*; the apology after he tried to kiss her in the courtyard: *the night's sent me mad*.

"Stop!" Beatrice was being too loud again, but she couldn't help it now. "Please, just stop. This could never happen. *We* could never happen. I'm the Matriarch. That's what I want"

"No, it's not. You can't stand your coven, and you're miserable being stuck here. You said so."

It didn't matter that he was right. In that moment, Beatrice wanted to fight. Her anger needed an outlet.

"That's not true. And the Blackwells aren't a single entity. There's Gigi, Albert, my parents, even Rett and Gabriel are decent."

She expected Oliver to argue. He'd been accusing Rett of murder just a few moments earlier.

But the warlock didn't give her the satisfaction of a fight. He held up his hands once again. "I'm sorry. You're right. I won't take the money. I'll stay here while you remain Matriarch. I just want to be with you."

Oliver reached forward to take Beatrice's hand.

She pulled away.

"You're not listening to me. It's too late." Beatrice wanted to run, but she couldn't disappear with Albert upstairs, so instead, she dropped back to the couch and clutched the cushion. She held it like a shield between her and Oliver, digging her fingers into the fabric in an effort to keep her own emotions under control.

Oliver stared at her, eyebrows pulled low in confusion.

The silence burned Beatrice's ears.

"Do you know when I fell for you?" she whispered, staring at one of the tassels on the cushion.

It wasn't a real question, but at the corner of her vision, Oliver shook his head.

"It was my first day of middle school. When you saved me from all the kids who were bullying me."

Beatrice looked up and saw the blank expression on the warlock's face, just as she'd expected. It should have come as a relief. Instead, it made her heart ache worse.

"I made the mistake of saying magic was real, and everyone in my class kept picking on me. Then, you came over and picked up a lily. You turned it black in front of all of them, and they stopped."

Beatrice waited for recognition to dawn on Oliver's face. She knew the interaction had meant more to her than it did him, but surely, the memory was in his mind somewhere.

The warlock stared at her, brow furrowed in confusion. "I did that?"

"You did."

And I've kept the lily ever since, while you don't even remember.

"For over seven years, I've thought you were Prince Charming. Seven years, you could've asked me out, but you didn't."

"B, don't listen to your brother, okay? I don't care that you're Matriarch now. This isn't a powerplay, I swear."

"I know." There were plenty of insults she could hurl at Oliver in that moment; *gold digger* wasn't one. "But you're not Prince Charming, and this isn't a fairytale." Or the timing would be right, and the warlock wouldn't have added *I think* in front of *I love you*. "So take Tabitha's money and go. You'll forget about me in a few weeks, guaranteed."

Beatrice glanced up, hoping he'd argue. She wanted Oliver to tell her that she was wrong, profess his undying love, promise to think of her every day they were apart.

Of course, he didn't.

The warlock stood, staring out the window, so still his eyes didn't even blink. No hint of an objection whispered from his lips.

So even he agrees. He will forget me.

Beatrice buried her face in the cushion. Her cousin had died, her brother was poisoned, yet this was the closest she'd come to crying for the day. It was pathetic.

But nothing hurt quite as much as realizing that, despite everything he said, her fears were true. Forget fairy-tales, Beatrice and Oliver wouldn't even go down as a tragic romance. She'd be just a fleeting fancy. He'd be the boy she forced herself to forget.

————

"A little help here?" Rett's voice called from the bottom of the stairs.

Beatrice flung the cushion onto the other side of the loveseat, sprang up, and rushed toward him.

Oliver followed, movements stiff, like a bulky, heartless robot creaking behind her.

Rett crouched so that Albert's arm could sling around his neck for support.

Beatrice grabbed her brother's free hand. There was no sign of any black in his veins.

"Thank the Goddess," Oliver whispered.

"Thank Rett," Beatrice said, turning between her cousin

and brother, uncertain who to address. "You saved him—Are you okay?—How did you manage it?—Can you stand?"

"Of course," Albert's voice slurred. "The silver killed the black. But B, I have to tell you—" He slumped forward.

Beatrice caught him.

"He's fine, just wiped out from the antidote," Rett assured her, slouching free from Albert's arm to let Beatrice take the weight. "Your brother could've died. That's the same poison that affected Tabitha and Bean. It's dangerous stuff. Especially when it enters into the bloodstream directly. Do you have any idea how Al got exposed?"

"We found a vial in the study," Oliver answered before Beatrice could. He rested his hand on her shoulder and squeezed. It wasn't affection. He wanted to make sure she didn't dispute his lie. "Tabitha must've saved it for some reason."

"That would be like her. She must've found a way to extract some from Bean." Rett wiped his forehead. Deep lines furrowed his skin and black half-moons shone beneath his eyes. They aged him. He could've been the ghost of a middle-aged man. "I'm just glad I had enough silverbloom for an antidote. I couldn't take losing Albert too, not right after—"

He closed his eyes and held up his hand in apology, unable to speak Elle's name.

So he's not heartless. Meanwhile, I've barely thought of her as more than a puzzle to solve.

Weighed down by guilt and her stumbling brother, Beatrice left the house.

She expected Oliver to at least help carry Albert back to the manor, but he stopped the moment they reached the path in the woods.

"Now I know that Al is okay, I have to leave."

Bean, who'd hidden in Beatrice's pocket for most of her last exchange with Oliver, peeped his head out now. He pawed at her hip, apparently wanting her to say something.

But what?

"Abandoning us already then." Beatrice tried to keep the bitterness out of her tone.

I told him to take the money and do just that. I can't be angry when he listens to me.

If only emotions were so logical.

"I've been with the Blackwells too long," Oliver said, muscles in his jaw growing tight. He pulled the collar of his dark green jacket higher and turned away, his voice cold and unconcerned. "I have my own coven matters to deal with."

And just like that, he disappeared into the darkness, leaving Beatrice to stumble through the forest and carry her brother's weight alone.

38

OLIVER

The subway had stopped running by the time Oliver arrived at the station. He caught the last bus traveling south on 70th Street and walked two blocks west to his family's home.

He needed to talk to his mother.

For the entirety of his journey, Oliver had tried to remember his first day of seventh grade at Dashmoor. He recalled snippets of the summer before— being scolded by his mother for getting the couch sticky with watermelon juice, playing witches vs. fairies in the Blackwell woods with Albert, Rett, and Gabriel, learning botany alongside Sophie despite being four years older.

And then, Oliver's mind hit against a wall. Suggestions swirled within. He could just make them out: school, Beatrice, a black lily. But it was only because the witch had told him what they were. When he tried to reach for his own memories, they were water in his fingers, slipping away before he could drink.

I should remember.

The Wyrmwoods lived a few blocks south of downtown

in a two-story brick home on Ivy Street. It was a chunk of red clay history wedged between glass beasts, five times its height. Metal snakes twisted in wrought iron bars around the windows. The coiled serpent of their coven stared at Oliver with deep-set emerald eyes from the brass knocker.

He banged it against the wood. "Lucille! Wake up!"

"What are you doing?" There was an annoyed whisper as the door opened, and Sophie appeared. Her curls frizzed around her head, wild and tangled, but she wore a long green witch's dress.

Oliver pushed his way past his sister and into the building.

While the family lived upstairs, the space below functioned as a shopfront. Bottles and vials held cheap, easily sourced potion ingredients like oak leaves, rabbit tails, and summer rain. Almost no one bothered purchasing those items, but Lucille claimed they gave the shop a legitimate feel.

The store waited in darkness, but light shone from a door behind the register. It led to his mother's potions den and records room. Was she already downstairs?

"Mom, get out here. We need to talk," Oliver said, charging toward the room as he went.

"Can you be quiet? Holy crap!" Sophie hissed at her brother, following close behind him. "Mom will realize we're down here."

"That's the point." Oliver stepped into the den and paused for a second. A brass cauldron bubbled in the center of the room and a smorgasbord of supplies cluttered the table, half with their lids off as though the potion's creator had been debating which to use.

Sophie fiddled with the sleeves of her dress. "All the Blackwells at school are claiming I'm a desperate, pathetic wannabe who stole their Matriarch's familiar for a selfie, and I maybe said something stupid in front of Bailey as retaliation, and now she's threatening to tell Raven Cherith, and I thought—"

Oliver held up his hand to silence his sister. He got the gist. "You can't drug people with forgetting potion without their consent, Sophie. Even if they're bullying you."

"I know. I wasn't going to use it." Sophie scoffed, voice growing high and condescending like only a teenage girl could manage. But then she stared down at her feet, scuffing her toes against the wooden floor. "I just wanted to see if I could get it done without Mom's help. I think I did."

She walked toward the cauldron and stared at the white potion within. Her eyes flicked toward her brother, likely hoping for praise.

Oliver barely noticed. He scanned the rest of the room. More expensive ingredients, the ones not for sale, like shadowmoss, were hidden in his mother's den. There was also a large filing cabinet.

"What's in there?" He pointed at it.

Sophie turned to look at the green-painted metal drawers. As a witch, she'd been given the privilege of working in the store under Lucille. "Business records."

My memory was wiped seven years ago. Tabitha's murderer was invisible.

The two things weren't related.

Except for the fact that Lucille Wyrmwood sold both spells.

It was a long shot, but what if the information he needed to understand everything was stored in her records?

A lump rose in Oliver's throat as he walked toward the cabinet. He grabbed the top drawer and pulled. It wouldn't budge. In a desperate bid, he kicked the base, hoping to shake the lock free.

"What are you doing?" A voice, cold and calm, came from the doorway.

Sophie squeaked. Oliver was too annoyed to feel guilty. He turned and faced his mother.

Lucille strolled into her den, broad hips swinging beneath an emerald robe, a black towel tied around her hair. She tilted her head, lips pursed as she considered Oliver, whose hand was still wrapped around her record cabinet. Annoyance flashed in her eyes.

"Looking for more information to give the police about me? I already told you that overzealous Sergeant appeared twice with questions thanks to you telling him that I sold something to Wilburn."

Because you did, and I was being accused of a murder I didn't commit.

Oliver wasn't about to defend his choice to tell Amos the truth. The Sergeant wasn't the problem in this scenario.

"Someone used a forgetting potion on me when I was a kid," Oliver said, staring at his mother. "Did you know that?"

The only reaction was a gasp from Sophie, who stood in front of the cauldron, arms spread and leaning against the rim as though she could hide the bubbling. Lucille could've been made of stone.

His mother's lack of response sent a chill through Oliver's blood. He looked into her dark, unblinking eyes and knew. It was exactly what he'd feared.

"It was you, wasn't it?"

That was the only answer that made sense. Lucille knew the Wyrmwood forgetting potions better than anyone. She'd have recognized the effects if someone else had used one on her son, and she could've found a way to undo it.

Still, an irrational part of Oliver hoped his mother would deny the accusation.

"Yes."

Oliver's chest tightened.

"No way!" Once again, the shock came from Sophie. She crept closer, likely realizing that her secret late-night potion-making was the least of any of her family's concerns. "You wouldn't wipe your own child's memories."

"I had no choice." Lucille clicked her tongue, flicking her gaze to her daughter. "On Oliver's first day of seventh grade, he went to play on the Blackwell Estate with Albert, and that evening some warlock brought both of them here and demanded I wipe their memories."

"Why?" A lump rose in Oliver's throat as he tried to walk into the swirling wall within his mind. "What happened?"

"I don't know."

"You didn't ask?" Oliver couldn't believe it. The cold in his veins turned hot, and the muscles tightened in his shoulders and jaw, trembling as he tried not to explode. "What if they'd done something to me? You didn't care? Instead of protecting me, you just blindly obeyed some Blackwell warlock?"

"He wasn't a Blackwell, just married into the coven," Lucille said, as though that was the important part. She pushed past Oliver and grabbed the handle on the third drawer of the cabinet. It slid open at her touch to reveal a series of files within. She removed a thin, unassuming beige, and shoved it against Oliver's chest. "I did protect you. And Albert. You knew something the Blackwells didn't want you to know. Trust me, you're both safer having forgotten."

"What's in the file?" Sophie asked, leaning closer and peering over her brother's shoulder.

"Anything I felt safe enough writing down about my exchanges with him," Lucille answered. She clicked her tongue again, and her eyes finally landed on the bubbling cauldron. "Your potion is well past burnt. It's presumptuous enough to steal my ingredients without wasting them."

Sophie yelped and ran toward the cauldron. The white liquid was brown and smoking.

Oliver left his mother and sister to worry about that. He opened the folder and skimmed the contents. "There's no name."

"I never write them down. Can you imagine if the police raided and discovered a list of my clients?" Lucille waved her hand, likely to clear the smoke rising over the cauldron. "Anyway, I thought you'd remembered him."

"Obviously not." Oliver's jaw clenched, and his voice turned into a growl.

Lucille sniffed. "I doubt it matters anyway. He was no one significant, and he's since died or gone bankrupt."

"Why would you—" Oliver started to ask, but he had his question answered as he reached the end of the paper.

The man in question had done more than force two children to drink forgetting potions. He'd bought an invisibility ring.

He'd returned every six months to have the magic renewed until four years ago. Then his visits and payments had stopped.

It made sense that his mother assumed the man was either dead or broke. Without refreshing the invisibility spell, the ring was useless. Anyone who could afford to pay for the magical upkeep of such an item would.

But there was another option. Something his mother wouldn't have considered.

One of the Blackwells figured out how to renew our invisibility spell.

And they'd used that power to murder Tabitha.

39

BEATRICE

B eatrice lay in the massive four-poster bed that she'd inherited, drowning in crimson pillows and black satin sheets. Bean snuggled in her hair, little breaths warm against her cheek. She envied his ability to sleep.

Her eyes burned from dryness. She stared at the dark shadows on the canopy of the bed, thoughts tumbling from Oliver's confession, to Albert's poisoning, to Elle's death, to Tabitha's still unsolved murder, then back to Oliver.

Always back to Oliver.

Which was frustrating because the Wyrmwood warlock was the least important. He shouldn't even enter the Blackwell Matriarch's thoughts.

Beatrice's only focus should be finding the killer and stopping them before they could strike again.

There had to be a clue she was missing.

"I'm sorry I didn't find the truth before you died, Elle," Beatrice whispered to the shadows. "I promise, if you were murdered too, I'll find who did it."

Not that it will do you any good at this point.

Beatrice held her breath, waiting to see if the shadows whisper back. Tortured spirits could linger after death.

No response came. Elle was gone. The banshee had severed her soul and carried it to the reaper.

"Of course, even if you were here, you might not help me," Beatrice muttered.

She sighed and rolled onto her side, pushing away returning thoughts of Oliver. He'd rejected her, and she'd sworn never to be with him anyway, so what did it matter?

Focus on the murders.

Two attempts had been made on Tabitha's life. Rett had cured the poison, but then an invisible assailant stabbed her. So the killer was either very talented or independently wealthy enough to purchase powerful spells, and they must have had something to gain from Tabitha's death.

But what about Elle?

No one benefited from her death, at least as far as Beatrice could tell.

So could it have been suicide like she'd originally thought? A guilty conscience?

Maybe because... because she and Rett...

Beatrice's thoughts vanished as she drifted to sleep.

———

Her eyes fluttered open.

She was back in the woods, dressed in a soft pink witch's gown. It hugged her waist and highlighted her curves, falling in lacy waves to tickle the grass. Her feet were bare; her hair fell loose around her exposed shoulders.

The moon hung low, large and swollen in the sky, shining on

Beatrice like a spotlight in a theatre production. Wind shook the trees and caught the fabric of her dress. But there was no chill on her skin.

I'm dreaming.

Of course. That explained why she was outside with no shoes in the winter, why there were no scents, no sounds.

A shriek pierced the silence.

Beatrice felt the noise in her stomach, rattling her body from the inside out.

The banshee emerged from the darkness and stepped into the spotlight. Her long white dress remained still despite the breeze, and her hair blew in the opposite direction, fanning behind her. Her prismatic eyes studied Beatrice, who trembled before her.

"You're the new Blackwell Matriarch?" Her breath was visible in the air before her. A white whisper that danced in the wind. "Where's the grimoire's power? You feel...average."

Excuse me? *Beatrice had never been labeled anything quite so offensive. She opened her mouth, ready to list her many accomplishments and talents. Her lips turned cold.*

There was only one reason for the banshee to visit her in a dream, and it wasn't to debate her matriarchal capabilities.

"Good point. Perhaps there's been some mistake." Beatrice licked her lips and stepped away.

"No definitely not! And don't even think of telling my master that when you see him. I'm in enough trouble as it is. Can't be late, or the time of death's wrong. Can't be early, or there's people trying to rob you! I mean, do you have any idea how difficult it is for me to live my life and collect souls? Honestly, I don't think anyone has it as bad as I do," the banshee said. She huffed and it echoed through the trees. "Anyway, as per the arrangement between your coven and my master, I've come to warn you. Your death is imminent, Beatrice Blackwell."

———

Bean's frantic pawing woke her.

Beatrice jolted upright with the familiar clinging to her hair. She grabbed the bilby from the tangled nest he'd created and held him before her.

He squeaked, large ears twitching. There was an anxious wildness in his eyes. Did he know about the banshee's visit?

Of course he does. He's my familiar.

At least she'd gotten something she'd always wanted, even if it was only for a short time. Only the most talented witches attracted familiars.

"I'm going to die, Bean. Soon." The words felt heavy in Beatrice's mouth. Her chest tightened, but she couldn't let her emotions overwhelm her. She needed to say this before she lost the ability to speak. "But you don't need to die with me. I don't want you to. You've been a good and loyal familiar to me. You can do that for another witch. Or warlock."

Bean's ears stopped twitching. His body went rigid for a moment. Then his tail rose and twisted around Beatrice's wrist. He squeezed. It meant *we're in this together.*

Which was sweet, but ridiculous. There was absolutely no benefit to both of them dying. Still, Beatrice's eyes filled with tears, and she pulled the bilby to her chest, hugging him against her.

"You are the best familiar to have ever existed, Bean."

He nuzzled against her for a moment before wriggling free. The bilby settled on his haunches beside her, body drooping as he stared up at her with sad, guilty eyes.

"People die. That's life. Doesn't make you a failure to lose two witches."

Bean's head straightened. He grunted an objection and shook his head.

He still thought there was a chance to save her.

"Once the banshee marks you, that's it. The chances of surviving after that must be minuscule. I wouldn't even know where to start trying to outwit death."

Bean's ears shot up. His tail pointed up toward the canopy.

No, toward the tower.

The familiar leaped off the bed and toward the door. He squeaked, waiting for Beatrice to follow.

They needed to consult the grimoire.

————

Bean rode on Beatrice's shoulders as she climbed the stairs. The familiar had ignited a dangerous flicker of hope within her.

There were dozens of protective spells in the Blackwell grimoire. Could there be a way to ward off death hidden among them?

The door to the study was open.

Had Beatrice forgotten to close it in her rush to get Albert help?

She stepped in and pulled the cord of the nearby lamp. The dim light flickered on, and Beatrice assessed the area, skin prickling, expecting an invisible hand to strike at any moment.

No attack came. There was no sign of anyone hiding behind the door or under the desk. The chair and all her papers remained just as Beatrice had left them.

She was just beginning to relax when the familiar let out a panicked squeak.

Beatrice's gaze followed Bean as he raced across the study. She gasped as he scurried up an empty lectern.

The grimoire was missing.

40

BEATRICE

It was impossible.

Beatrice had bound herself to the grimoire when she became Matriarch. Its power coursed through her, and hers through it. Only she could handle her coven's spellbook.

So how had someone stolen it from the study?

Beatrice stopped halfway down the stairs. She pressed her hand against the stone wall.

Bean gave her a curious look, but he remained silent.

She focused her will into the manor. *Wouldn't you be so much prettier if you were glowing?*

It was a contrary behavior for stones to display. But as Matriarch, she was master of the house. The grimoire's power was enough that she could force it to comply, if only for a second.

A tiny light flickered under Beatrice's palm. Then, it vanished.

Winded by the effort, she collapsed against the far wall, clutching her chest.

I've lost the grimoire's power. The banshee even said it in my dream.

But how was that possible? And what did it mean?

Beatrice turned the thoughts over as she descended the tower and returned to her room.

She opened the door, stepped inside, and froze. A dark figure stood beside her bed.

Is this the person who stole the grimoire? Have they come to kill me?

The figure turned a pair of green eyes toward her. They filled with recognition.

Beatrice stumbled back, searching the sleeves of her robe for a spell. She had to have something she could use.

A scream caught in her throat as the figure lunged.

Bean leaped from her shoulder onto her attacker. The familiar bit down on the person's hand.

"Ow! Stop!" A familiar voice shouted as the figure shook its arm in an attempt to dislodge the bilby

Beatrice found the light switch and flicked it on. "Albert?"

Her brother still wore the red bathrobe that she'd put him to bed in. He scowled at the familiar as Bean bounced back. "First poison, now a rat bite? It's a dangerous job being your brother."

Could be worse. You could be about to die.

Beatrice contemplated telling her brother about the dream, but knowing the truth seemed more burden than blessing. Albert couldn't help, and it would only make him panic.

Bean grunted, and Beatrice scooped him up, translating the familiar's offense. "He's not a rat, and he wouldn't have bitten you if you weren't creeping around my room in the middle of the night like a weirdo. What are you doing here?" Then, seeing the scowl deepening on her brother's face, she hurried to add, "Not that I'm not relieved to see that you're okay. I was really worried. How're you feeling?"

"Fine." Albert stared at his hand, rubbing where Bean had bitten. Then, he dropped onto the bed. "The antidote worked."

"We owe Rett a huge thank you."

Albert's eyes snapped up to his sister. His face turned white. "No, I don't think we do."

Beatrice's chest tightened. "What do you mean?"

But she had an idea. Her brother wore the same expression Oliver had when he'd last mentioned Rett.

"He had a test tube in his fridge," Albert said, eyes flicking around as though he felt guilty even saying it. "He tried to close the door fast, but I'd already seen it. And I wouldn't have made a mistake. Not with the color and strange movement from liquid to solid. Rett has a sample of the poison."

Was that what had her brother so panicked?

Beatrice sighed and sat beside him on the bed. "Tabitha probably sent some when she asked Elle for a cure. Rett would've needed it to make the antidote."

"But that doesn't make sense. The syringe didn't work. When you tried to extract some, it just got angry." Albert took a deep breath as though he needed to prepare for what he was about to say next. "I'm telling you, Rett made that poison. I think he might be capable of more than we realized."

41
OLIVER

When Oliver awoke the next morning his first thought was of Beatrice.

He needed to speak with her.

As the Blackwell Matriarch, she should be informed about the unknown member of her coven who'd purchased an invisibility ring. And if anyone could figure out how to return Oliver's missing memory, it was her.

Plus, he wanted to see her.

She needs to know why I forgot about giving her a lily all those years ago.

It had been too late to return to his dorm. Despite his anger with his mother, Oliver had slept at his family's home, in his old room. The bed was still there, pushed into a corner to make room for two large closets. His mother and sister were capitalizing on the extra space.

Oliver climbed out of the bed, pulled on his clothes from the day before, and went to the door. He hoped to sneak out before anyone in his family spotted him.

Unfortunately, his sister had other plans.

Sophie waited in the hallway outside, already dressed

in dark tights and a blue sweatshirt, hair pulled into an almost-neat ponytail. She'd slung a brown bag over one shoulder and carried her winter jacket in the other.

"Absolutely not."

"Oh, come on," Sophie hissed, following him down the stairs. "I'm not staying here. I'm pissed at Mom too. What're you doing that's so important I can't tag along?"

"Going to see Beatrice."

A burnt smell lingered in the shop downstairs, courtesy of Sophie's failed experiment the previous night. Oliver had a feeling that his sister's rush to leave the house had little to do with the fact that their mother had once wiped his memory. He covered his nose and stepped outside.

"I totally didn't think about the fact that we now have an in with the new Blackwell Matriarch," Sophie said, in a tone that suggested just the opposite. She jogged to keep up as he walked down Ivy Street.

Oliver raised his eyebrow at his sister. She and Beatrice were acquaintances at best.

"And she's living on the estate now, right? Some of the girls at school said there's an enchanted room that lets everyone fly once they enter." Her voice grew reverent. "I'll definitely join you."

Oliver snorted. "Too bad you're definitely not invited."

Not only was he trying to solve a mystery and get his missing memory, he also needed to talk to Beatrice about their relationship. She'd pushed him away the other night, and he couldn't understand why. Was it his suggestion they run away? Poor timing given Albert's condition? Or did she just not believe him?

He couldn't blame her if that was the case. Oliver had been blind to Beatrice for so long, but now he saw her, he couldn't imagine a life without her in it. He needed to prove that to her.

How was another question. But he didn't think Sophie's presence would make it easier.

"Well, that's your loss," his sister said. "Because you need me. Because I have this." She pulled a glass bottle out of her jacket and held it before him.

Oliver's eyes narrowed at the burned liquid within. "Your ruined potion?"

"No. Well, sort of, but it's exactly what you need if you want your memory back. Our forgetting potions essentially build a wall in the individual's mind. This"—she waved her potion in her brother's face—"will burn that wall. If you add the right ingredients." She grinned. "So, am I invited now?"

———

An hour later, the two Wyrmwoods waited by the Blackwell gates. Beatrice was either ignoring Oliver, or her phone had died. It was difficult to tell with the constant magic on the estate. The guards refused to allow them entry, but the message came that Beatrice would meet them outside.

Sophie was not impressed with the turn of events. She leaned against the black wall, arms crossed, lips stuck in a permanent pout. "Do you think she's upset with me for posting that picture with Bean? She didn't say I couldn't."

Oliver turned his attention from the gates just long enough so that his sister could see him roll his eyes. "This has nothing to do with you."

"Well, is she mad at you? Cause we need her help."

Although Sophie's potion provided a base, Oliver needed to add something linked to the missing memory if he hoped to regain it. His sister thought that a lock of Beatrice's hair might work.

"She'll help," Oliver said, turning back to the gate.

There was no trace of doubt in his mind. He knew Beatrice. She'd want his memory restored as badly as he did. It could be the key to solving the murders.

And fixing things between us.

Oliver just needed the chance to explain everything to her, confess his feelings, and prove that they were genuine. The atmosphere would be improved by a lack of dead bodies and poisoned brothers. His biggest obstacle would be Sophie.

Or so Oliver assumed until the gates opened, and Gigi emerged.

The old witch grunted as she pushed her chair onto the sidewalk. The extra weight on her arms trembled beneath her long gray sleeves. She'd needed to pin them back so the fabric didn't catch on the wheels. She turned her seat toward the two Wyrmwoods. Her eyes flicked over Sophie, dismissed her with a sniff, and focused on Oliver.

"Right on schedule," Gigi said, her lips curving in a tight frown. She unzipped an exposed pocket, no hint of secrecy, and pulled out a silver key. "Your money is in a lock box with the leprechauns at Castor's Bank. They're expecting you."

Sophie stepped away from the wall to peer around Oliver's shoulder. "What money?"

"I'm not taking it. It's not worth the conditions," Oliver said, elbowing his sister away and addressing the old witch. "Now where's Beatrice? She's who we came to speak with."

Gigi tapped her fingers against her wheels, studying Oliver with pursed lips. "Conditions can be amended. If it's your friendship with Albert you're reluctant to give up—"

"It's not just Al."

The old woman's eyebrows rose, stretching the skin around her eyes and adding extra creases to her forehead. She sighed—deep and heavy. "It's as I've feared. You've fallen for Beatrice."

Oliver didn't deny it.

Behind him, Sophie barely suppressed a giggle. "Have you? I always said you denied being interested in her way too much."

Oliver shot his sister a look from the corner of his eye. This wasn't the time.

Gigi clicked her tongue and looked at Sophie. "There's a restaurant on Wicklow Street, Very Good Food. The Black-wells have a tab there. Order anything you want while you wait for your brother. On us."

"But—" Sophie started to object, glancing at Oliver, likely hoping for support. She found none and closed her mouth back into its pout. Another glance at the old witch's steely gaze had the fifteen-year-old staring at the ground and nodding meekly. "Yes, ma'am."

"Good." Gigi nodded in approval.

They watched Sophie as the fifteen-year-old finally crossed the street, scuffing her feet on the road and earning an annoyed honk from an impatient driver. The noise seemed to break the temporary silence between Oliver and the old witch.

"Come," Gigi instructed. "I want to check the perimeter."

Oliver's jaw clenched. He didn't see what that possibly had to do with him. The old witch had always thought her grandchildren too good for a Wyrmwood. She'd been against his friendship with Albert from the beginning. Gigi would only try to convince him to take the key and get out of the Blackwells' lives for good.

"No. I need to talk to Beatrice."

"Please," Gigi said.

The word was a shock to Oliver's system. The old witch issued commands, not requests.

But now Gigi's voice softened, and she slumped in her chair with an uncharacteristic weariness. "You deserve to know the truth."

———

Oliver pushed Gigi's wheelchair along the gray stone sidewalk as they walked the perimeter of the Blackwell Estate. The old woman held her left arm out to the side, fingers skirting the smooth black wall. He wasn't certain how she could inspect the protective spells and speak at the same time, but he wasn't brave enough to question her ability to multitask.

"You might not have known it, Oliver, but Tabitha had her eyes on you for quite some time," Gigi said, voice slow and heavy as though there was a weight attached to each word. "Beatrice's talent was identified from young. That's why her father was allowed to remain a member of the Blackwell coven, why I moved into their home, why I taught her myself."

Oliver nodded. Beatrice and Albert's situation had always been unusual. "My mother always said Tabitha had a reason for wanting them to remain Blackwells."

"Yes, Lucille has always been clever. A rather dangerous quality at times." Gigi leaned back against her seat, fingers still tracking the wall. "Your mother knew what she was doing by sending you to Dashmoor, encouraging your friendship with Albert. She hoped you and Beatrice would fall in love. I did everything in my power to dissuade such a tragedy, but here we are."

Oliver wished he could defend his mother from the accusation. But she'd never hidden her scheme.

"Look, I'm as annoyed as anyone that it worked," Oliver admitted, pushing the wheelchair faster and more roughly over the sidewalk than was probably wise. "But I'm not the greedy, opportunistic monster you believe me to be."

"To the contrary." Gigi gave a soft, huff of a laugh. "Outside of a momentary lapse of judgment where I believed you'd killed Tabitha, I've always quite liked you. You remind me of my late husband. Same adventurous spirit. He was a Cunningham."

Oliver almost tripped over an uneven stone on the sidewalk. The Cunninghams were a minor coven of even less significance than the Wyrmwoods. They had no spells of any note, and a Blackwell marrying one sounded ludicrous.

"That's why I tried to keep you away," Gigi continued. "The moment Tabitha realized how close you and Beatrice were, your life was at risk. She would never have allowed anything to happen between the two of you."

A strange chill prickled the back of Oliver's neck. "What happened to your husband?"

"He got sick. I tried to save him, but the potion I brewed backfired. Cost me my legs." There was a slight tremble in her voice. A truth she wouldn't speak.

But Oliver would. "Tabitha killed him."

They turned the corner. Gigi began her inspection of the North wall, silent for a long while. When she finally spoke, it was in a whisper, as though to herself. "Maybe Tabitha killed him. And maybe she swapped the labels of my ingredients to ensure that my attempt to save him failed. She warned me against trying to cure him."

Oliver's shoulders grew heavy as he took in the old woman's words. But what did they have to do with him? "You think Tabitha wanted to kill me."

"I know she did. It took all my effort to convince her there were better, subtler ways to keep you and Beatrice apart."

"Like bribing me." Oliver guessed.

"And making Beatrice swear a blood oath when she became Matriarch." Gigi pulled the brake to her chair, forcing them to stop. She spun to face Oliver, grabbed his hand, and pressed the key into it. "You two can never be together the way you want, Oliver. Give up on that dream. Otherwise, Beatrice will die."

42

BEATRICE

Beatrice waited in the woods, among a thick grove of trees, her back pressed to an old oak. She clutched the skirt of her red dress, holding it up to avoid the mud. It had been designed to wear with heels, not the black sneakers she had on.

Terrible outfit for sneaking around.

But she'd had Matriarchal duties that morning. It was only when Gigi left to do her usual patrol of the perimeter that Beatrice had the opportunity to summon Albert so they could execute their plan.

They'd spent most of the previous night discussing what to do with the information about Rett. Albert wanted to arrest their cousin straight away. But, without the grimoire to boost her power, Beatrice knew better than to try. Rett was the golden child of their coven. The rest of the Blackwells would never accept such an accusation against him.

Not unless they had undisputable proof.

Like the murder weapon.

Bean dashed over the raised roots and blades of grass, a

blue-gray blur on the forest floor. He stopped before Beatrice, sat up on his haunches, and squeaked.

That was her signal to move. She opened a pocket that had been sewn into the waist of her dress, allowing her familiar to hop in before making her way through the trees.

Rett knew the estate better than anyone. He'd have no shortage of options for places to hide a knife. But if the weapon could connect him to Tabitha's murder, he'd likely want to keep tabs on it to be able to ensure it remained undiscovered.

There were two places Rett frequented. Beatrice and Oliver had already searched the greenhouse. That left only her cousin's room.

Beatrice crept against the wall until she reached Rett's house. Once there, she pushed open the downstairs window. Albert had unlocked it for her.

In order to investigate, Beatrice had needed to ensure the house would be empty. Her Aunt Elba enjoyed a lengthy and expensive, booze-filled brunch with other Blackwell witches every Sunday. Today's meal would feature an ostentatious tribute to Elle, and their mourning festivities would likely stretch until midnight.

Beatrice had tasked Rett with the arrangements for Elle's funeral. It meant meeting with the embalmer and the police, which would hopefully keep him off the estate for most of the day.

Albert had taken care of Gabriel by inviting him to join Gigi on a patrol of the estate.

That left the house empty.

Beatrice had also begged her brother to take both their grandmother and cousin strolling around the city after. Albert had reluctantly agreed. He didn't mind hanging out with Gabriel, but failed to understand why Gigi would be a hindrance to a murder investigation. After all, their grand-mother didn't live in Rett's house.

But no one was as focused on the grimoire as Gigi. She'd notice it missing soon, fly into a rage, and blame Beatrice.

I'd like to be dead before that happens.

Bean grunted from her pocket, almost as though he could hear the dark humor in her mind and objected. The familiar still hadn't given up on the idea of saving her.

"The important thing," Beatrice assured him as she climbed through the window, keeping her voice low despite knowing the house was empty, "is that we solve the murders and find a way to get Albert all the details to give Amos. I want to be the last Blackwell killed."

Bean grumbled. He was not impressed by her self-sacrificial talk, but Beatrice would rather die doing something important.

My ego couldn't survive accomplishing nothing and being killed in my sleep.

She wondered what Oliver would say about that. He'd always said she was too conceited. Perhaps she was proving his point.

Thoughts of the warlock crept into her mind as she tiptoed past the couch where they'd been last night when he invited her to run away with him.

I could've accepted after all.

Beatrice was going to die anyway. Why not from a broken vow? At least that way, she might get to enjoy a week with Oliver before the magic caught up to her.

It had to be better than being murdered.

But Beatrice couldn't abandon her coven like that. She needed to catch the killer. Even if it was quite literally the last thing that she did.

43
OLIVER

Oliver stumbled along Wicklow Avenue, silver key dangling from his fingers. The thought looped like a broken record in his mind: *If we get together, Beatrice will die.*

Gigi had pressed the key into his hand before he could object. She'd kept talking, assuring him that choosing to pursue his own dreams was an admirable choice in this instance. That it would be best for Beatrice if he never spoke with her again.

Ever?

That couldn't be right. Oliver couldn't agree to that. Even if he couldn't have the relationship with Beatrice that he'd begun to imagine, he still wanted her in his life. They were friends, in their own way, and they had a murder to solve, a memory to recover, a killer to catch.

Oliver didn't have the chance to explain all that to the old witch, however.

His mind had still been processing the significance of Beatrice making a blood-oath to never be with him when two brown heads had appeared around the corner of the estate's east wall: Albert and Gabriel. They'd called to their grandmother and started to approach.

Oliver didn't have the stomach for another confrontation. He'd fled, still holding the key that he'd intended to reject.

He pulled open the door to Very Good Food, stepped into the small restaurant, and searched for his sister.

Sophie sat in the corner, nose wrinkled as she stared down at the menu.

Oliver weaved through the plastic seats, soaked in the scents of cheese and pizza grease, and dropped into the chair opposite.

"You know, when she said *Very Good Food*, I didn't realize she meant the name of the restaurant," Sophie complained, not looking up from the menu. "I thought the Blackwells would eat somewhere fancy and classy. Not a cheap, fast-food place. Do they even have anything healthy?"

"Salad," Oliver suggested, barely registering his sister's complaints.

Sophie scoffed. "I bet they drown it in dressing." With a dramatic huff, she dropped her menu. Her brow furrowed as she noticed the expression on her brother's face. Her eyes flicked to his hand, which was palm-up on the table, and her fingers scrambled for the key. "You accepted their money?"

Her tone was disapproving, but excitement glinted in her eyes as she examined the key. She waved it before Oliver, taunting him to take it.

He didn't have the energy.

Sophie sighed and lowered her hand. "What happened? I thought we were getting your memory back, and weren't you desperate to talk to Beatrice? I thought you'd fallen in love with her." She gave him a small, sly smile. Another attempt to goad him into responding.

"Do you want to eat here or not?" Oliver couldn't find it in him to care much either way. He had no desire to stay at the restaurant, but he didn't want to leave either.

"Yes. I'm not going to pass up using the Blackwells' tab." Sophie grew annoyed. She tapped the key against the table, staring at Oliver for a few seconds before she tossed it at him. "Fine. Don't tell me what's going on. Not like I care anyway."

Oliver caught the key with a sudden sense of guilt. He hadn't intended to upset his sister, but how could he explain something he hadn't fully wrapped his head around yet?

"Beatrice will die if we get together. She swore an oath. And now the Blackwells are bribing me to go away and never talk to her again." He waved the key in explanation.

Sophie's eyes widened, and her mouth opened in an 'o.' The corners of her lips twitched.

"Mother, maiden, and crone. Are you smiling?" The annoyance Oliver felt was a comfort, burning through the numbness of Gigi's news. "Sophie, this isn't funny."

"No, I know. I know." She was still clearly trying not to smile. "But you're kind of admitting that you like Beatrice. And I didn't think you would. At least, not to me. But I've always thought—And especially in the hospital, you asked about her like a lot, and—"

"That's not the main thing to take away from what I just said." Oliver glared at his sister.

Sophie took a sip of the water before her. Her lips left a shimmer of pink gloss on the plastic. She appeared more composed when she rested her cup back down. "Okay, so, what are you going to do about it?"

"What do you mean? Did you hear what I said? Beatrice swore an oath. She'll die. That's it. There's nothing to do."

"Seriously?" Sophie raised her eyebrows. "You didn't quit when the Blackwells were coming for us, or after they tried to kill you. But you're going to give up now? I know you're a warlock, but haven't you ever heard there's no such thing as an infallible spell?"

Oliver opened his mouth to protest. Technically, his sister might be correct. But uncovering and exploiting a magical weakness was near impossible in certain instances. The spell controlling Beatrice's oath would've been cast by Tabitha. Oliver could never figure out a way to break it.

But B could.

She was the most impressive witch Oliver knew. But if it were that simple, why wasn't she attempting to undo the spell now?

Because she doesn't believe we're worth fighting for.

"How do you convince a girl that you mean it when you say you like her?" Oliver fought the urge to bury his face. He couldn't believe he was asking Sophie that question. But his sister was the closest thing around to a girl.

"A big romantic gesture. I can help you plan one. I really like the idea of having a Matriarch for a sister-in-law"

Absolutely not. Asking a fifteen-year-old for advice was bad enough. Oliver had some dignity to maintain. And he hadn't said anything about marriage!

I mean, in the future, I assume—

No. Oliver shook his head. What was he doing? He'd sound like his mother soon. There was a murder to solve, a memory to recover, and definitely a spell to break before his mind started wandering in that direction. Oliver opened his mouth to object to his sister's statement when something caught his eye at the window.

Gigi had finished her perimeter check and was now being pushed down Wicklow Avenue, seemingly against her will.

Albert's fists clenched around the handles of his grandmother's wheelchair as though the cold had frozen them in place. The two were arguing; the old witch's arms waved as they exchanged quick, sharp sentences.

Gabriel walked beside them, disengaged from the conversation. His gaze turned toward the Very Good Food window, and a chill went through Oliver. Gabriel's eyes shone with the same bewitched expression they'd had on the night of Tabitha's death, after seeing the banshee.

"Welcome to—oh, it's you," a familiar voice said beside Oliver. He turned to see the waitress, Kenya, with her notepad and pen at the ready. "Hope you're here to thank me for helping you and your girlfriend sneak into that estate. She already did. Where is Beatrice today anyway?"

"Yeah, where is your *girlfriend*?" Sophie echoed the question, placing a very obvious inflection on the last word.

Oliver kicked his sister under the table, which finally got her to stop smirking for a second while he answered the waitress. "She's busy today. But don't worry, I'm sure she'll bring Bean back for some food soon. He refuses to eat anything else."

An expression of concern flashed over Kenya's face. "She shouldn't bring Bean here."

That was weird. Oliver had been under the impression that the waitress liked the familiar.

"He might get sick."

Oliver didn't understand. "Sick from what?"

"From..." Kenya's brow furrowed. She blinked as if trying to remember something, then pressed her hands to her temple and shook her head. "I don't know. Sorry. Can I take your order?"

Oliver stared, uncertain what to say. Not because he had yet to look at the menu, but because he recognized what had just happened to the waitress. After all, it had happened to him too.

Kenya had tried to retrieve a memory and found it blocked by a magically induced white wall, courtesy of a Wyrmwood potion.

44

BEATRICE

RETT MUST HAVE USED MAGIC. THERE WAS
NO OTHER EXPLANATION FOR HOW HE'D
MANAGED TO CRAM SO MANY ITEMS INTO
THE SMALL SPACE. ROWS OF WOODEN
SHELVES JUTTED FROM EVERY WALL,
THREATENING TO SNAP UNDER THE WEIGHT
OF A HUNDRED DIFFERENT BOOKS, PLANTS,
AND POTION BOTTLES. THERE WAS A BED ON
THE FAR END, A MINI FRIDGE HUMMING
BESIDE IT. NEXT TO THAT A SMALL,
MAKESHIFT CAULDRON APPEARED TO HAVE
BEEN SPLATTERED WITH PAINT IN AN
UNSUCCESSFUL ATTEMPT TO HIDE THAT IT
WAS CONSTRUCTED FROM PAPIER-MÂCHÉ.
PAPERS, PENS, AND A VARIETY OF MUGS
CLUTTERED A DESK NEAR THE DOOR.
BEATRICE GLANCED IN A TEACUP AND
SPOTTED SOMETHING GLOWING WITHIN.

REMNANTS OF SILVERBLOOM.

B ean climbed out of her pocket, scurried across the desk, and inspected the other mugs. He squeaked and tapped one with his tail.

Beatrice stepped closer and saw a collection of deathcap mushrooms. Rett must have stolen them from the greenhouse.

That must be the base for the poison.

Beatrice should have guessed. Silverbloom was particularly effective against deathcap. They originated from the same forests in Germany.

Her chest tightened. The mushrooms were enough proof for her.

Rett created the poison. He's the murderer.

But she'd need more to convince her coven.

Albert had seen the poison in the fridge. It couldn't hurt to take as extra evidence, and maybe Beatrice would find the knife hidden within too.

She held her breath, wary of traps as she crossed the rest of the room. It would be just like Rett to bewitch his belongings to throw spikes at intruders. Thankfully, Beatrice made it to the fridge still alive. She opened the door, and her eyes grew wide.

There had to be fifty different potions within. Had Rett made all of them himself? How? No one would have taught him. Warlocks weren't supposed to be this adept with magic.

A mixture of envy and begrudging admiration shot through Beatrice. Even she had needed to learn the basics from Gigi. Her cousin really was more talented than she was.

Too bad he'd chosen to use his natural ability for evil.

Albert hadn't imagined it. A vial of dark poison hissed near the back of the fridge. The coalescing black mass was impossible to mistake.

She reached for it and then hesitated. It had broken the glass when her brother grabbed it.

I need the antidote.

Albert had described it to her, though she wasn't sure how useful his memory would prove: "*Sorry, I didn't really see it. Rett said he had to inject it on the opposite side, and I was staring at the poison. But I think it looked like silver light.*"

Strange. Bean remembered drinking the antidote. But

with her impending death, Beatrice didn't have time to question the significance of that difference.

Magic often glowed. Beatrice spotted more than a few shining concoctions in her cousin's fridge.

Only one was silver and already placed in a syringe, needle sterilized in a plastic container at the top. It only needed to be torn off, and it could be injected.

Rett thinks ahead.

Beatrice grabbed the antidote and slipped it into the pocket of her sleeve, careful to secure it so that the plastic cover wouldn't break and allow the needle to poke through.

She reached for the poison next, but a loud squeak from Bean stopped her.

Beatrice rose from the fridge and hurried to her familiar, who'd climbed onto Rett's bed.

The bilby's tail poked out from underneath the pillow. For a moment, Beatrice wondered if he'd gotten stuck beneath it, but in a second, he crawled free, pushing a large black leather tome before him.

"The grimoire!" Beatrice gasped.

This was exactly what she needed. Once she'd bound her soul to the spellbook again, there would be no need to worry about any more proof. She'd have power. Her word that she'd discovered the poison in Rett's room would be enough to apprehend him.

Beatrice stretched her hand forward. Her palm hovered over the empty ruby.

I don't want to be the Matriarch.

It was a stupid, childish thought. Gigi would be furious. Every witch dreamed of being Matriarch, especially when she belonged to one of the city's most powerful covens.

And Beatrice was about to die, so what did it matter if she seized power again for a few hours or a few days prior?

But what if I don't die, and this becomes my life?

She hadn't understood what it meant when she bound her soul last time: spending her days in pointless meetings, managing the Blackwell's petty squabbles, constantly worrying her coven would turn on her.

What good was power if Beatrice couldn't use it to do anything worthwhile?

And what if the very reason she died was because someone wanted the grimoire from her? That's why they'd killed Tabitha after all, wasn't it?

Beatrice was mulling over the decision, palm still hovering over the ruby, when blue powder floated into her view. She had just enough time to register the magic before something heavy struck her from behind.

45
OLIVER

Once Oliver realized that Kenya had been given one of his family's forgetting potions, things started clicking into place.

The poison had been the first attempt on Tabitha's life. But she wasn't the only one who'd been affected. Bean had needed some of the antidote too.

Given how the poison had entered Albert, it was tempting to believe that it had been a similar situation for the former Matriarch and her familiar. But even without being aggravated by the needle, the black lines spread quickly. Perhaps Tabitha would've had time to seek help, but Bean was tiny. And the familiar hadn't recognized the poison.

What if that was because he and Tabitha had ingested it? The toxin might spread slower if it entered through the digestive system instead of directly into the bloodstream.

And there was only one type of food Bean ate.

It all made sense. Tabitha must have known a hundred different protective spells. But why would a Blackwell Matriarch waste time checking for malicious magic in a greasy human establishment like Very Good Food?

The killer must have seized the opportunity and slipped something into her meal.

But Kenya saw.

Why else would someone block her memory?

Given the illegality of the situation, amnesiac powder wouldn't work. The government would ask questions. A Wyrmwood forgetting potion was their best option.

But the killer hadn't risked buying one direct. Instead, they'd turned invisible, slipped into Wilburn's study, and taken some of his. That was why he'd accused Beatrice of stealing it and why he'd placed a new order.

That had to be what happened. Oliver felt certain. But he remained at a loss as to the murderer's identity.

There's an easy way to find out.

Sophie had the base potion they required. The restaurant was full of objects the waitress would've interacted with on her forgotten day. Adding one would be simple.

"So you hold her down, and I'll pour it in her mouth," Sophie suggested. "You're strong. You could threaten her into telling us what she remembers."

Oliver's jaw clenched. "That would be wrong, Sophie. We can't give her a potion without her consent."

Sophie rolled her eyes, but there was a hint of guilt under her defensiveness when she responded. "Fine, but she's not going to be able to consent. She's a human."

Which meant that explaining the situation to Kenya would be illegal. They'd need to wipe her memory again when they finished, but two spells in quick succession on a human might be dangerous. Plus, Oliver didn't carry amnesiac powder or forgetting potions. He doubted his sister did either.

"Still. We're not pouring something down her throat. She has a right to know what we're giving her."

Oliver stood and walked across the restaurant to where Kenya was taking a different order. Sophie followed.

The waitress spotted them coming toward her. She excused herself and approached them. "Your pizza will be out in a second. Stuff here's quick."

"We need to talk to you about something, please. Outside, preferably?"

Kenya's nose wrinkled as she considered it. "Yeah, I know you're not quite a stranger, but I don't really know you, and—"

"Please. It's about the day that Bean got poisoned. The one you can't remember because there's a big white wall blocking you when you try."

The waitress' eyes widened. She leaned closer, glancing between Oliver and Sophie. "How do you know that?"

"Because the same thing happened to me," he told her truthfully.

Kenya nodded. She dropped her notebook into her apron, tucked her pencil behind her ear, and shouted to a short man behind the counter. "Ed, I'm stepping out for a minute. Come look for me if I'm not back in five."

————

Ten minutes later, the waitress leaned against the Very Good Food van in the same alley where Oliver and Beatrice had convinced her to sneak them into the Blackwell Estate.

"I still think you're playing prank," Kenya said. Her hand reached for her pencil. When she discovered it missing, she twisted her hair instead. "I mean someone giving me something to block my memory? That's like the sci-fi stuff my dad likes."

Oliver shrugged. He'd been careful not to mention magic in his explanation, and luckily, the waitress' imagination had gone in completely the wrong direction. When Kenya agreed to give Sophie her notepad and pencil, she'd asked if she could see the device that was going to be used to scan them. The idea that the young girl before her was a witch about to enchant the items and add them to a potion didn't appear to have crossed her mind.

"How else do you explain the wall blocking your thoughts?" Oliver asked.

"I don't know. Maybe I'm just forgetful. Maybe everyone has blocks like that." Despite her protests, Kenya remained, twirling her hair and flicking her eyes in the direction that Sophie had vanished.

The waitress' eyebrows rose the moment Oliver's sister returned.

"So, let's guess, you've got some sort of chip for me to stick in my ear? Or do I get to choose a red pill or a blue pill?" Kenya suggested.

Sophie shook her head. She pulled the glass vial out of her pocket. The liquid retained its burned brown color. Not exactly what Oliver would call appealing.

Kenya's eyebrows rose. "You're joking. I'm not drinking that."

"It's totally safe," Sophie said, pulling the stopper out of the top. The liquid released a curious scent. It was grease, and cheese, and a hint of sweat, like the young witch had managed to bottle Very Good Food and turn it into a perfume.

To prove her point, Sophie dipped her finger into the potion and licked it.

"And it'll let you remember what you saw and possibly help us solve a murder," Oliver reminded the waitress.

Kenya's eyes narrowed at the brown liquid. She shook her head, stepped forward, leaned back again, hand twitching.

Was she reaching for her lost pen or toward the potion?

Oliver held his breath as he waited to see.

46

BEATRICE

A strange chill crept up Beatrice's right wrist.

On instinct, she tried to cradle it to her chest, but a sharp rope dug into her skin.

She'd been captured.

Beatrice cracked her eyes open and squinted up at a dark stone ceiling, trying to get a sense of her location.

It appeared to be an old potions den, not dissimilar to the one in her own house. But where her basement had always felt vibrant and full of life, this felt heavy and dangerous. Long shadows crept toward her from the candles on the walls. There was a glint of threatening silver from the blade of a knife in the corner. Spiderwebs clung to cabinets full of bottles with eerie green glows.

But perhaps Beatrice's opinion of the place was tainted by the fact that she was tied to a stone slab in the center of it. She was seeing what a witch's room looked like not to a practitioner, but to an ingredient.

A lump rose in her throat.

This can't be how I die.

There was supposed to be some heroism in her demise, a moment of glory where she sacrificed herself for the greater good, or, at the very least, some sense of satisfaction that she'd outsmarted Rett and the truth would be revealed after she was gone.

Beatrice hadn't even managed to recover the grimoire. Her murderous cousin would seize power for himself now, and there would be nothing she could do.

The cold continued to rise in her wrist.

She turned her head and saw the black poison, bubbling under her skin as it crept toward her throat.

The antidote.

There was some in her sleeve. She could save herself still. If she could just get her hand out of this rope to recover it.

Beatrice's wrist tugged against the restraint. Something stirred in her pocket.

Her heart stopped for a moment before Bean's nose poked through. The familiar must have been affected by the same spell that had knocked Beatrice unconscious. But now, he'd awoken too.

They made eye contact. Beatrice flicked her gaze toward the ropes at her wrist.

Bean's ears twitched in understanding. He scurried over Beatrice's red dress, hiding in the fabric. His teeth chewed through the cord that held her left arm down with little issue before scurrying to free her right.

Beatrice breathed a sigh of relief the moment her hand was free. She'd have a chance to make a difference before she died after all. She twisted her wrist, fingers slipping into the pocket of her sleeve, searching for the antidote.

It wasn't there.

Her pocket, previously full of an assortment of spells, had been emptied.

A short sharp, bark of a laugh burst from the air above Beatrice's head, followed by a loud, panicked squeak as an invisible force hefted Bean into the air.

Rett was in the room with them.

47
OLIVER

Kenya insisted on returning to the restaurant if she was going to drink some mysterious concoction, but once they were seated at a table where her boss could see, the waitress took the glass vial from Sophie.

"This is the stupidest thing I've done in my entire life," she said. "Cheers."

Kenya threw back the small bit of brown liquid and rested the bottle on the table. She wrinkled her nose. "Tastes like chowder, but I—"

Her voice broke off as her eyes grew wide. The whites of her irises glowed, highlighting flecks of yellow in the waitress' dark eyes.

Is she human?

She certainly didn't know anything about magic. Oliver didn't have time to consider before cracks appeared in Kenya's irises, like a wall breaking. She pressed her hand to her forehead and squeezed her eyes closed. When she opened them, they were normal again.

"Oh my God," Kenya whispered. She licked her lips, expression turning anxious as she flicked her gaze between the two siblings sitting across from her. "You were right. I... I remember."

Oliver nodded, encouraging her to continue. His own chest felt too tight to allow him to speak.

"It was a boy. One of the Blackwells. He put something in her chowder. It was so strange. He was dressed as a cook, and no one else seemed to notice him in the kitchen. But I did. I knew he didn't belong."

Oliver and Sophie exchanged a look. He suspected that they were thinking the same thing. In theory, witches could sneak into human spaces using magic. Castors tended to notice impressions. But Grovers were predisposed to ignore anything out of the ordinary. Dressed in the right clothes, you could enchant yourself and fool most of them. But there was always a risk.

Anxiety or simply a heightened intuition made certain humans more alert to the deception. The chances of being caught must have been about one in five, not good odds if you were attempting something as sinister as murder.

It was probably better than trying to sneak into a crowded kitchen invisible, Oliver supposed, given the likelihood of bumping into a cook or a waiter or any number of dishes and causing obvious pandemonium. Tabitha might've grown suspicious if she'd heard something break behind the door. But Oliver still would have expected Rett to have a more refined plan, even if the Blackwell warlock had armed himself with the forgetting potion.

"I saw him add something to Tabitha's chowder when I was coming to collect it," Kenya continued. "So I confronted him, and then... I guess, I forgot. And I brought the order out anyway." She curled her hands into fists and pressed them against her cheeks, staring at the table with a panicked expression. "Does that make me an accessory to murder?"

"Probably," Sophie said, shrugging.

Oliver elbowed his sister's ribs. He managed to find his voice to reassure the waitress, "No. It doesn't. The poison didn't kill Tabitha. But tell me, the boy you saw disguised as a chef, was he tall and thin, with light hair?"

"No, the opposite," the waitress said, shaking her head, and looking slightly calmer now her conscience had been cleared of murder. "He had the same dark hair, round face they all have." She snapped her fingers as though remembering something important. "He was a twin."

"There are no Blackwell twins," Sophie said.

"Well then I've never seen a pair of brothers more identical in my life," Kenya said. "Every single one of their features was the same, even their eyes." A shudder went through her. "I could never forget those. They were so eerie and unfocused. They looked haunted."

Oliver's breath caught. He knew the eyes she was describing.

But Gabriel wasn't a twin. And he'd been in his house that night. The only way he could have been responsible for killing Tabitha was if he could be in two places at once, which was impossible. Unless—

A pain shot through Oliver's head, and his thoughts hit against the white wall that sealed his memory.

48

BEATRICE

B ean twisted in the air, gnashing his teeth as he struggled to free himself. There was a sharp sound, like the crack of metal.

"Dammit!" Gabriel Blackwell appeared, dressed in dark jeans and a black sweater. He stared at his hand, but his strange, unfocused gaze made it appear as though he were looking beyond. "You've broken my ring."

In two steps, Gabriel crossed the floor. He raised his hand, still holding Bean by the tail. With a flick of his wrist, he slammed the poor, small familiar against the wall.

"No, Gabe, stop!" Beatrice's shout came too late.

There was a loud squeak of pain as the bilby's head collided with the stone. Gabriel released his grip, and Bean dropped to a wooden table beneath. He didn't move.

Beatrice stared at his small blue-gray body. Her chest tightened to the point where it hurt to breathe.

This is wrong. This is all wrong.

Bean wasn't supposed to die. And Gabriel wasn't supposed to be the killer.

"I never did like rodents," her cousin said, his lips

curling into a frown as he glanced down at the familiar's body. He turned and tilted his head, studying Beatrice with his haunted gaze. "I am sorry to have to kill you though, B. I've actually always quite liked you. Better than Elle certainly. That's why I went to all the effort of finding a way to let you live. But then, you had to go snooping around and try to take the grimoire back. At least you've given me the chance to summon her again."

The cold poison crept into the crease of Beatrice's elbow.

She shook her head, trying to take in her cousin's words, but unable to look away from Bean. Was Gabriel working with Rett?

Bean's tail twitched. His little body rose and fell in an unsteady rhythm. He was injured, but alive.

Beatrice's eyes watered with relief. Maybe it wasn't too late to do something worthwhile before she died.

"I don't want the grimoire back, Gabriel, I swear," she said, turning her head to look at her cousin. "Rett can keep it. He can bond with it and take the power. I'll make a vow, swear it on anything your brother wants. Just let me go, please."

Then I can grab Bean and get him out of here. Give him a chance to keep living.

"Anything Rett wants?" Gabriel frowned, thick eyebrows furrowing above his small nose. "You think he's involved in this?"

"Well, I mean, you didn't do this alone. You couldn't have."

He had been in his house when Tabitha was murdered and in Beatrice's study when the banshee came for Elle.

"Hah!" Gabriel scoffed. It was an angrier noise than Beatrice had heard him make before. His wild eyes focused long enough to shoot her a disdainful glare. She'd offended him. "You truly believe Rett capable of murder? Do you know him at all? He's not cruel or power-hungry. He deserves to rule this coven, but he won't take it for himself. That's why I stepped up. Just me."

Beatrice stared at her cousin, unable to believe what he was saying. Gabriel wasn't offended because she'd accidentally implied he was incompetent. He was upset that she'd falsely accused his brother.

But if Rett really was innocent, then did that mean Gabriel truly had worked alone? It was impossible. He'd have to be able to...

Be in two places at once.

Beatrice's eyes widened. She stared up at her cousin, recognizing that strange, wild unfocused look in his eyes now: madness.

"Please, Gabe, just let me go. I won't tell anyone, I swear."

I'll just write it on a piece of paper and pass it to Albert and Gigi and any other coven member who might believe me.

Her cousin sighed, and, for a moment, he appeared the same sweet, vacant boy Beatrice remembered. "I really am fond of you, B." He reached into his pocket and pulled out a syringe full of glowing silver.

The antidote. Her pleas had worked. Gabriel was going to release her after all. She just needed to be ready to grab Bean once he did.

"So I won't make you suffer." Gabriel removed the plastic tube that kept the needle sterile. "We'll summon her quickly."

"What are you talking about?" There was something heavy and apologetic about his tone. "Who are you summoning?"

"You'll see," her cousin said.

Then, he pressed the needle into her vein, right at the point in her elbow where the black mass had reached.

The metal aggravated the poison. It hissed in her blood, and the cold began racing, climbing ever closer to Beatrice's heart.

49
OLIVER

Oliver paced the corner of Wicklow and 71st Street, feeling an irrational fury toward every brunette family that passed by that wasn't the Blackwells. He couldn't get ahold of Beatrice. Albert had blocked him. Talking to Gigi was probably his best hope.

"Would you stop?" Sophie said, looking up from her phone. It had refused to turn on for a few minutes when she'd first tried, likely the result of holding it too close while she'd added to her potion, but it appeared to be working now. She'd been texting on it for the past ten minutes. "If you want to find a moving target, the best strategy is to stay still."

"Sorry I'm not calmer," Oliver snapped, taking his frustration out on his sister. "My best friend and his grandmother are walking around with a murderer."

"You don't know it was Gabriel."

Except, I do.

Oliver's memories were still blocked, but the headaches that trying to access them caused were a hint in themselves. After hearing Kenya's story, he had begun piecing together what had happened when he visited the Blackwell Estate on his first day of seventh grade.

Rett had been starting to experiment with magic, teaching himself simple spells by spying on witches. Although Oliver and Albert praised him to his face, both privately agreed it was a waste of time. Neither expected the older boy to ever achieve much.

Did we challenge him? Say he wasn't good enough?

The wall that blocked Oliver suggested that they had.

Rett's ego wouldn't have stood for any insult, however innocent it might have been. He must have wanted to prove himself to the younger boys, regain their awe.

"Casting a spell that would allow someone to split in two is practically impossible," Sophie said, voice rising and falling in a nervous laugh. She was trying to convince herself. "It's forbidden magic. The last known recipe to do so was burned over a century ago and even then, few witches had the power to brew such a potion. Rett would have to be the most talented warlock in history."

"Maybe he is."

Sophie's phone buzzed. She read the screen and worry filled her eyes.

Oliver stopped pacing long enough to see who the message was from. "Really?" He sneered at his sister. "You're messaging Mom?"

Sophie pulled the phone away, pressing the screen to her chest so he couldn't read it. "For your information, I was asking her about the man who bought the invisibility ring and had your memory wiped. Which is a bit more useful than pacing the street corner."

Oliver stopped. "What did she say?"

"You were right." The defensiveness slumped from his

sister. "Your description of Rett and Gabriel's dad matches perfectly with what she remembers."

Oliver resumed his pacing, scanning the street for any sign of a Blackwell.

The information only confirmed what he'd already guessed. Rett and Gabriel's dad, a warlock by the name of Malcolm, had been a quiet man, independently wealthy but with little influence in any coven. Exactly the sort that Lucille Wyrmwood would have forgotten.

"I get that he couldn't risk you and Albert knowing if his son performed a forbidden spell. But why did he buy an invisibility ring?" Sophie asked, chewing her lip as she read the message on her phone again.

"For Gabriel, so no one would notice when he split in two and realize what Rett had done." Oliver was no expert on magic, and he knew almost nothing about forbidden spells, but he doubted a child like Gabriel would've had an easy time controlling such an ability.

"Do you think he went mad from the spell?" Sophie asked, voice soft.

"Well, he's killed two people, so what do you think?"

Sophie hugged her phone tighter. "Poor Rett. I know you're not a fan of his, but I can't imagine watching you lose your mind and knowing that I caused it."

Oliver scoffed. "Trust me—"

He was going to say that Rett's ego was great enough to survive but, when Oliver had seen him more recently, the older warlock hadn't acted like the overconfident, brash leader from their youth. Rett seemed quieter, more contemplative, and more subdued. He hadn't taken the power of the grimoire for himself, hadn't gloated when he saved Albert's life, hadn't even taken credit when he saved Tabitha.

"—Rett might be a better person as a result."

Ironic that the very thing that proved his talent might also make him doubt it.

But Gabriel's faith in Rett had never wavered. Even before the spell, he'd idolized his older brother with an obsession that bordered on unhealthy.

Now, he'd killed because of it.

Oliver suddenly understood why Beatrice spoke so much. It was torture having all these ideas in your head. He started explaining his theory in full to his sister.

"I don't think Gabriel ever meant to kill Tabitha with the poison. If he had, it would've been faster to inject it into her veins, like he did with Elle. He must have always intended for his brother to save her."

"Why? I thought you said Rett made the poison. So wouldn't that just make him look suspicious?"

"Yes, to you and me. Because we know Rett made the poison, but if Tabitha didn't, she'd have assumed that whoever saved her was incredibly talented. And it wasn't exactly a secret that Tabitha wanted to leave the Blackwells in the hands of her most powerful descendant." Not that Oliver had known until after the former Matriarch's death, but it wasn't farfetched to assume that Gabriel, who lived on the estate, had heard rumors. "What better way to prove Rett's ability than by saving her life?"

Oliver paused as he caught sight of dark hair further down the street. It was a couple in blue jackets, holding hands. Even at a glance, they bore little resemblance to the Blackwells. No one on the street did. Oliver was just getting jumpy.

"Except, Rett didn't take credit for the antidote. He gave it to Elle," Oliver continued, running his hand over his curls. "So Gabriel met with Tabitha on his own to tell her the truth, that Rett was the one who saved her and that he should lead the coven."

"Except he couldn't because he's a warlock, not a witch," Sophie said. She gave her brother an apologetic shrug. "I mean, I've never heard of a male Matriarch, have you?"

"No." And Tabitha would've said the same thing. Except with considerably less tact than Sophie had. "Which is why Gabriel must have decided to just kill her, so the grimoire would be available for Rett to take."

Sophie pursed her lips. "I suppose. But what about Elle? She never took the grimoire, so why would Gabriel need to kill her?"

Oliver opened his mouth, but he didn't have an answer for that part of things just yet. Maybe Beatrice would have an idea.

He stopped at the corner again and peered down the length of the Blackwell Estate's western wall. Passersby drifted along 71st street, parking their cars, slipping in and out of stores, calling to one another with obnoxious voices. It was a picture of human normalcy in the city.

But something was off.

There was a tall, blonde walking among the rest, long hair flowing behind her in the opposite direction to the wind. Instead of winter clothes, she wore a long, white dress, and a pair of strappy, black heels that clicked against the ice on the pavement where she stepped.

Oliver's breath escaped him, visible for a moment in the cold air. The sight sent a shiver through him.

Why had the banshee returned?

50
BEATRICE

"I am sorry, but we can't be too quick either," Gabriel said, staring at the black mass as it spread into Beatrice's upper arm. He pressed the needle into her vein a few millimeters ahead of the poison's path. "Or else I might miss her when she arrives. I almost made that mistake with Elle."

A stab of ice seized in the center of Beatrice's shoulder as the poison stopped. She felt it bubbling within her vein, coalescing in a large clump. The needle blocked its path to the heart, but it wasn't enough of a threat for the poison to retreat.

Beatrice closed her eyes, trying not to scream at the pain. She took a few shaky breaths. At least, she was starting to understand things a bit more.

"You killed Elle to summon the banshee. Because..." Beatrice's throat was dry, it took her a second to continue. "... you needed banshee's breath. To sever my connection with the grimoire."

It was so obvious, she didn't know why it had taken her until now to deduce. She'd bound her soul to the Blackwell's spellbook. Only banshee's breath had the power to sever such a connection.

Beatrice would simply never have thought to use it. Most witches or warlocks wouldn't. Banshee's breath was dangerous to capture and unpredictable once released. No one in their right mind would risk it.

Still, it's a bit embarrassing that it didn't occur to me.

"Almost, but you're wrong about one thing," Gabriel said, letting out a nervous giggle. "Elle killed herself. See, after you became Matriarch, Elle realized how foolish she'd been to try to take the grimoire for herself. It was nothing personal against you, B, just that we both knew Rett would be superior in the role. I mean, you needed our grandmother to control the coven, but my brother is a natural leader and talented. The magic he's mastered? It's stuff you couldn't even begin to comprehend. He outclasses every witch in the city."

Gabriel's voice took on a hushed, reverent tone as he spoke of his brother. He lifted his hand, and the needle left Beatrice's skin.

The poison wasted no time rushing forward. It spread, dispersing into different veins and numbing her shoulder.

"Elle was part of the problem though. No one's ever understood how brilliant Rett is because she's always stolen credit for his accomplishments. So I offered her a chance to redeem herself," Gabriel continued as though unaware of the black lines creeping along Beatrice's shoulder. "The plan was to poison Elle and keep her in a state of near-death long enough to fool the banshee. Once she arrived, I was going to catch her breath, and then save Elle with the antidote. It might have worked. Except that Elle chickened out. She snatched the antidote from me. But she was never a very good witch. She didn't think about how the poison worked, and she injected herself wrong and ended up dying anyway."

She grabbed the antidote.

Now there was an idea.

Beatrice's eyes fluttered open and flicked toward the syringe of glowing silver in her cousin's hand.

Thanks to Bean, her left wrist was free, but a rope higher on her arm limited her mobility. She couldn't reach the syringe but perhaps, if her cousin leaned closer, she might have a chance.

"You already severed my connection to the grimoire," Beatrice said, trying to ignore the cold inching closer to her heart and focus on one last chance of salvation for herself and Bean. "Why do you need more banshee's breath?"

Gabriel frowned, blinking at her with his mad eyes as though he thought the answer should be obvious. "To fix myself."

The response caught Beatrice off guard. For a split second, she shifted her gaze from the antidote to her cousin.

"When we were children, Rett brewed the most incredible potion. I drank it, and it allowed me to split myself into two. It's an amazing gift, you know, I'm very grateful to him for granting me such an ability." A smile spread across Gabriel's face, so wide it looked like it would crack his skin. "But I've had as much of power as I can handle. Do you know how painful it is? Tearing yourself into two, experiencing two realities simultaneously, then compressing yourself into one body again and forcing it to accept an impossible scenario. That you were in two places at once."

The madness turned in Gabriel's eyes, making it look like he was burning from the inside out. Perhaps he was, in a way.

"You can stop, Gabe," Beatrice whispered. Lowering her voice was a ploy to get her cousin to lean closer, but she found that she truly wanted him to listen to her. "You don't have to keep splitting yourself."

"I can't stop!" he shouted, stepping backward, flinging his arms up, and moving the antidote even further from Beatrice's reach. "The feeling of ripping your soul and reconnecting it is torture. But it's intoxicating. And it's the best way for me to help Rett. I can't give it up, B. Not until he's achieved everything he deserves. But then, thanks to your sacrifice, I'll be able to."

He drew close, trembling. Beatrice got the impression he wanted to apologize to her again.

But she didn't wait to hear.

The antidote was only a few inches from her left hand. Beatrice grabbed it from her half-mad cousin and stabbed the needle through the fabric of her dress and into the top of her arm, praying it would find a vein.

Gabriel was slow to react. He blinked at the empty space in his hand where the syringe had vanished.

Beatrice felt a prick as the needle went into her skin, followed by a rush of warmth as she pushed the antidote in. The silver liquid shot toward her heart.

Would it make it in time— or would the poison arrive first?

Her answer came less than a second later when her cousin breathed a sigh of relief and turned to look at something behind her head.

"A valiant effort, but it's made no difference," he said, patting the top of Beatrice's head. "You're still set to die. The banshee's arrived to take your soul."

51
BEATRICE

"Not you again." The banshee's voice reached a high, cruel pitch, just shy of a shriek. The sound floated down into the potions den as though she were at the top of a flight of stairs.

Beside Beatrice, her cousin fell into a deep bow. He slid his hand into his sweater. "You've come early. Thank you."

"I have not," the banshee hissed. There was a clicking sound, like heels on stone. A few seconds later, her pale face and long, unmoving hair appeared above the Beatrice's head. "Boo."

Beatrice couldn't have screamed, even if she was afraid. Her chest was spasming, half burning, half freezing, causing her to convulse. She coughed instead.

"Dammit." The banshee's lips curled in a frown and her prismatic eyes narrowed. "Why aren't you dead yet? This coven, I swear! Some of you rush to death and some of you keep clinging to life." She stomped her foot. "Just don't tell my master when you meet him in..." She pressed a French-tipped finger against Beatrice's forehead. "I'd say, about a minute."

"Will you gift me another one of your breaths while we wait?" Gabriel asked, holding the thin glass vial that he must have had hidden under his sweater.

"Go away." The banshee rested her hand on his face and pushed him back. "I'm not letting you steal from me again. Eek!" A sudden yelp, not quite a shriek, escaped her. She pulled Gabriel back, holding his shoulders and positioning herself behind him as though he were a shield. "What is that?" She pointed to something on the table beyond.

Beatrice tried to focus through the pain so that she could see what had upset the banshee.

It was Bean! The familiar had managed to get back on his feet.

"Is that a rat? I absolutely hate rats," the banshee said, peeping out over Gabriel's shoulder.

"Oh? I can take care of him for you if you're willing to trade. What do you say, dead rodent for your breath?"

No, he's not a rodent, he's a marsupial.

Beatrice wanted to shout, but her body betrayed her. She froze, watching in silent horror as her cousin managed to grab Bean once more. In his weakened state, the familiar could barely resist.

I'm not going to make it. I can't help him.

The chill reached the center of her chest. Beatrice had a split second where she understood what that meant, and she used it as best she could.

With her final breath, she gathered what remained of her strength and pushed her will toward her familiar, hoping her belief in him would be enough.

Then, the poison won. It seized Beatrice's heart moments before the antidote arrived. She felt a shock of cold through her body, then pain, and then—

Nothing.

Beatrice Blackwell was dead.

52
OLIVER

Oliver's heart pounded in his chest as he hurried toward the shell of an old windmill on the corner of the Blackwell Estate.

He'd left Sophie with Amos' number and instructions to call, then had raced after the banshee, following her through the wall, just like the morning of Tabitha's murder. Only this time, Oliver hadn't let the creature out of his sight. He'd kept a cautious distance, tracking the bright white of her dress through the mud and leaves of the forest floor.

But now she'd vanished.

Oliver had seen her step into the interior of the old mill, but it was empty.

Moss grew on the dark gray stones and dust covered the floor. The banshee's heels had left little circles of mud, leading toward a section of the wall.

Had she used magic to pass through it again? That seemed odd. There was no magical protection on the wind-mill itself.

A secret passage?

The suggestion made Oliver's head spin. He refused to stop considering it, and once more his thoughts slammed against the white wall.

Definitely a secret passage. One I've used before.

Oliver followed the banshee's tracks. He studied the stones before him. Only one was moss-free.

He pressed his hand against it and pushed.

The wall ground against the floor as it moved backward, revealing a hole with a staircase leading down.

———

Oliver raced down the stairs. Glowing torches illuminated the room beneath.

It was an old potions den, full of dusty vials and stone tables. They were peripheral to Oliver's focus.

Beatrice lay on a slab in the center of the room, legs and arms bound with rope. Her red dress flickered in the torchlight, casting streaks of dark auburn in her hair, which fanned behind her in waves. Her green eyes stared up at the ceiling.

They didn't blink.

Her chest didn't rise and fall; her fingers didn't even twitch.

It was exactly what Oliver had feared most when he'd seen the banshee returning yet again to the Blackwell Estate.

Beatrice is dead. I'm too late to save her.

Oliver's body was slower to react to the realization. His legs kept running, moving him closer to two individuals it was in his best interest to avoid.

The banshee looked at Gabriel, who stood by one of the tables, holding something small and gray in his hand.

"Told you. One minute," she said, voice smug and haughty. But there was the slightest hint of a tremble beneath, as though she wasn't as in command of the situation as she sounded.

Or maybe that was Oliver's wishful thinking.

"Don't know where you're going next, but you can't stay here," the banshee said, turning toward Beatrice. Then, her expression softened into an actual smile. "This part won't hurt. At least, I don't think it will. I've never had my soul severed. But none of the corpses I've handled have ever complained."

The creature inhaled, her chest expanding, and Oliver's body finally stopped, right at the bottom of the steps.

He was about to have a front-row seat as Beatrice's soul departed from her body.

53
BEATRICE

Beatrice's soul clung to its warm, familiar home within the witch's mind.

It watched through her unblinking eyes and heard with an acuity that made Beatrice worry she'd been deaf her whole life. But it didn't feel.

There was no pressure from the table against her back, no softness from the velvet dress, no stifling cold from the poison in her heart. She wasn't even certain she still had limbs.

Otherwise, she would have willed them to move and shove the banshee away as the creature drew closer.

Or at least, Beatrice would have opened her mouth and objected.

I'm still here!

But not for much longer.

The banshee opened her mouth and inhaled. Little flecks of white light spun in the darkness at the entrance to her throat, like stars swirling in a galaxy. They gathered in the center: an airy mass of visible breath, ready to sever Beatrice's soul.

Gabriel shouted. Something small and gray leaped across the room and landed on the banshee's shoulder.

"Aah! Aah! Get it off!" The banshee's breath flew from her mouth, sailing almost a foot above Beatrice's head.

There was a clatter of noise as Gabriel came running.

"Help! I can feel its paws!" The banshee's voice was high and distressed.

Gabriel made no effort to assist. His eyes were as focused as they'd ever been, locked on the breath that floated through the small space. He brandished his glass bottle before him, swiping like he thought he was chasing butterflies with a net.

The banshee flailed her arms and managed to knock Bean off on her own.

But even wounded, the familiar seemed to have found new life. He hissed and squeaked and grunted, lunging at the terrified banshee and backing her into a corner.

No, just run and save yourself! Beatrice wanted to shout to him. *I'm already dead.*

And there was nothing that could change that.

But of course, Bean wouldn't care. As her familiar, he could sense her soul, still lingering, and he wouldn't abandon her. Even if it was futile, he would die trying before he gave up.

Well, perhaps we'll end up wherever we're going together.

Another noise, beyond Bean's hissing and the banshee's yelps of fear, reached Beatrice.

Someone was coming down the stairs. She recognized the footsteps.

But it couldn't be—

Oliver appeared at her side, still dressed in the clothes he'd worn the day before.

He leaned forward, studying her with dark eyes,

muscles in his face clenched with worry that only served to highlight his chiseled jaw and strong cheekbones. The light danced on his skin, making the sweat glisten.

Why is he here? Didn't Gigi say she was handling his payment?

But Oliver hadn't come for money. He'd come for her.

"Beatrice," he whispered her name and stroked his hand over her cheek.

She wished she could feel it.

"Bean, keep holding her back," Oliver shouted.

The familiar squeaked in agreement.

"No, call him off! Do you know how many diseases rats carry?" the banshee cried. "You're only wasting time and prolonging the inevitable. She's already dead. If you don't let me do my job, her soul will end up stuck here, haunting this place forever. Is that really what you want?"

"No," Oliver said. He looked back at Beatrice and rested his hand on her cheek once more. "I want to save her."

The words would have made Beatrice smile, if she had lips to move.

She would never get over Oliver Wyrmwood, would she? Even now she was dead, he was still her knight, coming to her rescue.

Only her tormentors weren't some sixth-grade kids now. They were a murderer and a harbinger of death.

The odds were not in Oliver's favor this time.

But just like Bean, he'd decided to try.

I should've taken you up on your offer to run away when I had the chance, Beatrice thought at him. *I never needed to become Matriarch. I would've been a million times happier traveling the world with you. You may only think that you love me, but I know.*

I've known since we were kids.
I love you.

54

OLIVER

Some part of Oliver, the logical part, knew that the banshee was right. He was only delaying the inevitable.

And yet...

He couldn't accept that.

This wasn't how his story with Beatrice was supposed to end. He'd already begun planning for the next time they met, what he would say, how he would prove to her that he loved her, how he would fill a room with a thousand black lilies and convince her that there was a way to break the spell that kept them apart.

But you already found one.

Death meant the end of Beatrice's oath.

It was a sick sort of irony. But Oliver couldn't give in to the numbness. Not again. Sophie was right. He couldn't give up. As long as Beatrice's soul was still here. There had to be a way to bring her back.

Oliver just needed to figure out what it was.

But how? Even for a warlock, his magical ability was

limited. If a spell existed that could wake the dead, he certainly didn't know it.

Oliver stared into Beatrice's unblinking eyes.

Our roles should be reversed. You'd know how to save me.

The witch always had an idea. She'd look around this dusty old den and find some random pair of items and somehow enchant them to save the day. Like when she'd used seawave root dust and the spindle to create a sleeping spell.

How had she thought to do that?

Fairytales.

Beatrice had said they revealed fundamental truths.

Oliver's breath caught. He recalled the stormy day back when they'd been bored teenagers, and Beatrice had convinced them to put on a performance of *Snow White.*

There was one thing that could bring someone back from the dead.

But was Oliver powerful enough to pull it off? He couldn't even perform a botanical enchantment.

That's not true. I turned a lily black once for Beatrice, even if I don't remember. I can do this as well. For her.

Oliver closed his eyes and gathered his will, amplifying his own small source of magic with his belief.

"I love you, B," he whispered, then leaned forward.

55

BEATRICE

Oliver's lips pressed against hers.

And Beatrice felt them, humming with magic, sending a sudden warmth spreading through her.

Her heart thumped. A silver glow emanated from her chest, visible even beneath the red of her dress.

The antidote.

Oliver's kiss had reanimated it.

The cold poison fled to the tips of Beatrice's fingers and toes, trying to escape the warmth flooding through her. But it was no good. The antidote flooded her veins.

Beatrice's body was alive once more, glowing with a silver light. Her soul was safe within.

She closed her eyes and brought her hand forward, grabbing Oliver's collar and pulling him close. The magic was still on his lips. It tasted like honey and almonds, and a light fragrance clung to the air around them, earthy and spicy and sweet, like lilies in full bloom. The scent made Beatrice's head feel light and giddy.

She'd never felt, or tasted, or smelled anything quite so wonderful.

Oliver brushed his hand over her cheek and pulled away, a hesitant smile spreading across his lips. "You're alive." His voice was soft, like he could barely believe it.

"Because of you," Beatrice said, light-headed as she returned his smile. Her heart beat, quick and excited, like it wanted to skip now that it was functioning again. "You saved me."

Bean launched himself onto Beatrice and burrowed against her neck, squeaking in excitement.

"That's right." Despite still being bound to the table, Beatrice giggled, using her left hand to hug the familiar as best she could. "You saved me too, Bean. The greatest familiar in all the world!"

The bilby gave a squeak that sounded almost bashful, then he scuttled from her embrace to chew through the rest of the ropes. Beatrice looked up at Oliver.

He stared at her, his smile open-mouthed and goofy. Somehow, it was even more attractive than his usual statuesque perfection.

Beatrice had never seen him look at a girl like that.

"Next time," a high-pitched and annoyed voice said, interrupting the moment, "I'd prefer you let nature take its course."

Bean finished chewing through the bindings on Beatrice's right arm and jumped onto the table, positioning himself between her and the banshee. Oliver stepped forward too.

"Relax." The banshee held up her hands, but she took a step back, keeping her eyes on Bean. "I was only sent to collect one soul. I'm not going to get a prize for returning with a second."

A stab of worry tightened in Beatrice's chest. *What does that mean?*

It occurred to her that there was someone she hadn't heard in the past few minutes.

Gabriel.

Beatrice managed to tug the last rope on her upper body free so that she could sit up. She twisted, looking around the old potions den until his shape came into view.

Her cousin sat on the floor near the base of the steps. His chest rose and fell, but his eyes were white. Drool dripped from the corner of his mouth.

Beatrice's stomach lurched at the sight. She turned back to the banshee. "You stole his soul."

"Excuse me?" The banshee flipped her blonde hair over her shoulder. "He's the one who went chasing my breath." She pointed at the floor beside him.

The glass jar had dropped from Gabriel's hand and shattered. Its sharp edges flickered in the torchlight.

A lump rose in Beatrice's throat.

"Why do you look so bothered?" The banshee gave a disdainful sniff. She seemed more relaxed now that Bean had resumed his task of chewing Beatrice's ropes and was no longer hissing and snarling at her. "He was going to kill you, you know."

"I know." But Beatrice's heart still felt heavy as she looked at her soulless cousin.

Gabriel had been driven mad by a power he couldn't control. How long had he been suffering without any of his coven realizing?

Beatrice recalled how desperate he'd sounded, talking about finally severing his connection to the magic that allowed him to split his body into two.

Had Gabriel run into the banshee's breath on purpose?

"What about the other half of him?" she asked, swinging her legs from the table. They trembled with pins and needles as she stood. "Is there another Gabriel out there, still running around?"

The banshee scoffed. "I'm not in the habit of collecting only half a soul." Then, seeing Beatrice still looking at her, she sighed and flipped her blonde hair again. "No, there isn't. Whatever perverse magic allowed him to keep tearing himself in two was taken from him. His soul is tattered and ripped, but it's whole."

That was some relief.

The banshee tapped her foot for a few seconds, glancing between Beatrice and Oliver. Her eyes rather purposefully ignored the familiar on the edge of the table. She seemed to be waiting for something.

When it didn't come, she clicked her tongue on the roof of her mouth and threw her hands in the air. "God, I hate this job. I come all this way to collect a Matriarch's soul, have to settle for a damaged one, and get attacked by a rat." She shuddered, brushing her skin as though trying to wipe off the memory of Bean's paws. "And not even a thank you? Honestly. You'd think witches would have more respect."

With those parting words, she glided up the stairs and, Beatrice hoped, out of their lives for at least the next several decades.

———

Beatrice and Oliver climbed the stairs. A black bone handle protruded from his pocket. It belonged to a silver knife—the original murder weapon. Discovering it now almost seemed a cruel joke. They'd already solved everything.

But the knife would help Sergeant Amos close the case for good.

Beatrice stepped out into an empty circular room, with gray stone walls and a wide-open archway that faced the trees.

"Is this the Blackwell Estate?" she asked.

It must have been. No other oaks and birches still had their leaves at this time of the year. But Beatrice didn't recognize her current location.

Oliver nodded as he climbed from the stairway to join her in the room. "We're in an old windmill near the corner. Here, check this out."

He took her hand and placed it on a smooth gray stone just beside the stairs.

At her touch, the wall started to move, scraping along the floor toward them.

Oliver took Beatrice's hand and pulled her back. From a safe distance, they watched the room shrink and the stones hide the entrance to the underground den.

"I think Rett found the den when we were kids. He's the one who cast the spell to allow Gabriel to split in two."

Beatrice knew that, but how did Oliver?

She glanced down at her hand, held tight in the warlock's own. The sight made her chest flutter more than it should have.

Given that she'd already died, Oliver was no danger to her life. But what about her heart? His kiss may have saved her, but Beatrice had no idea how.

She cleared her throat, trying not to lose herself in his eyes. "Sounds like you've solved even more of this mystery than I have. You're quite the detective, Mr. Wyrmwood."

A smile flitted across Oliver's face before disappearing. He dipped his head, lowering his gaze to the knife. "Not really. I got some information last night. There's a spell I think I need your help with."

"Doubtful," Beatrice said, twisting her head so that it was within his line of sight. She smiled. As horrible as she felt for her cousin and the people he'd killed, she refused to wallow. Not now. There were too many things to be grateful for. "You've obviously been holding out on me. You brought me back from the dead! I can't even imagine casting a spell so powerful. How did you manage it?"

Oliver laughed. If Beatrice didn't know better, she'd think he sounded almost embarrassed. "Come on, you know how."

Beatrice shook her head. She really didn't.

"Well, it was your idea," he said, laughing again. "Fairy-tales hold the answers and all that. I figured how else do you revive a sleeping princess?"

Beatrice's heart pounded. He couldn't mean—? But what else could it be?

She gazed into Oliver's brown eyes, soft and unusually shy, and her smile grew broader. "True love's kiss?"

He laughed again, embarrassed, but he didn't look away. "True love's kiss."

Beatrice stood on the tips of her toes, wrapped her arms around Oliver's neck, and pulled his lips to hers.

She kissed him, deeper this time, tugging on his lower lip, letting her hands slip beneath his jacket and under his shirt to feel the light sweat on his muscles. There was no honey or almonds or lilies. Instead, Oliver tasted like soda, and the scent of pizza clung to his coat.

It was just as perfect.

Oliver wrapped his arms around Beatrice. His fingers tangled in her hair, brushed the small of her back, and pulled her body toward his. She let her own hand trail over his chest, enjoying the slight dip between his pectoral muscles.

When they finally separated, Beatrice's sleeves had slipped down, and two of the buttons had popped open on Oliver's shirt.

She smiled. "I always wondered what true love's kiss felt like. I like it."

"I do too." Oliver gave her that same goofy, open-mouthed grin that he'd had down in the den. "But maybe we can keep that part of the story to ourselves? I don't think your brother or my sister will let me live it down if they know how I saved you."

Beatrice laughed and took the warlock's face in her hands. Her thumbs stroked either side of his chiseled jaw, and he leaned into her touch, likely expecting another kiss. She tiptoed and brought her head closer, but whispered into his ear instead.

"Have we met? I will be telling absolutely everyone that part of the story."

56

BEATRICE

Gigi, Albert, and Sophie were in the downstairs foyer with a group of guards when Beatrice and Oliver returned to the Manor.

"Two of my grandchildren, dead in the space of a day." Gigi's voice was loud and anxious. They must have only recently returned. Through the crack in the door, Beatrice could see her grandmother moving from her wheelchair to her broomstick, her hand like a talon, digging into Albert's shoulder for support. "And no one can find our Matriarch? Go! Search the grounds!"

The guards rushed out the door, and almost collided headfirst into the witch they were searching for.

One of them, a shifter with close-set orange eyes and short brown hair, opened his mouth and pointed. "Well, she's right here! We've found her. And Mr. Wyrmwood!" He took a step back and eyed Oliver warily. "Don't knock me out this time, please sir."

Beatrice had no idea what that was about. And before Oliver could respond, the doors burst open.

Albert stood in the center, staring at them, eyebrows

lowered and forehead wrinkled. Behind him, Sophie tapped her foot to the rhythm of the grandfather clock in the corner of the room, and Gigi adjusted her grip on her broomstick, hovering in the air above a glass coffee table, surprisingly modern amongst the black and gray gothic chairs and cauldron-motif rug.

At the sight of Beatrice and Oliver, the stress fell from Albert's face. He let out a long breath, and his mouth opened in an unsteady smile. Then he rushed forward and pulled them both into a hug.

They wrapped their arms around him as well.

"Told you they'd be fine," Sophie said, running forward. She didn't rush to embrace her brother, but there was a large smile on her face, and the nervous tapping of her leg seemed to have stopped. Her hand rested on her hip, projecting a slightly exaggerated confidence. "Did you kill Gabriel?"

"Of course not," Beatrice said, extracting herself from Albert's embrace. "He ran into the banshee's breath himself, I think—" Her voice broke.

Oliver wrapped his arm around her shoulder and squeezed.

Beatrice rested her head against his chest, enjoying the momentary comfort. Then she looked at Sophie once again, confused. "How do you know Gabriel's dead?"

"He was with us when it happened," Albert explained. "Well, half of him was, I guess. We were walking back here, and he suddenly let out this weird half-laugh, half-scream and dropped to the street. His body flickered for a moment and then he just vanished." Albert's jaw clenched, and he shuddered at the memory.

"The humans thought it was a magician's performance

and started applauding," Sophie explained. "Whole thing was really loud. That's how I found them."

"Is it true, B?" Albert asked, eyes heavy as he looked at her. "Did Gabriel really kill both Tabitha and Elle?"

Beatrice sighed and nodded. She wanted to cling to the joy of being alive and being in love, and for a few blissful minutes, walking through the woods with Oliver, discussing everything that had happened and starting to make plans for the future, she'd been able to.

But now the tragedy of everything had to be faced.

She slipped her hand into Oliver's for comfort and guided him to the couch. They sat beside one another as Beatrice launched into the story.

"You brought B back from the dead with true love's kiss?" Albert interrupted the story as she came to the end, raising his eyebrows at his friend, an amused expression on his face.

Technically, it wouldn't have been that simple. True love's kiss couldn't really wake the dead, but the magic of it had reinvigorated the antidote already within Beatrice, which in turn had cleansed her heart of the poison and allowed it to start pumping once more.

But explaining all that made it seem much less romantic.

So instead, Beatrice smiled and kept quiet, turning to watch Oliver splutter. Despite his embarrassment, that goofy grin returned to his face.

Albert laughed, apparently finding that more amusing than an answer. "Guess I owe you an apology for thinking you were after B's title. Sophie explained everything. But you could've just told *me* that you liked Beatrice." He glanced at his sister and made a face. "Not that I see the appeal."

Beatrice stuck her tongue out at him. "You also don't see a Matriarch."

Three confused faces stared at her. Only Gigi's own gave her pause. But everyone—even Beatrice's grandmother—would learn the truth soon enough.

"Gabriel used banshee's breath to sever my connection to the grimoire. I'm no longer the Matriarch, and I don't plan on taking up the title again." She stood and stared at her grandmother. "I'm sorry, Gigi."

The old witch's eyes widened.

Beatrice braced for her grandmother's impending rage, which would likely be masked by a thick layer of disappointment.

"Banshee's breath? I would never have thought. He was a genius," Gigi said, making the sign of the maiden, mother, and crone as best she could manage with only one hand.

"That's it? That's all you have to say?" Beatrice stared at her grandmother, almost annoyed. All week, Gigi had been lecturing her on the importance of her role, the honor that had been bestowed upon her, and now she was fine with her giving it all up?

A small, sad smile flickered across Gigi's face, but her mouth remained closed in its tight-lipped frown.

"Well, I have something to ask." Sophie stood from her armchair, hip cocked to the side. "If you're not the Blackwell Matriarch anymore, then who is?"

———

The five of them made their way through the manor's twisting corridors, heading toward the back exit. There was no choosing a new Matriarch without a grimoire, and Beatrice had been so wrapped up in her discussion with Oliver that she hadn't thought to retrieve the spellbook from Rett's bedroom.

Sophie trailed at the back of their procession, trying to peep into every door. Albert had been stuck with the unfortunate task of answering all her questions, and Oliver kept stopping to scold his sister for trying to snoop.

That left Beatrice and Gigi guiding their way at the front.

A loaded silence hung between them. And soon, Beatrice gave up waiting for her grandmother to speak first.

"Oliver told me what you said to him earlier. You were supposed to be Matriarch before your accident, but Tabitha killed granddad and sabotaged your potion when you tried to save him. She's the reason you can't walk or brew potions now."

"You're telling me things I already know," Gigi observed, her voice stiff as she maneuvered her broom through a particularly tight corner. The bristles swept the dark stone wall.

Because I'm waiting for you to explain why you never told me!

"Well, you tell me something that I don't know then," Beatrice suggested, squeezing between two suits of armor that faced one another and shrunk the already narrow passage. "After Tabitha did all of that, why were you loyal to her? Why did you agree to groom me to take her place?"

Gigi flew over the soldiers, taking advantage of the manor's high ceilings. Her lips twisted for a moment, and then she sighed. "After the potion exploded, I was left with no legs, no husband, and no title. I had no desire to lose my coven as well. And of course, there was you."

She stopped, chin quivering. Beatrice had never seen

such an expression on her grandmother's face. Gigi was holding back tears.

"My granddaughter with the greatest magical aptitude," she whispered, staring straight ahead at the torches flickering beside the door. "I knew Tabitha would select you the way she had done with me. A selfish part of me believed that I could groom you to be the type of Matriarch this coven needs. And I thought that having one of my descendants ascend to the title might give purpose to my suffering."

They stopped before the door, waiting for the other three who had been waylaid near the statues. Sophie was trying to get the suits of armor to follow, convinced they were bewitched.

"I'm sorry Gigi," Beatrice said, casting her gaze down to the floor. "I wish I could've done that for you. But we both know I make a terrible Matriarch and—"

"Can you ever be quiet, child?" Gigi raised her hand and pressed a finger to her granddaughter's lips. A fond smile crept across her wrinkled face. She sighed, and pushed a lock of hair behind Beatrice's ear, her touch tender. "You have no reason to apologize. I want your story to have a happier ending than mine. I'd never condemn you to a life of misery just to have one of my descendants as Matriarch."

Beatrice reached up and took her grandmother's hand, holding it to her face for a moment. But she really couldn't keep silent, not when she'd had a brilliant idea.

"You know, Gigi," she said, hiding a smile. "I'm not the only grandchild you have left."

57
OLIVER

Oliver dragged his sister away from the statues, which were never going to start moving, no matter how many times she had them turn around to check.

"But I heard Bailey say," Sophie insisted. "They all come to life."

"Yeah, and I'm sure she'd never utter a word of untruth. Isn't she the one who burned *worm* onto your neck?"

Sophie didn't answer. Further down the corridor, the others were already opening the door and stepping outside on their quest to retrieve the grimoire.

Oliver hurried to catch up to them.

"Who do you think will be the next Matriarch?" Sophie asked. "Gigi can't perform spells anymore, right? And Linda is out since she tried to kill you. What other old witches are in the Blackwell coven?"

"Maybe you should ask Bailey," Oliver muttered, pushing open the door. But the truth was, he was curious to know too. The Blackwell Matriarch held a lot of power in Castor's Grove.

"Ha. Ha. I think—" Sophie began to say, but she cut herself off as they stepped outside onto the green lawn that surrounded the manor.

The entire group stood on the cobblestone path in silence. Oliver followed their gazes to a lone figure in a black cloak, emerging from the trees.

Rett threw his hood back and stepped out of the shadows.

He was a skeleton: skin pulled tight, cheeks hollow, and face pale. Dark shadows under his eyes made them glow like two green orbs in empty sockets.

His head lowered, casting his gaze to the grass. His shoulders stooped.

Yet, even in mourning, with the glisten of tears still on his cheeks, there was something commanding about Rett's presence.

It wasn't the fine black silk of his shirt, visible beneath the cloak, or the long stride of his legs. It wasn't even the grimoire, metal edges and leather cover blending with Rett's clothing so that the ruby seemed to float in the air before him, a beacon of his arrival.

There was just something about the warlock.

A sense of power, perhaps.

He doth bestride the narrow world. Like a Colossus.

The quote was from Julius Caesar. It was spoken by Cassius, whose idea it was to murder the play's namesake. There was a bitterness to the line that Oliver normally related with when thinking about Rett.

He was surprised to find it gone now as he watched the boy he'd once admired.

Rett didn't ditch me and Albert because he thought he was better than us. He was being haunted by his own demons.

"It's not what it looks like," Rett said, holding up a hand and offering the group a wan smile, perhaps mistaking the reason for their silence. "I'm here to return this to its rightful owner." He held up the grimoire so that they could see the gleaming ruby. No blood swirled within.

"Rett, it's not that," Albert stepped forward, wringing the end of his large gray sweatshirt. "I'm so sorry to tell you this, but Gabriel—"

"—is dead." Rett cut him off, holding up his hand. "I know. He left me a note with the grimoire explaining everything." He turned to Beatrice. "I'm so sorry. I take full responsibility for everything that's happened."

Recalling the sight of Beatrice, dead on the stone table, Oliver felt suddenly protective. He drew closer to the witch, wrapped his arm around her shoulders, and pulled her body to his.

He was ready to forgive Rett. But the first part was knowing the truth, once and for all.

"What happened that day when you gave Gabriel his power?" Oliver asked, turning to Rett. "Were Al and I there?"

"Of course we weren't," Albert said, looking at Oliver as though he were mad.

"You were." Rett rested a hand on his cousin's shoulder. "My father paid Oliver's mother to wipe your memories. I'm sorry about that too. But my father said that if the truth ever got out, I'd be thrown in jail and Gabriel in an asylum. In hindsight, perhaps that would have been the best outcome." His sunken eyes drifted to the woods. He took a deep breath and started to explain.

"I found a potions den hidden beneath the old windmill when I was eleven. There was an old handwritten spellbook made by a former Blackwell witch and expensive ingredients, the type no one had ever even told me existed as a warlock. And I was curious and arrogant. I started using the books within to teach myself how to brew proper spells. None of the other warlocks my age cared much about potions. *Leave that danger to the witches*, they said, *we can buy them once they're perfected.* But you two"—Rett paused to look at Albert and Oliver—"and my brother, you guys hung on my every word."

From there, the story went as Oliver had assumed. They'd goaded Rett, and the older boy had decided to impress them by casting the most impressive spell he'd discovered.

"We were all going to drink it. But Gabe insisted on going first. He wanted to prove he believed in me." Tears filled Rett's eyes for a moment. He blinked them away. "It was horrible. His body ripped in two, and he kept screaming about how much it hurt. We went to get help and found my father. You know what happened from there."

Forgetting potion for Albert and me, creeping madness for Gabriel, and a lifetime of guilt for Rett.

Maybe Oliver's mother was right. She'd given him the best of the three options after all.

"That doesn't make anything that happened your fault though," Sophie said, stepping forward into a patch of mulch near the base of a hedge of black roses. There was a flash of horror across her face as she glanced at her shoe, but she hid it quickly and looked at Rett with big, sympathetic eyes. "You couldn't have known what would happen."

"I've had more of a hand in it than that," he admitted, turning away from Sophie and beginning to pace along the edge of the woods. "I kept renewing the invisibility spell on Gabriel's ring. I mean, I hid it when I thought he intended to poison Tabitha. But he managed somehow anyway, and I never told anyone and instead gave him back the ring. I really convinced myself that he'd never intended for her to die. I didn't think he was capable of murder."

"None of us did," Albert reassured him.

But Rett continued to list all the ways he was at fault. "The poison I invented killed Elle and almost you as well, Albert. And using banshee's breath to break the Matriarch's connection to the grimoire was my idea. I pitched it as a last resort when we thought there was a chance of Linda or Wilburn managing to steal it."

Beatrice and Gigi shared a look. A few feet away, even as she tried to covertly wipe the mud from her shoe onto the grass, Sophie was staring at Rett with a little too much admiration.

"I'll accept whatever punishment you want to give me," Rett said, stepping forward and holding the grimoire out for Beatrice to take.

Beatrice stepped out from Oliver's embrace. She tapped the metal binding of the spellbook. "Obviously, I'm incredibly talented. But Tabitha wanted the *most* powerful member of our coven to take her place. I don't think that's me."

Oliver's eyes widened. *She can't mean—what's she trying to say? A Matriarch is supposed to be a witch.*

Beatrice pushed the grimoire back into Rett's hands.

"No." He stared at the spellbook, a hint of excitement in his eyes quickly snuffed out by guilt, then attempted to give it back to the witch. "People are dead because of choices I made. I don't deserve a reward."

"Oh, trust me," Beatrice said, stepping away and

putting her hands behind her back so that it was clear she wouldn't take the grimoire. "Leading this coven is a punishment! You're going to spend the rest of your life dedicated to protecting the Blackwells. You won't get to make any decisions based on what you want. You'll be stuck in meetings, and managing finances, and pretending to care about everyone's petty squabbles. You'll barely be able to leave the city. I would never consider that a reward."

Gigi flew toward Rett, placing herself between him and Beatrice.

She was going to object.

There was no way the older witches like her would accept a warlock as their leader.

"Beatrice is right." Gigi's response was so unexpected that it took Oliver a moment to register it. The old woman lifted one hand from her broom and placed it on Rett's shoulder. "What you've accomplished on your own may have had terrible consequences, but it's also a sign of an incredible talent. Tabitha recognized Beatrice's aptitude, but was blind to yours."

Maiden, mother, and crone. The Blackwells are going to have a male Matriarch!

"As was I," Gigi continued. "And for that, I carry some of the blame too. Perhaps if I'd noticed sooner, I could have trained you and saved you a great deal of pain. It won't make up for everything, but for what it's worth, I'd like to guide you now, going forward. I think you could be one of the greatest leaders our coven has had."

Rett stared at her. Beneath the pain and guilt, there was a flicker in his eyes, an expression that reminded Oliver of Beatrice. It hinted at something powerful, something brilliant.

"I'll do my best to be worthy of such praise," he said.

Then, Rett raised his palm and rested it on the grimoire's ruby. His blood seeped into the gem, flooding the woods and the sky around him with a dark crimson light.

58
OLIVER

*S*ix months later

Oliver walked up the stairs and onto the platform.

A dark train with hints of purple waited before him. The emblematic tree of Castor's Grove had been engraved in gold, the city's motto beneath: *HERE, ALL ARE WELCOME.*

The sight sent a slight twinge through Oliver's chest. In all his dreams of traveling, he'd never thought about feeling homesick.

"Maiden. Mother. And Crone." Sophie huffed as she trudged up the last step and onto the platform. She barely made it to her brother before she dropped the small duffel bag she'd offered to carry. "What do you have in that thing? Books?"

"Yes, and I'd thank you not to be so careless with them." Oliver crouched down and unzipped the duffel bag, checking that none of the paperbacks had opened in his sister's dramatic drop. It would be difficult to get the pages to lie flat again if they folded funny.

"I can't believe you made me lug those up the stairs." Sophie gave the inside of the bag a fleeting, disdainful glance, then pulled a tube of lip gloss from her purse.

"No one made you come all the way to the station. You could've said goodbye at the house like Mom and Dad."

"I told you, I'm meeting friends near the beach afterward." She flicked the gloss over her lips then slipped the tube back into her purse, looking around the platform. "Is Rett coming?"

And there it was. The real reason she'd come to see him off.

"You know he's an adult and the leader of a coven." The Blackwells hadn't settled on an official title for Rett just yet. Some had pointed out that the male version of Matriarch was Patriarch, but that had been quickly vetoed. A warlock controlling the grimoire was difficult enough for many to wrap their heads around without adding a masculine moniker to the mix.

"Yeah, duh." Sophie said, rubbing her lips together to ensure the gloss was evenly applied. "What's your point?"

Oliver rolled his eyes. He was quite certain that his sister understood, even if she was acting like she didn't.

But he didn't have a chance to confirm because Beatrice arrived a moment later, Albert and Rett in tow.

Oliver grinned at the sight. If Sophie thought his bag was heavy, he could only imagine what Beatrice had in hers. Both Albert and Rett were bent over beneath one of the witch's suitcases.

Beatrice had a much smaller white bag slung over her shoulder. Bean rode in one of the pockets, upper half of his body hanging over the side, ears twitching in excitement.

Oliver went to greet her, and Beatrice wrapped her arms around him, pulling him into a kiss.

It was sweet and gentle, her lips soft on his. The slight scent of vanilla drifted from her hair, and Oliver reached his hand up to caress it. He swore he'd never felt anything quite as soft.

"Blech." Albert made a puking noise as they pulled apart. He slapped his hand on Oliver's shoulder. "No need for that now. She's not dead."

Oliver coughed, glancing around to ensure that no one else on the platform had heard. "You're never going to stop making that joke, are you?"

"He can't," Rett said, grinning as he rolled a very large, very pink suitcase toward one of the train's nearby doors. "Every time we think the joke is dead, it comes back to life."

The others laughed, Sophie with an unnecessarily high-pitched giggle.

Oliver didn't think the comment all that amusing, but at least Rett was able to make bad puns about what had happened now, even if his shoulders seemed to sink afterward. He couldn't have managed that a couple months ago.

"Do you both have the itineraries I made?" Rett asked, turning to Oliver and Beatrice.

"All up here." The witch tapped her forehead. Seeing the anxious expression on her cousin's face, she added, "And in my phone."

"I wrote it all down." Oliver patted the pocket of his jeans, where the piece of paper lay. He'd read it every night for the past week so that Rett's script was already starting to fade. The first leg was the train out of Castor's Grove. It would take them to the airport. Their first flight got them to Florida, and a second one to the Caribbean, where they would begin their world tour by hunting for seawave root and whatever other mysteries hid amongst reefs.

"Good," Rett said, giving Beatrice an annoyed glance. "You're going to be handling magical items. There's a good chance your phones end up dead or disconnected for long periods. You two need to be prepared."

Bean squeaked in objection.

"Sorry, you three. How could I forget you, Bean? I'm expecting you to be in charge." Rett smiled at the familiar. "Make sure they check in when they're supposed to and don't get distracted."

"Yeah, this isn't a romantic trip," Albert said, punching Oliver's arm. "You two are acting as Blackwell ambassadors. You can't be making out everywhere you go."

"B is the Blackwell ambassador," Oliver corrected him. "I'm just tagging along to write down all the things she does."

Beatrice slipped her hand into his. "You're a lot more talented than you think," she said, then grinned. "Don't worry, Rett. Together, Oliver and I are going to be the greatest traveling witch and warlock duo that the world has ever seen. We're going to help so many creatures who are living without the modern magical conveniences of a city. Oliver's going to come back with a massive collection of short stories about all of our amazing work."

"Sure. Just be certain that everyone you help knows that the Blackwell coven from Castor's Grove sent you as a show of goodwill to all our foreign brethren," Rett said, glancing toward the train as the doors finally opened and the other passengers began making their way in. "And remember that your primary mission is collecting specimens of rare flora and fauna. The PR is secondary."

Rett was the leader of the Blackwell coven, not a philanthropist. He wasn't funding Beatrice and Oliver's travels for the next year out of the goodness of his heart or an innate desire to help the less fortunate. He expected a return on his investment.

"You can count on us," Oliver reassured him. He hefted his large duffel bag over his shoulder and looked at his sister. "Helping with my smaller one?"

"Absolutely not. I'll take one of Beatrice's," Sophie offered. She went to the small pink suitcase that Albert had carried, lifted it two inches off the platform, then placed it back down at once. "That's worse than Oliver! Don't tell me you packed a ton of books too."

"Some," she said. "But those are in the one Rett has. That's got a collapsible cauldron, bottles for specimens, and a couple of essential potions' ingredients of course." She rattled off a rather long list as the others helped lift their bags onto the train.

When it was time to leave, Oliver pulled his sister into a tight hug. He recalled an earlier farewell, cramped in the small bathroom at The Museum of The Mystic. Then, he'd imagined himself going on the run for years, hiding alone in shoddy apartments.

He looked at Beatrice saying farewell to Albert, and a smile spread across his face as she caught his eye.

Exploring the world with the girl I love is so much better.

AUTHOR'S NOTE

Thank you so much for visiting the magical city of Castor's Grove!

If you enjoyed *Banshee's Breath*, please tell your friends, or leave a review in the place where you purchased it. It would mean so much to me!

Please visit Plotworks Publishing to keep exploring the Castor's Grove universe! Sign up for the newsletter and get a discount!

You can also follow me on Instagram: @aj.renwick

Now turn the page for a sneak peek at the next title in the Castor's Grove universe—

CASTOR'S GROVE

CHANGELING'S DAGGER

a young adult
paranormal
romance

A.J. RENWICK

CHANGELING'S DAGGER

Kenya Davidson's lime green sneakers pounded across the pavement as she turned south on 76th Street. Heart racing, she twisted to peer over her shoulder as she ran. There was no one there. So why couldn't she shake the sensation that she was being followed?

Wow, I don't know. Maybe because I'm paranoid this morning?

Her parents' fears were becoming contagious. Despite living in a safe area, so far to the north of the city her mother claimed it should be classified as a suburb, both Courtney and Reuben Davidson were petrified of something bad happening to their only daughter. It wasn't just imaginary muggers and hypothetical thieves that concerned them. What if Kenya tripped over the uneven sidewalk and hurt herself right before a big race?

But I know every inch of these streets. I'll be fine.

Plus, Kenya was an adult now. She'd turned eighteen two weeks ago. It was her decision if she wanted to stretch her muscles. And this morning, it was a necessity.

She'd woken up with her heart already pounding, her

limbs already trembling. The qualifiers were today. She couldn't lie in bed waiting. She needed to move, to prepare, to run.

While her parents were still in bed, she'd donned her sneakers, repositioned her curls so that they were safely atop her head, and slipped out the door. She'd be back before they had a chance to miss her.

Near the corner of Underwood Avenue, Kenya swore she heard footsteps a few paces behind. Her breath caught. Without breaking stride, she turned her head. Was that a shadow disappearing between two of the houses?

The toe of Kenya's shoe caught on a pebble, and she stumbled forward before catching herself.

Oh, well done! I can fall, twist my ankle, and get mugged.

Then she could listen to her parents say *I told you so* for the rest of her life.

And maybe they were right. Running in the dim light, alone, hours before a race wasn't calming Kenya the way she'd hoped.

But she refused to give in to the fear. Instead of slowing and speed-walking home, she took a deep breath and turned around.

See?

The sidewalk was empty—no footsteps, no shadow, no vicious mugger. She'd imagined it all. The most dangerous thing on the street was the pebble.

Kenya kicked it toward the road, feeling satisfied as it disappeared down a grate and into the sewers.

You're welcome, Castor's Grove. 76th Street is safe now.

"Excuse me," a female voice shouted from across the street, waving a map. It was a woman about her mother's age, with a round face and rosy, pink cheeks. She wore pair of tortoise shell glasses, a bucket hat, and overalls.

A tourist.

Rare, but not unheard of, in this area of the city. Certainly not a reason to be afraid.

Kenya breathed a sigh of relief. She didn't know what was wrong with her this morning. She wasn't normally so quick to panic.

"Would you be able to help me?" the tourist asked, unfolding her map as she crossed the street. As she drew closer, her height became more obvious. Despite the hunch in her back—as though she'd spent years of ducking under doorways—the woman was close to six feet.

"Always happy to help." Kenya smiled and closed the space between them.

Too late, she noticed the glint of silver flash behind the woman's map.

The tourist, who probably wasn't a tourist at all, grabbed the front of Kenya's white shirt and plunged a blade into her chest.

Kenya screamed.

Not because it hurt, but because it seemed like the correct thing to do when a stranger stabbed you in the middle of the sidewalk.

The woman shoved her map into Kenya's mouth, trying to silence her.

The air around the blade burst into a blaze of energy. Red and blue flames licked at Kenya's skin. Heat spread through her veins and washed across the backs of her eyes. The houses, the street, and the woman vanished, Kenya's vision consumed by the fire.

"Counterclockwise thrice," the woman's voice echoed through the flames. She began to twist the blade.

Kenya's muscles burned, contracting and pulsing in a way she'd never known possible. The map fell from between her teeth. She gasped for air and breathed in only fire. It filled her mouth, burning into her throat and chest, transforming her from the inside out as her body began shrinking, rippling and morphing into an unfamiliar form.

With a third and final twist, the woman pulled the blade free.

The flames vanished, and Kenya's vision returned as she dropped to the sidewalk.

She landed on four furry orange paws. Something strange was attached to the bottom of her back. Kenya turned her head and saw it: a long, fluffy tail. She swished it, and it moved at her command.

What the actual hell?

Kenya had no idea who this strange woman was or what bizarre abilities her knife had, but she knew one thing with shocking certainty.

I've just been transformed into a cat.

* * *

"Don't be afraid," the woman said.

"How could I not be terrified?" Kenya asked, spinning her head. Instead of her voice, she heard a high-pitched yowl.

This wasn't real. Kenya must've been dreaming.

The woman crouched onto her knees, bringing her face closer. Her storm-colored eyes still seemed a mile away. The blade that she'd just stabbed Kenya with balanced on her knees. "This is going to seem very confusing, but I promise, I'm going to guide you through it."

Thanks, but no thanks. I am going to wake up.

Kenya lifted what should've been her right hand but was instead an orange paw. She slapped it onto her left. Five claws extended, sinking into the skin.

She yowled.

"Kenya Davidson, your life is about to—"

Before the woman could finish, a dark figure sprung from between two of the houses.

Kenya leaped back, the rest of her claws extending on instinct. The fur rose along her spine, and her tail froze.

This is real?

Before her, the dark figure came into view—a man dressed in black; his face hidden by a hockey mask. Only his hands, large and olive-toned, were visible.

Whatever was going on, he must've been the villain. Only someone with sinister intentions would bother to wear a black turtleneck in the middle of summer.

Which made Kenya's stabber... the hero?

That didn't sound right.

The woman faced down the masked man. Her ears had sprung loose from beneath her bucket hat. They stuck out from her head, large and pointed like a creature from a folktale.

I have got to get out of here.

What was the best direction to run?

Left toward her home.

As Kenya turned, she glimpsed her stabber pulling something new from the pocket of her overalls. It was a small pink cube, as though someone had made strawberry flavored chicken stock. The woman dropped it.

The air filled with powder and the scent of flowers. A heartbeat later, a hand wrapped around Kenya's neck.

"No, put me down!" she mewled, paws flailing through the blur of pink, vision obscured. She didn't know who'd grabbed her until they escaped the powder, and the woman's pointed ears came into view.

Footsteps pounded behind them. The masked man was in pursuit.

Kenya's brain rattled in her skull as they raced in the wrong direction, slipping through narrow side roads. The signs blurred. She lost any sense of where they were.

The woman turned through a twisting alley, only to find the path blocked by a gray stone wall.

"Drumbeat!" she loosed the word as though it were a curse and spun around. The masked man blocked her retreat.

The woman was trapped, which meant Kenya was too.

Oh no. This is bad.

Whatever was happening, Kenya was not part of it. She needed out of this alley. Now.

The woman's grip slackened as she retreated to the wall. Her focus was on the masked man, not the girl-turned-cat wriggling in her arms.

Good.

Kenya took advantage of her neck's new flexibility, twisting her head and sinking her teeth into her stabber's skin.

"Ahh!" With a scream, the woman flung Kenya away— straight toward the masked man.

This was not the plan!

At least, it hadn't been Kenya's. Her stabber used the opportunity to jump.

While the woman cleared the wall, Kenya landed like a furry grenade on top the masked man's head. Her claws scrambled for a grip, scratching at his short black curls.

He grabbed her tail, trying to yank her away, but the pain made Kenya's claws sink deeper into his scalp. As he pulled, her back left foot raked over the strap of his mask.

The fabric ripped.

Kenya was flung once more across the alley. She twisted in mid-air, watching as the mask fell to the ground.

Beneath was a square jaw, a pair of pale pink lips, and deep brown eyes. Kenya knew that face.

The masked man was Camilo Lopez, her family's landscaper.

PLOTWORKS PUBLISHING

And now turn the page for a peek at another A.J. Renwick series, *The Warlock's Homeowners Association*, a comedic suburban fantasy!

the
WARLOCK'S
HOMEOWNERS
ASSOCIATION
presents...
BOOK
ONE
SUB
DIVISION
BATTLES
OF THE
DEAD
AND
UNDEAD
A.J. RENWICK

SUBDIVISION BATTLES OF
THE DEAD AND UNDEAD

On a cold night in the middle of June, at exactly 10:57 pm (though when the story was retold, the time would be changed to midnight for dramatic purposes), a dead man strode into The Clover Motel.

A brown messenger bag hung from his shoulder, and beneath his arm, he clutched a black chrysalis. It shimmered with iridescent light and radiated with the heavy heat of the underworld.

Bartholomew Whitlock wasn't dead in the traditional sense, or even the untraditional sense. His heart still beat. His breath was steady. He had no desire to moan, hold his arms stiff before him, or eat brains. His death was a metaphorical one.

Gone was Bartholomew Whitlock, exalted among the Acquisitions Department of The Bearded Syndicate, in his place was—

"Bartholomew Bartlow?"

Rebecca Willis, the woman stuck working the night shift at the motel's front desk, peered at the identification card through a pair of pink-rimmed spectacles. Had she looked closely, she might have noticed a curious sheen on the plastic, like it was turning brown in a pattern of lines and dots. But the news was reporting on a plane crash, and Rebecca took a morbid delight in listening to tragic stories, even if only so she could inform her husband the next day and chide him for his lack of empathy when he remained indifferent. She was eager to get this new guest checked in so that she could get back to the television.

Still, she attempted to make what she considered polite conversation as she typed Bartholomew's information into the old computer. "I'll bet school was tough for you."

Rebecca cracked a sympathetic smile and looked at the man before her desk.

He stared back, dark eyes serious beneath a pair of thick black brows that matched the curls on his head. His lips were drawn in a tight thin line. "No," he said, "I was an excellent student."

Rebecca stared at him. There was something unsettling about his voice. In the moment, she couldn't place what it was, but when she recounted the meeting later, she'd realize. Though Bartholomew's face was smooth, not a day over thirty, he spoke like a radio-announcer who was pushing seventy.

"No, I meant— Right, well..." Rebecca waved her hand in dismissal and continued entering the information. "And do you know how long you'll be staying with us, Mr. Bartlow?"

"Who? Oh that's me." He nodded. "No, not yet. But I'll need a pet-friendly room. I'm about to get a cat." For some reason, he shifted the black chrysalis in his arm as he spoke. An arc of light shimmered around it, as though it were wrapped in a rainbow.

Rebecca blinked. She'd never seen anything like it,

which wasn't surprising. Most people, even magical and undead ones, hadn't.

"Very good, Mr. Bartlow. Pets are only allowed in rooms on the first floor. We have one still available." The Clover Motel in fact was mostly empty, but Rebecca had been instructed to say otherwise by her boss, who was under the mistaken assumption that the lie gave the establishment an air of desirability. "We'll keep your credit card information on file until then. Wi-Fi password and information are in a binder on the side table when you go in. Room is right down the hall, second on the left. Here's the key."

She dropped it into Bartholomew's waiting hand. Like the rest of his body, his fingers were long and thin. Unlike the rest of him, they had a tendency to twitch like the limbs of a dying spider. They curled around the key with a snap.

He turned, took two steps toward the hall, and stopped. His fingers flitted into his pocket and retrieved a green bill.

As a habit, Rebecca's interest in guests ended the moment the room key was exchanged. She'd already begun switching the computer tab back to the news. However, the glint of green caught her eye.

It wasn't often that guests bothered to tip her.

And it wasn't a one-, or five-, or even a ten-dollar bill that Bartholomew was crinkling in his fingers. Rebecca recognized Benjamin Franklin's shiny forehead, and even if she hadn't, the two zeros beside it could have only meant one thing.

Bartholomew had her interest once more.

He rested the hundred-dollar bill on the desk. "If someone with a beard shows up, tell me."

"Absolutely!" Rebecca grabbed the money before Bartholomew could change his mind. She would have responded just as eagerly to a ten.

Of course, she would have been just as inefficient if he'd given her a thousand.

Two bearded men would visit the motel in the next week, and Rebecca would inform Bartholomew about neither. Not due to malice, but because the entire encounter slipped from her mind, replaced instead with facts about the night's disaster.

The private plane had exploded mid-air, killing three individuals: the pilot, co-pilot, and a single unnamed passenger. His face flashed across the screen: a man in his thirties with a black beard, long, slicked back hair, and dark eyes that seemed strangely familiar.

I bet he'd be handsome if he shaved, Rebecca thought, and then immediately imagined a new, and incorrect, face for the deceased passenger, which drew more than a little inspiration from the hero on the cover of a romance novel that currently waited beside her bed.

It would be years before she realized that she'd rented a room to a dead man, or even remembered Bartholomew's request. And even then, it would be only for a second before a bearded man plucked the memory from her mind.